FAMILY SKELETON

About the Author

Family Skeleton is Carmel Bird's ninth novel. Carmel's other works include short fiction and non-fiction.

Other Books by Carmel Bird

Child of the Twilight
Cape Grimm
Red Shoes
The White Garden
The Bluebird Café
Cherry Ripe
Unholy Writ
Open for Inspection
Crisis
My Hearts Are Your Hearts
The Essential Bird
The Common Rat
Automatic Teller
The Woodpecker Toy Fact (USA title Woodpecker Point)
Births Deaths and Marriages
Fair Game
Dimitra
The Mouth
Dear Writer Revisited
Not Now Jack - I'm Writing a Novel
Writing the Story of Your Life
The Stolen Children - Their Stories
Red Hot Notes
Relations - Australian Short Stories
Daughters and Fathers
Home Truth
The Penguin Century of Australian Stories
The Cassowary's Quiz
Fabulous Finola Fox

FAMILY SKELETON

Carmel Bird

UWA PUBLISHING

First published in 2016 by
UWA Publishing
Crawley, Western Australia 6009
www.uwap.uwa.edu.au

UWAP is an imprint of UWA Publishing,
a division of The University of Western Australia.

THE UNIVERSITY OF
WESTERN
AUSTRALIA

This book is copyright. Apart from any fair dealing for the purpose of private study, research, criticism or review, as permitted under the *Copyright Act 1968*, no part may be reproduced by any process without written permission. Enquiries should be made to the publisher.

Copyright © Carmel Bird 2016

The moral right of the author has been asserted.

National Library of Australia
Cataloguing-in-Publication entry:
Bird, Carmel, 1940– author.
Family skeleton / Carmel Bird.
ISBN: 9781742588902 (paperback)
Family secrets—Australia—Fiction.
Australian fiction.
A823.3

Typeset in Bembo by Lasertype
Printed by Lightning Source

uwapublishing

Author's Note:

I am grateful to the Australia Council for the Arts which awarded me a Writing Fellowship. Family Skeleton is one of the projects I was able to pursue as a recipient of the Fellowship.

Australian Government | Australia Council for the Arts

'The Storyteller knows what the Storyteller knows;
the Storyteller tells what the Storyteller tells.'
CARRILLO MEAN When Where Why How

PROLOGUE BY THE STORYTELLER

Imagine you have a talking skeleton in the wardrobe. That's me. I still have my own teeth.

Once upon a time, in the years between the great wars, there was born a baby girl named Margaret. This happened in the artistic atmosphere of Eltham in the shire of Nillumbik, twenty kilometres to the north-east of Melbourne. Margaret's childhood was happy, although during some of it the whole world was at war for the second time. When Margaret grew up she married Edmund, who was a very distant cousin, and she went to live in the wealthy atmosphere of Toorak in the city of Stonnington, five kilometres to the south-east of the Melbourne Town Hall. And lived happily ever after. You think so? There was happy and there was sad. Life's like that. Even Cinderella died in the end. Margaret and Edmund had four children, and in the way of things, before he was quite seventy years old, Edmund died. So Margaret lived alone in the lovely old house built by Edmund's father. She was known as a philanthropist and patron of the arts, and people from the news media would sometimes come round with various recording devices and would then tell stories about her and her good works and her pretty family life in Toorak. These stories didn't get very far beneath the surface. How could she possibly be as good as she seemed? One morning she said to her faithful housekeeper, Lillian: 'I think I'll write my memoirs.'

Now we're getting somewhere.

Let me tell you a few things about Margaret and Lillian. Margaret has led a life of privilege. She grew up in Eltham where her father was the local doctor. She trained as a nurse, but when she married she retired to have four children and look after her husband who was in the funeral business. Lillian, much the same age as Margaret, came from lower down the social scale. She has always worked as a housekeeper, also has four children, and her husband also is dead. For many years she has been Margaret's housekeeper, and as you can see they have formed a warm understanding. Lillian knows her place, and Margaret knows she knows. But when Margaret needs a shoulder to cry on – and this is not often – she turns to Lillian. When she needs – well – someone to talk to, she turns to Lillian, housekeeper, mainstay. Margaret is the matriarch of an influential family, yet without Lillian she possibly couldn't manage the smooth performance that is her public and private life. Patron of this, president of that, mother, grandmother, volunteer. Margaret is a good woman. And so is Lillian. You can easily tell the difference between them: one is tall and leonine with Italian spectacle frames, the other small and simian with glasses from her local pharmacy. One has her own teeth; the other doesn't. And Lillian comes from the other side of the river. Thus may class divides be identified in this little patch of the animal kingdom.

'I don't know what Mr O'Day would think of you writing memoirs,' Lillian said.

'He would turn in his grave.'

'I believe he would.'

'Then he will just have to turn, won't he?'

Margaret laughed again, but it was a kind of forced laugh.

The Book of Revelation

'Death is the golden key that opens the palace of eternity.'
E. R. O'Day

Lillian just smiled. Margaret smoothed her hand over the blue linen cover, ran her fingers across the surface of the first page.

'Yes. I'm calling it *The Book of Revelation*.'

Lillian smiled again.

'Well, why don't you say something, Lillian? Is it a good idea? Or not?'

'Oh, I think it's an excellent idea.'

'What do you think about the title, then?'

'It sounds rather gruesome. Violent is it, the story?'

'I don't think so. I don't quite know yet. I haven't started actually writing. For some reason I keep thinking of my father. In the war. But it's really just a journal, Lillian. Or a memoir.'

'You might have to decide which. And I wondered: is the title a bit, you know, blasphemous, sacrilegious?'

'Oh, I don't think so really. I think that by the age of seventy-eight nothing's blasphemous any more.'

'You made that up, Margaret.'

'And by this age I can also make up anything I like.'

'So will it be truthful, the story you tell? The journal – or the memoir? Or do you plan to make it up?'

It was Margaret's turn to smile. In fact, she laughed.

'Oh, you know me, I wouldn't dream of writing fiction, Lillian,' she said.

You will have the pleasure of reading a few of the pages of Margaret's *Book of Revelation* in the course of this narrative. One other thing before we really get going here: every little chapter of the story is preceded by a pithy saying attributed to E. R. O'Day, Margaret's late husband. He was of course the patriarch, the boss of the family, but I am pleased to say that I am the boss of the story; I will guide you, will tell you where to look, and will suggest various ways of thinking about the things you see. Do not imagine that Margaret headed her section of *The Book of Revelation* with Edmund's sayings. No, that was all the work of the skeleton in the wardrobe. I might say: 'Trust me, I'm a fiction writer' – but that would be a bit silly, wouldn't it?

Heavenly Days

'Go to a funeral – catch your death.'

E. R. O'Day

Eddy O'Day was a philistine, but he was not a fool. He was even something of a philosopher, particularly when he had had a drink or two, which was quite often. He kept an incredibly comprehensive cellar. When his father died in 1968, Edmund took over the family funeral business and it never looked back. It had always been steady, but Edmund turned it, people said, into not just a business, but an art form. It was Edmund who bought the large unpromising property on the outskirts (he loved the word, and so do I) of the city and developed the Heavenly Days theme park where you could be married or buried or even baptised. Eighteen-year-olds revelled in celebrating their birthdays at Heavenly Days where there were rides such as the Spooky-Kooky and the Tomb of the Unknown Zombie. Bucks nights were a speciality; not so much hens, although for a time it was fashionable to hold the baby shower in the Goo-Goo Conservatory. The food, I should point out, was excellent, likewise the drink. Edmund was no fool. There was a Roman Catholic bias to the overall theme, although, as Eddy would say, the heathen was as welcome as any other sinner. The genius of it all was not really the small ferris wheel at the centre, although that was perfectly splendid, but the fact that people were encouraged to buy large family plots, places they could decorate in life, and where they could enjoy family picnics. Somehow Eddy was able to convince people that they were going to need a great chunk of land in eternity. The plan was called 'Here-and-Now-Here-After'.

Yes, Heavenly Days was an art form, a great installation. Above the doorway inside the reception area was a replica of a Chinese ivory skeleton from the family home. In the house the original of the strange little thing, the size of your pinkie, hangs inside the front door, beside a small statue of St Michael. People seldom notice the quiet presences of these figures, but they are the protectors of the household. The skeleton is known as George. 'Our personal *memento mori*,' Edmund would say, 'as if we needed one.'

Edmund said he probably should get an arts grant for creating Heavenly Days. That was a joke. Eddy was something of a humorist in his way. Every morning he presented his staff with what he called the Epitaph of the Day. These were pithy sayings on the topic of death, quoting for example the words of Goethe or Christ, but always signed E. R. O'Day in fine red lettering. The staff called them headstones. When they opened their computers first thing, there it was, the Epitaph of the Day. 'Death, where is thy sting? In the hip pocket.' Or 'A man who won't die for something is not fit to live.' And so forth. Of course they were not really epitaphs, but Eddy was free with language, and generally free with the truth.

He used to say that the four things to consider were sex, women, wine and death – you could forget the old death, judgement, heaven and hell nonsense. Sex is the initiator, he said. The entrance gates to Heavenly Days were a giant iridescent butterfly which Edmund liked to point out was a sexual symbol. He couldn't see a black mantilla without thinking of lace knickers. Although many of his staff were women, they seemed to be happy enough to take his philosophies on board. Without sex, he said, you wouldn't have death – well, you wouldn't have anything, would you. What

Edmund had, first and foremost, was charm. He was handsome, rich and charming – what more do you want?

Edmund had a wife and family: well, in fact, he had two families. There was Margaret, his wife, who was what is known as a virtuous woman, and there was Fiona, who was what is known as a mistress.

Here is a sort of diagram of the 'family'.

Margaret and Edmund had four children: Joseph, Paul, Rafaela and Isobel.

Joseph is married to Charmaine (children: Orson, Oriane, Orlando, Ophelia).

Paul is gay and his partner is Gerard (no children).

Rafaela is married to Jean-François (no children).

Isobel is married to Hugh (children: Rupert and Gustav).

Edmund and Fiona had two sons: Frederick and Julian.

Margaret plans to leave the house to Isobel and Hugh, mainly because she can not bear the thought of what Charmaine might do to it.

You can see that the family tree is branching out quite nicely here, one way and another. Naturally we will be looking at the love/sex lives and the procreations of the younger members of the family. You could call it an extended family, what with Fiona and the boys.

Edmund and Margaret were in fact related. He came from the business side of the family, and she came from the more artistic and professional side. These things happen. He was a 'funeral' O'Day and she was a 'medical' O'Day – two areas of interest that are not necessarily so very far apart. The official funeral O'Day residence was in the old Toorak home, Bellevue, where Edmund had grown up, and the house where Fiona and the boys lived was just a few blocks away. Smaller, more modern, but a place of comfort and luxury. The quickest way to describe Bellevue to you is to show you the advertisement for it that would appear in 2020. I realise that the eye of the reader can easily slide carelessly across such elements of the text. However, I suggest you take your time and study this little document carefully.

FORTHCOMING AUCTION

Landmark Toorak Georgian Family Home

'*Bellevue*'

Number 10 George Avenue

Style & comfort   21st Century Living

Two Hectares Prime Residential Land

Six Bedrooms + Ensuites; Italian Marble Reception Hall
Gracious Drawing Room; Generous Dining; Perfect Kitchen; Studio;
Studies; Sitting Rooms

Tennis Court; Butler's Pantry; Silver Strongroom; Conservatory;
Billiard Room; Wine Cellar

Supercinema Screenroom; Children's Suite + Games Room;
Monitored Security; Gymnasium; Five-car Garage
River Access + Boathouse; Pool + Cabana; Landscaped Gardens;
Heritage-Listed Trees

Immaculate Condition from Attic to Cellar

Inspection Strictly by Appointment
www.realestateaustralasia.com.au/july2020.html

The O'Day family, well known as funeral directors to the Melbourne establishment, built Bellevue in the nineteen twenties. The house goes up for sale for the first time in ninety-five years.

Margaret was not only virtuous but, as you know, rather wise, or perhaps cunning, and she treated Fiona and co. as part of the larger family. Edmund had lots of other women off and on, but they didn't really count. Yes, you'd have to say his charm was considerable.

All good things come to an end, and eventually, when he was seventy, Eddy O'Day himself died. He had always said he would. ('A man who lives fully is prepared to die at any time.' E. R. O'Day.) So virtuous Margaret became a widow, and so did mistress Fiona. And in the normal course of events, Margaret herself died.

So let's begin with Margaret's funeral, this being a tale about a family of funeral directors, and then we can go back and see how things got to the point they got to.

Two Minutes of Fame, July 2014

'All stories, if continued far enough, end in death.'
E. R. O'Day

The funeral of Margaret, matriarch, widow of Edmund Rice O'Day of O'Day Funerals, took place on a winter morning in Melbourne in 2014. Before the church service, as the hearse was leaving the family home in Toorak, a glittering flock of tropical turquoise butterflies, bred for such occasions, was released into the chilly air. A few of the creatures fluttered swiftly away to disappear in an ethereal zigzag flash, but many seemed bewildered, reluctant to move far from their boxes. Some stuck like jewels to the family's clothing, others remaining huddled in their containers, refusing to move until the boxes were shaken and they were forced to come out. 'I shook it and shook it and shook it and still it just stuck in the corner of the box. So I picked it up in my fingers but I think I squeezed it too tight and it got crushed, ick,' said one of the children afterwards, flicking her finger and thumb to demonstrate how she had flicked the broken thing onto the gravel. Charmaine, who had thought of having the butterflies, was quite disappointed in their performance.

If the sun had been shining more brightly, the butterflies might have been more active. A sense of anticlimax hung in the air. The whole funeral event was in due course routinely produced, in a somewhat outdated format, as a 'deluxe' DVD. O'Day Funerals specialised in those. The butterflies were recorded on the gardener's phone and immediately tweeted, and were recorded also on an ancient video camera operated by the housekeeper, Lillian. They will live on in a family archive of poor quality videos, and will flutter forever on Facebook.

Lillian, now. You will like Lillian – or at least I hope you will. The gardener's phone clip turned up on YouTube where it had sixty-five seconds of fame that have entered the possible eternity of the internet. Images of butterflies had always been a motif in Margaret's life, a kind of signature, rather in the way that some people seem to attract images of frogs or cats or pigs. There is no real meaning to these little fetishes, when you come down to it, but throughout the life the motif persists. And there it was, the motif, following Margaret into the hereafter. Eternity with Butterflies on a YouTube clip. Don't try to make too much out of it all now, will you? If Freud had thought of it he might have commented that sometimes a butterfly is just a butterfly. A funny thing was that, although Edmund frequently drew attention to the butterfly he called the Great Fanny of Eternity at the entrance to Heavenly Days, Margaret never really caught on. A giantess of Catholic respectability, she seemed to be capable of sealing off the reality of the thing, the possible symbolism of the insect's form. Perhaps it was her 'coping mechanism'. Or perhaps she was so finely tuned to nature, so much of a butterfly on legs herself, that she simply *lived* the meaning of it all. I find it a bit enigmatic really. You can decide.

The Summer Before the Funeral

*'Black horses, black carriages, and fast-fading flowers.
Why not the colours of a sunset?'*

E. R. O'Day

Yes, it was a hot summer, long and hot. Margaret, still very much alive at this point, stood at the window looking out onto the scene in the garden. The umbrella of early summer oak leaves cast its shadow in dappled sunlight soft as honey over a long table. Around this table sat family and friends. Margaret's chair at the far end was momentarily empty, a pale green shawl draped over its back. There were cane armchairs and elegant smaller tables around the periphery. It was a charming group, picture perfect, the emotional focus being a baby girl. The antique cradle swathed in fine net rested on its tall frame beside the baby's mother. The cradle was, as you might have guessed, a family heirloom. The christening cake, iced in gleaming white, was decorated with the fresh petals of the palest pink roses. This baby was Margaret's second grand-daughter, fourth child of son Joey and his glamorous wife Charmaine. The occasion was the celebration of the baby's baptism and, truth to tell, Margaret had withdrawn to the house for a few moments in order to preserve her good temper. She had been on the point of making a sharp remark, the kind of remark she very seldom, if ever, would make in public. She was a woman of considerable self-control, known for her goodness, indeed for her virtue, as I have already said. She generally concealed most of her own more unpleasant emotions behind a face and demeanour of charm, even of sweetness.

Margaret wanted to comment on the baby's name, but didn't. Charmaine was already aware of her thoughts; and anyway, it was now pointless to say anything. Charmaine had gone ahead, against the wishes of many, but of Margaret in particular, and called the baby Ophelia Rose. A doomed name, Margaret said. But Shakespearian argument meant very little to Charmaine.

'It's such a pretty name,' said Charmaine. 'I've always loved it, you know. There was a girl at school whose aunt was called Ophelia and she always used to come to school concerts and things and she was incredibly pretty and had this amazing singing voice and she used to sing my song to me sometimes, you know, "Charmaine", my song?'

Paul, who was fond of Charmaine, supplied the first line in the style of a Welsh tenor, and everyone laughed with delight.

Margaret considered Charmaine to be an idiot, but she fulfilled her function as an excellent breeder of O'Day children, and didn't seem to pass on her own empty head, although she did pass on her rather delicious facial features. All to the good. Charmaine would sit at the piano and play and sing the song – of course she had no irony – trilling on about how the man in the Charmaine story was hoping for Charmaine to come back to him along with the mating bluebirds. Mating bluebirds! You can catch the song for yourself on YouTube. I like the version by the Silver Masked Tenor, from an old recording made by the Silvertown Cord Orchestra long, long ago. It's worth noting that Margaret's father (of whom much more later) had a vinyl record of this very version in his collection of seventy-eights. Margaret's mother used to sing the thing to her children as a lullaby. Well, it is a pretty melody. In fact it irritated Margaret that her daughter-in-law had taken ownership of the song. There was much about Charmaine that irritated Margaret – but of course she seldom showed it. Edmund had found Charmaine highly entertaining, and naturally he loved the very look of her. Legs, tits, eyes, teeth, hair – and arse, of course. She was the real thing. Personality. That was it, personality. He's not wrong. And shrewdness and cunning. That's Charmaine. There's a certain amount of evidence to suggest that Eddy was the father of Charmaine's daughter Oriane. Imagine! Margaret hadn't actually caught a whisper of this, but I do wonder what she would have done, at the time, if she had known. What do *you* think? I don't suppose it would make much difference to the family tree thing. Eddy used to make loud comments about what he called Charmaine's 'stuffed shirt howling half-wit family of millionaire dry-cleaners'.

'How did they come to get you and KayKay, Charms?' he'd say. It wasn't so much the lowliness of dry-cleaning, as Charmaine's lack of *taste* in general that strangely fascinated him, that got to him. Eddy was fond of – what would you call it? – the glamour of the arts, I suppose. Prided himself on his taste, yet could never resist the call of lust. Perhaps he was more complex than he appeared. He had after all plucked Margaret – pretty but not very sexy – from the arty/medical Eltham branch of the family. Charmaine's lot were *crass*. (What a word! Crass. It's like spitting.) And while we're at it with the nasty words, Charmaine and KayKay were both well known as sluts. Although Charmaine didn't really look like one most of the time. Eddy's sons were quite different from him. Paul was a gay musician; Joseph was a rather dull businessman, respectable husband and father. Perhaps Eddy's genes will pick up again in the grandchildren.

'Ophelia,' said Charmaine, 'it really works with all the children's names'.

These names were: Orson, Oriane and Orlando. Was Ophelia consistent? Yes, it probably was. Margaret held her tongue and turned a blind eye to this somewhat comical list of names. She had suggested the possibility of 'Olivia' for the second daughter, but this was quickly dismissed as being too popular, and also the name of a pig in a picture book. Privately, Margaret hated the notion of all those 'O. O'Days', and what any routine joker could make of them. The art master, Clive Bushby, at Loyola College where the boys of the family were at school openly called them the 'Ooops O'Daisies'. Margaret herself would sometimes say to Lillian: 'The Ooopsies will be here for lunch on Sunday.' Then they would both laugh. Lightly. For Margaret adored the children, and the word was spoken with affection. Spoken to Lillian, you will have noticed. I can tell you now that Lillian was in fact Margaret's closest human being. I say 'human being' rather than 'friend' or anything else. Margaret did have friends, naturally she did, but I think a better word for them might be 'acquaintances' really. She would never open her heart to them. If she could be said to open her heart – well, perhaps not her heart so much as her mouth and mind – to anyone, it was to Lillian. Oh, all right – sometimes she opened her heart, such as when Edmund died, say. Lillian was perhaps more like the sister Margaret had never had and always longed for. 'Consider yourself lucky,' said the acquaintances (at lunches and gallery openings and in theatre foyers and so forth), 'that they're not named after towns in the United States, or after peculiar tropical plants or popular songs.' Remember Charmaine? The local pharmacist's children were, for instance, called Dusk, Acapulco, Sylph and Tytonidae. The acquaintances said that celebrities were to blame for this fashion in naming children. Maybe. The late Peaches Geldof, for one. She had set the benchmark high. The internet is pretty vague and messy about the meaning of the name 'Charmaine'. Is it a feminine form of 'Charles', or does it just mean 'charm'? Not to worry. The names of Margaret's other grandchildren, Rupert and Gustav, sons of Isobel and her husband, Hugh, are perfectly good names, aren't they? A relief. There is, however, their nanny to consider; she's called Smith, which is short for Smithereen. Yes, her name is Smithereen Garvey.

'The received meaning of Ophelia is "help",' Margaret said to Lillian one time during Charmaine's pregnancy.

'Help?' said Lillian, who loves to listen to Margaret when she's on her high horse. 'How do you mean, help?'

'Oh, I've never been sure on that point. It could mean the child is meant to be useful around the house, or is – um – calling for assistance.'

Lillian couldn't really see what the fuss was about, but that was Margaret for you, always holding an opinion, always wanting control, the last word, elegantly resenting it when she didn't get her own way.

As soon as the disapproval about Ophelia was gently but firmly put to Charmaine, early in the pregnancy, all hope of changing the name was lost. When Charmaine dug in her Jimmy Choos, they were stuck fast. It was not Charmaine's first victory over the O'Days, but it was to be one of her most significant and lasting. Although she was not particularly intelligent, she was mischievous, with a certain sly natural wit, which she usually paraded as innocence.

She brought round to Bellevue, one evening, a coffee-table book about roses. Before dinner she produced the book, a ribbon marking the place where there was a gleaming photograph of a luscious pale pink bloom. Charmaine read:

'The Ophelia rose is a hybrid tea, urn-shaped, double, perfumed. The blooms are creamy pale pink, with sparse leaves which are deep green, glossy, ovate with finely toothed edges. Most of the pests and diseases – to which this rose is quite susceptible – can be controlled with good cultural practices.' She looked up and repeated, 'controlled with good cultural practices', grinning, as if she found the phrase amusing. Was the idiot developing a crude sense of irony after all? Nobody spoke. This was really the first time Charmaine had ever actually *put a case* to the family, and there was something unsettling, something faintly ominous flickering around the moment. In the past she had simply done things, wilfully ignoring the unspoken rules of the Toorak

O'Days, without ever actively reasoning her position. This was a new Charmaine; reading aloud from a book was, for one thing, very new.

Quietly, from her deep armchair, her back stiff and inclined forward, Margaret spoke.

'Yes, it is a very lovely rose. I have one on the lower terrace. Sometimes I think of moving it, since it has never really flourished there. Perhaps my cultural practices are not good enough. But the blooms are certainly urn-shaped, that's accurate. Urn-shaped.' Margaret pushed her lips forward as she pronounced the word – *urn-shaped*. Quite slowly she said it, her eyes wide, her gaze moving carefully across the assembled family. Charmaine appeared to ignore what Margaret was saying, and she continued to smile serenely, perhaps even smugly. The truth was that naming a baby Ophelia made Margaret nervous. She wasn't entirely sure why this was so, but there was definitely something about it that troubled her. There was the madness and the drowning in *Hamlet*, of course, and there was also a painting Margaret knew from childhood – Ophelia disappearing beneath the water.

So on the afternoon of Ophelia Rose's baptism, while the family and their friends were gathered on the lawn, Margaret was standing in the tapestry room, so grandly named for the faded silken image of the *Lady with the Unicorn* that hung on the wall. This room was Margaret's personal domain. It was on the opposite side of the house to the den, which had belonged to 'my late husband, Edmund'. The two rooms perhaps complemented each other, one so masculine, the other feminine – or maybe they accentuated the sharp differences that existed between Margaret and Edmund, and that somehow bound them together. She was composed and proper, he inclined to be loud and excitable, even wild. He had played full-forward for Melbourne in his heyday, and was known as a ladies' man. With good reason. And as I have said, he came from the business O'Days, while Margaret, sharing a surname which they believed signified a family relationship in the distant past, came from the medical and artistic O'Days. In a curious way they made a perfect couple, particularly in public. They had negotiated well in the power struggle that is marriage, and everything went along smoothly in their healthy, wealthy world. Then Edmund died, and all the power went over to Margaret. All the power and none of the fun. She missed Edmund – well, everybody missed Edmund. The sons took over the business, and things went on as usual, although the Headstones that used to come up on the computers every morning disappeared. The staff were really sorry about that. Some of them tried to do it themselves, but it wasn't the same.

Pause here to look briefly at the two branches, to continue the tree metaphor, of the family. There were the Toorak O'Days, and the Eltham O'Days. The suburbs in which they lived and breathed and had their beings were statements also of the divide between them. Toorak is the grandest suburb of Melbourne. It's where the most powerful, most wealthy, most established families tend to congregate. Where the houses are spread, tall and solid and set in large grounds, where the streets are lined with handsome and sheltering trees, where security cameras have operated in every nook and cranny since time immemorial (you can see I am getting carried away with the pleasure of talking about it). Video surveillance was invented for the people of Toorak. Where there are nannies and butlers and permanent gardeners and housekeepers and even window washers – so much glass. Where the gates are electronically operated, where the garages hold many, many cars, and are often located underground. Consider the nature of the vast vehicles that deliver the hundreds of tiny children to the gates of the walled schools in the area, children with giant backpacks and cello cases spilling like tragic hopeful ants from the mysterious depths of conveyances designed to withstand military assault on rocky mountain roads. Remember that thing Shakespeare said about the boy 'creeping like snail unwillingly to school'? And his boy didn't even have the backpack, etc. Well, yes, I am describing luxury of a kind, and also a sort of moated existence. It's lovely, Toorak. Or weird and a little creepy – depends on your point of view. These days wealthy foreigners have almost overrun the place, edging out people such as the O'Days. And you will see evidence of this in the advertisement for the sale of Bellevue. Turn back if you will and consider the fact that the house is being sold not by a local agent in an office in Toorak Village, but exclusively online, by realestateaustralasia.com.au. Perhaps prospective foreign buyers will either buy it sight unseen, or will fly in with a code for opening the gates and doors, and a set of instructions.

It's a bit different in Eltham, which is out in the hills on the far wooded edges of the city and given to wild life – by which I mean birds and kangaroos and wombats and so on. Whereas the streets of Toorak have been smoothly macadamised for what seems like forever, many of the narrow hilly streets of Eltham are made from clay and orange gravel. Once upon a time an arty fellow built a kind of gothic pseudo-monastery there, and this became a glorious centre for the arts – painting, sculpture, music, stained glass, poetry, dance. Theatre, I imagine. Secular it was, the monastery, a place for joy and laughter and love and sex and drugs and drunken behaviour – well, you know, the arts. I think they grew a lot of vegies. Maybe grapes. They drank plenty of wine, I do know that. In the winding roads around about lived artists of all kinds. It was vibrant! And it was here that the other O'Days, the medical/artistic ones, set up shop/home. Margaret's father was the local and beloved doctor. (Keep an eye on that word 'beloved'.)

So that was the two branches of the family. Uniting them in Margaret and Edmund makes a bit of a glitch in the tree thing, really. Now back to Margaret in her tapestry room in Toorak. You can see that she has transported more than a little bit of Eltham to her new setting.

Collections of pots made by Eltham potters, and in a tall glass-fronted cabinet in the tapestry room, her collection of Famille-Verte, her beloved Chinese porcelain, the first piece of which was given to her by her own godmother at her baptism. In a more motley cabinet of curiosities, among the bric-a-brac of souvenirs collected by various members of the family from visits abroad, were the dark and mysterious artefacts, mementoes of horror, that Margaret's father and uncles brought back from New Guinea after the war, being the Second World War, 1939–45.

On the table beside her, this day of the baptism of Ophelia, in her tapestry room, were her field glasses. These were handsome, decorated in brass, and had belonged to her father who had been a keen wildlife watcher. She loved them, loved seeing the magnified world with, as it were, her father's eyes. She was quite deeply attached to her father, you will find. She picked the field glasses up and focused on the party under the oak tree. Yes, there *is* something disturbing in this image of Margaret spying on her own family in her own garden, but it was something she often did. I suppose if your family fortune is in the business of death, you can get into various creepy habits. And there before her was her world, arranged around the party table, celebrating the life of the child, signifying the hope of the future, telling the story of how, in spite of anything and everything, life will go on, and the sunlight will dapple down through the leaves and the laughter will drift up into the skies. Out beyond the little banquet, beyond the branches of the oak, beyond the rose garden, the tennis court, the pool, the river – beyond everything was everything else, Margaret knew, was the big wide world that turned, that rolled on, that swivelled its big blind eye to matters of babies' names. Playing a sort of observer god, she watched and mentally recorded the interplay of the guests in the garden. Talk about surveillance. These people are mad for it, aren't they?

Margaret watched young Father Justin Rhys out in the garden. Here's a nice new character, then. Father Rhys was urbane and affable, sporting a fine new panama hat which set off his handsome features and clerical collar, traitor in the matter of the baby's name, having blithely dribbled water on the child's head while intoning in his rich melodious voice 'Ophelia Rose' – like a presenter on a TV garden or cooking show. He was supposed to be Margaret's friend, even her ally, but he was powerless in the face of Charmaine and the names. Margaret could recall an old priest from her childhood, Father Garvey – by insignificant coincidence the good father belongs to the family that has since given us the nanny Smithereen – who was a bit deaf. He sometimes ignored the secular names such as Sandra and Lorna that were whispered to him at the font, and instead graced the babies with the names of saints. Was there a certain playfulness at work when he misheard the name of the dentist's baby Valerie and said 'Apollonia'?

When Father Rhys's friend – his life partner, if you must know – art master Clive Bushby started eulogising about the beauty of the name Ophelia and quoting lines from *Hamlet* about rosemary for remembrance and pansies for thought, Margaret quietly left the party table. She wasn't about to get into another discussion of the baby's wretched name. Went mad and threw herself in the river, for heaven's sake. Why don't people think about what they're saying?

When Lillian went up into the house to fetch another tray of sandwiches she called into the tapestry room to check on Margaret.

'Margaret, do you want some tea?'

'Oh yes, that would be so nice.'

'What about sandwiches, do you want some sandwiches?'

'Do you know, I think I would. Cress. I like the cress.'

You'd have to say this is a pretty rude way to go on at a party in your own house – a little private scoffing of cress sandwiches while you spy on your guests. Lillian was used to it. Margaret was just keeping an eye on things, and it takes a pot of Lapsang Souchong and a few tiny sandwiches to keep an eye.

Faithful Lillian knew more than a great deal about Margaret. She knew nearly everything. She knew, of course, about *The Book of Revelation*, which Margaret started shortly after the arrival in Toorak from Florida of a distant O'Day relative, Doria Fogelsong. Doria came shortly before Ophelia Rose's baptism, and she was a guest at the party in the garden.

She was researching the family history of the O'Days. That's a reasonable and ordinary thing to do, but there was something about Doria that seemed somehow out-of-the-way, that was unsettling. If Margaret was a bit leonine, and if Lillian was simian, then Doria was distinctly vulpine. It was as if Doria, with all her emphasis on the importance of the recent and distant past, had startled Margaret into taking stock of her own life. So there was Margaret, busily writing every day, noting the passing of time. She was wise to note the appearance of Doria, but then Margaret had a certain amount of second sight. I mean that, she did. She had occasional second sight. She knew somehow that Doria was the archetypal stranger who rides into town – Doria was the harbinger of fate. Do I overstate the case? I don't think so. We must watch out for Doria Fogelsong. She has inserted her way into the action and with her has come not a little evil magic. How will Margaret cope? How will anyone? Doria was in the party tableau that Margaret scrutinised from her window – the family at the happy feast, with the newly arrived visitor making herself very much at home.

Doria, I should tell you right now, is going to disappear quite suddenly from the lives of the people at Bellevue. Well, she's actually going to disappear from the face of the earth. Now there's a revelation for you. Let me save time and trouble by putting it in the language of the journalist:

> In Melbourne, July 2014, visiting American historian Dr Doria Fogelsong disappeared without trace. She had failed to arrive at a ceremony in Hobart on July the fifteenth. Her passport and possessions were found in her riverside apartment, which appeared to be undisturbed. Her pocketbook and the key to the apartment were missing. Police discovered her phone on the pebbles underneath an aloe beside the front door to the apartment building. It had last been used on the night of July the second. She had sent a text message, a short shopping list, to a local supermarket, and another (CALL ME) to a man named Benjamin Ross, who was unable to shed

any light on her disappearance. Examination of prior calls, texts and emails, as well as incoming messages, yielded no apparently useful information. Water police established that no trace of Dr Fogelsong could be found in the Yarra River.

So there was Margaret every night in bed, propped up on a pile of pillows, jotting away. *The Book of Revelation* was the kind of journal that is sometimes only jottings, but that sometimes resembles a story the writer expects to be read, a story full of the writer's own private thoughts and frank admissions, as well as a considerable number of revelations. Secrets. Sometimes Margaret talked to her reader. Sometimes this reader seemed to be part of herself, sometimes not. The journal ranged freely across the present and the past. It was memoir as conversation. Often she wrote with such detailed care that surely she supposed there would one day be a reader, a stranger who required a certain amount of explanation about things. In some ways she was writing her own private version of her world, a version that might one day stand against the grand work of family history on which Doria was embarked. The journal was loose and informal, moving freely from past to present, from sharp observation of others to the exploration of Margaret's own feelings.

You don't want to read the whole journal, you know. Margaret might be a matriarch, might be a pillar of the Church, might be a highly educated and sensitive woman, loving mother and grandmother and so on, but she isn't really such a great writer. I don't mind giving you bits and pieces, but I will need to interrupt from time to time, since what Margaret knows is not necessarily as much as I know. Trust me, remember?

Margaret did return to her guests under the oak tree, in due course. Clive had the table, in particular the children, in a roar with a story of a bishop and a monkey. And after that people started to pack up and leave. By eight o'clock that night Margaret sat up in her bed, opened a lovely big journal covered in blue linen, took her fountain pen (yes) and began to write. Jottings to begin with. Then she started to get into the swing of it, and she would write it just about every night. I must remind you that the quotes from E. R. O'Day are my doing, not hers.

Readings

from

The Book of Revelation

'My life is not as happy as it was, now I am dead.'
E. R. O'Day

Where to begin?
    (She really wrote that. Well, I guess she was talking to herself.)
    I could start with when I was born. Then what? Edmund would think this was all hilarious. Me keeping a journal suddenly. I miss him. A light went out when he died. He was the most alive person. That's why he made such a success of the family business. He used to say: 'In the midst of death we are in life.' He was always joking about funerals; I suppose you have to when you work with them all the time. I still think of him every day. Pray for him, of course. (She ran out of steam on Edmund at that point. Well, to be fair, there is probably a skill to starting a journal, particularly at her great age. She moved on to talk about Father Rhys and Clive Bushby, who were probably at the forefront of her mind, mainly because Father Rhys didn't back her up in the business of the baby's name. As if it mattered. I rather like the sound of the Ooops O'Daisies – it's a great name for a band.)

I remember when Justin Rhys was new to the parish and he appointed me as his unofficial mentor. 'Guide me in the mysterious ways of the little world around us, Lady Margaret.' Was he mocking me? I think he was. He still persists in calling me Lady Margaret sometimes. I do find this irritating. But he is charming, yes, and definitely competent and immensely popular. As I write I realise it is a lifetime since he first turned up with his long hair, and installed his Harley and his drum kit in the presbytery garage. He was scarcely more than a boy, yet he was appointed to the position of parish priest. Not that this is in any way a difficult parish. And Justin was definitely up to the job, being urbane and very clever. He won the hearts of the parishioners early on with his celebrated football sermon, which came to be known as 'Between the candlesticks and the goalposts'. Once, perhaps I was dreaming or dozing, I thought I heard him say in the middle of the Litany of Loreto: 'Lawn and Garden, Pray for us.' Surely he didn't say that? I mentioned it to him later, and he laughed and said that it was exactly what he had said. He can be wicked. Then there's his partner, Clive Bushby, to consider. So witty and affable. And yes, I do mean 'life partner'. Once this would have shocked me, but I have grown accustomed. Perhaps I am wiser than I used to be. Clive can be very amusing, and is incredibly popular at Loyola, a fine painter, and an excellent art master. The parish generally turns a blind eye. The diocese turns a blind eye. I am happy enough to turn a blind eye myself. Once when I said this to Edmund, I remember, he said that one day the blind eyes would all come home to roost.

Most of the parish accepts Justin without question. But one time silly, oozing Sissy Bagwell came up to me whispering the way she does and asked me if it was possible they were gay, Justin and Clive. I said what a strange suggestion, Sissy. But really I wanted to say that obviously they are gay, you idiotic woman, and what of it? People can be such sanctimonious fools. Perhaps the fact that one of my own sons, Paul, is gay makes me more tolerant, but really! Sissy is one of those women who advertises their own spirituality and perfection by constantly reminding other people that she has them in her prayers, whether they like it or not. When things turn out well for them, she claims responsibility.

I feel a little uncomfortable, writing about Sissy and Justin like this. But I suppose that's what happens in a journal: one betrays one's secret thoughts and opinions. And I *am* calling it *The Book of Revelation*, after all!

With Sissy, when things are not so good, the fault would appear to lie with the *subject* of the prayer, or elsewhere, not with the prayer itself. Certainly not with Sissy. Not with God, or with one of the saints or anything. She acts as if it's impossible to wilfully resist the magical formula of the great Cecilia Bagwell, who has a direct line to God. He will do her will. Except when He doesn't. But she never remembers those times. I once had the misfortune to sit beside her on a bus trip to somewhere for the blessing of a new church, and I remember how I squirmed when she announced in a very loud voice to the whole bus that she was praying for our safety on the journey. *She* was praying. Forget the driver, forget the work of people who maintain the bus – we were in the praying hands of silly Sissy Bagwell. Heaven help us!

Naturally I wouldn't mind if *Justin* got up and blessed the bus. That's his job, after all. But Sissy is just one of God's busybodies.

I happen to know that Sissy purposely travels on public transport in order to hand holy cards to fellow travellers. She quietly explains to people that she is praying for them and that the Virgin will protect them. I'm inclined to think the cards represent an evil spell. She looks rather sweet and harmless, although her enormous green eyes, which resemble gooseberries, really should be an indicator of the dangers within. I have always suspected a streak of cruelty in her. Am not really sure why. But I believe people generally accept the cards she gives out, and tolerate her. She's just a loony old woman. The mad arrogance of her attitude is in fact quite deadly. I make a point of avoiding her, mostly, and when I am cornered I have a way of just drifting, never engaging. There's a thing I do with my eyes that kind of empties them, as if I'm either far away or maybe not even there at all. It's simpler that way. I think the

Queen does this too. It's different if you ask someone to pray for you, or if you want them to. But Sissy blunders into people's lives like a great blind stupid swaying elephant in big black wellington boots. Bludgeon. Blunderbuss Bagwell. It's so nice to be able to write those words. I couldn't ever utter them, unless I said them to Lillian, I suppose. Dear Lillian. What she puts up with from me. I expect Sissy prays for Justin to see the light and to stop being gay. Or maybe not, actually, since she also gets a lot of pleasure out of examining what she thinks of as the sinful lives of others. I imagine she sees herself as a paragon of virtue. Well, of course she does. Although if she thinks her priest is sinful, she will have a terrible dilemma on her spiritual hands. Sidling around and whispering and piously interfering will get her nowhere. But she enjoys it all. She's a truly hideous woman, to be avoided. Note to self: Avoid Sissy Bagwell. Lillian is a prayerful woman, but so very different from Sissy. Lillian reminds me of my mother. The way she wipes her hands on her apron, the way she tilts her head and smooths a lock of hair back from her forehead. I suppose the difference, the real difference, between Lillian and Sissy is the difference between humility and arrogance. Lillian's respect for others, Sissy's belief in her own direct line to God. It makes me tired to even think about Sissy. But I will. I'll write a little biography of her. Here goes.

 We were at school together; she was Cecilia Feeney, known as Sissy, one of a whole tribe of Feeneys from Mount Macedon. She was in the boarding house. In those days, as my aunts would say, butter wouldn't melt in her mouth. Twice she was cast as Mary in the Christmas pageant. Soon after she left school she joined the Carmelites, but she came out after about three years and suddenly married Mark Bagwell, who had been in training for the priesthood. In those days such cases were rarer than they are now, and Sissy and Mark were something of a curiosity at the time, but they gradually blended in to the scheme of things and had four children. He died quite young on a boating trip in Belgium or somewhere. Some people said there was a suggestion of suicide. Sissy could have been a factor, in my opinion. She's enough to drive anyone to despair. Something she did afterwards struck me at the time as being strange. She crossed Mark's name off the stickers on the back of her mail. Just simply crossed him out with texta, and the stickers lasted for years and years, every Christmas a card from Sissy with Mark obliterated by thick blobs of red ink. But apart from that, her misplaced piety and prayer surely belonged safely back in the convent where perhaps it could be retrained or at least contained. Even put to good use. But she's out in the world, bustling and bumping about like a lead balloon until she dies. Or like Richard the Third – he said he had the world to bustle in. That might be going a bit far. Sissy hasn't murdered anybody.

Yes, I am judgemental. I think it's a matter of self-preservation, actually. I forgive myself. There, then.

There is, I have understood since early childhood, an etiquette of prayer whereby you can, indeed must, pray for others, but seldom talk about it, and certainly not in the smug, bullying way of Sissy Bagwell. Prayer is a bit like money in a way. We never actually talk about money and probably shouldn't talk about prayer. Well, once upon a *time* we didn't talk about money, but nowadays there's a great deal of talk about it, and, for that matter, about everything under the sun, including people's intimate lives, which seem to me to be incredible, beyond imagining. And prayer might be as good a thing to talk about as anything else. All my children are on Facebook and Twitter and all the rest of it, as are several of my grandchildren, and many of my friends. And there it seems to be practically mandatory to rabbit on about every little thing.

I think I prefer talking to myself here in my journal. Am I afraid of something? Of being unmasked? But I don't think I am masked in the first place. Am I? Am I wearing a mask? What a funny thought. Should I just be baring my soul on Facebook? Would that do me good?

I had an aunt who would probably have loved Facebook. She was a great one for announcing that she was saying a novena for this one or that one, and even as a child I thought I could see that the ostentation of her carryings-on was some weird kind of self-promotion, something horrible. In her handbag she had a tiny red book where she would tick off the corporal works of mercy as she performed them. So she would be sure to feed the hungry, water the thirsty, shelter the stranger, clothe the naked, visit the sick, comfort the afflicted, bury the dead. The most significant feature of her appearance was not so much her stony, uncharitable and disapproving eye, but the grim and narrow horizontal line of her colourless lips. She appears sometimes in old family photos, a dreadful sanctimonious presence in dark clothing. There's one picture of her with a dead kangaroo. I remember that one quite vividly. One day I may find, tucked in a box or a drawer in an attic or a cellar, the handful of those red books. Would I have the strength to burn them? I wonder. I am pretty sure I would. I like to think I am quite tough and practical.

Are they the kind of thing Doria Fogelsong is looking for, those little red books? I rather think they are. I will keep coming back to Doria because she worries me. Edmund would say she has come here to upset the pigeons and put a cat among the apples in the applecart. I still enjoy thinking of his jokes, and making up jokes he might have told.

The aunt with the red books was Auntie Ruffle, one of a large number of aunts. She was from my father's side of the family. There were jolly fat aunts and mean skinny ones. Ruffle was one of the skinnies. Once when I was in bed with a sore throat she came to visit me. I remember a dark purple apparition with a nasty slippery black leather handbag from which she produced a packet of jelly beans for me. They had been in the bag for a long time, and their surfaces were crazed with faint lines. I actually saw her, as she was about to leave, take from her handbag the little red book which had the tiniest gilded pencil attached by a ribbon. She licked the pencil, licked her finger, flicked the pages and made a discreet tick – I suppose she was checking off 'visit the sick'. My father used to joke about her, saying that she was after all part of what he called the Funereal O'Days, whose actual business it was to fulfil the order to 'bury the dead'. He found it quite amusing when I married into the funereal branch of the family. But he and my mother were very fond of Edmund, my dear Edmund, who was so debonair. And handsome. And very clever too. He was the one who brought O'Day Funerals right into the modern world. He developed Heavenly Days out on reclaimed land that nobody wanted. He had a real flair for business. Our son Joseph is much the same, although I hope he is at least more faithful to Charmaine than Edmund was to me. I mustn't get started on Charmaine. Edmund's besetting sin was his unfaithfulness. I forgave him. I decided it was the best thing to do for all concerned. His flirting could sometimes be quite endearing in a way. Like when he ran off for the afternoon with the beautiful daughter of the Hungarian family who were having their regular musical picnic at their plot out at Heavenly Days. Oh, Edmund!

But back to the aunts – another time when I had tonsillitis, one of the fatties, Auntie Vera, brought me a box of coloured pencils and stayed with me all day. We drew pictures in a big blank book and drank pineapple cordial.

'See how fast you can draw a penguin, Margaret, and I will draw the ice. I do really good ice. Hurry up or it will melt before your eyes and the water will ruin the paper.' She was very kind and funny and wore floppy floral dresses. I loved the pencils. But Vera was a kleptomaniac and when she left that afternoon she had packed up in her very big leather bag two of my mother's treasured cups and saucers – periwinkle-blue Wileman Dolly Vardens from the late nineteenth century. My mother knew what had happened and said Vera couldn't help herself and we just had to be kind and understanding. I think this was a mistake, but I don't quite know what I think should have been done. Should we have actually confronted Vera with her crime and destroyed her? Would it have been for her own good if she had had to face the truth? I always regretted the loss of the cups and saucers, being so fond of china, but was never allowed to mention them. They sat in a glass cabinet at Vera's house, gloriously blue and twinkling, like a pair of princesses, alongside dozens of other different kinds of china pieces, none of them particularly valuable. Where did she get the others from, I wonder? Was the whole collection just a cache of stolen goods? I don't really know how we were related to Vera – I think she was married to a cousin of a cousin. She was on my father's side of the family, so there's an O'Day connection of some kind.

This would be Doria's territory again, the unravelling of the connections. I hate the thought of her unravelling. The past is all knitted up to produce the present what can be gained by undoing it and twisting it all up again? I actually think I am a true romantic, that I wish for the unfathomable past to remain unfathomable.

Aunt Vera had two sons who were much older than me. Trevor married an Italian girl, Sofia, and Malcolm was probably gay – he lived with a poet in the wilds of Tasmania and they kept bees. I think Trevor and Sofia went to live in South Australia where her family has vineyards. I have lost touch with all of these people, but I sometimes think of them in the context of how the family tree branches and fans out to a kind of infinity. The idea makes me dizzy. I can't follow family trees very well for some reason; I find them complicated. Although I like trying to puzzle out the histories of royalty, which are much clearer because they have been properly worked out for centuries. My father, being of Irish descent, had no time for the British royal family, yet he was fascinated by the Czars. And so am I. Mother, being originally Methodist, loved the King and Queen, and little princesses. I got a toy golden coach for the Coronation in 1953. It wasn't really a toy. I was too old for toys. It was a perfect miniature. It's in one of my cabinets.

Doria will take care of our family tree, so I don't really have to think about that. But Doria herself is another story altogether. I keep thinking about *her*. I hope she doesn't cause trouble somehow. There's something there I don't understand. I hope I'm not being unfair. I wonder what Lillian makes of Doria.

Going back to Vera, though: I remember with shame a day when her son Trevor was trying to say that something was 'obvious'. Twice he said 'ovbious', and both times I sniggered. I could be a bit of a prig. One time we went to Tasmania for a holiday and my loveliest memory is of the visit to Malcolm and the poet Noah Rhys (a distant relative of Father Justin. How things do connect sometimes). I don't remember Noah very well. He had a beard. We played in the wild orchard where big fat apricots were hanging from the trees. Underneath the trees there were boxes of bees, in rows like mysterious white dolls' houses, I thought. We had honeycomb and fresh scones for afternoon tea under a weeping willow. The branches hung like a fountain all around us. I'm getting a little poetic now. Perhaps memories do that to you. We ran in and out among the leaves. The honey had a smoky flavour, and Trevor said they achieved that by making bonfires of old cheque-book stubs and taxation returns. I wonder if that was really true.

So much of life is memory. That day under the willow tree in Tasmania frequently comes back to me in a lovely glow, and I wonder, was it so beautiful at the time? Or does distance lend it an artificial glamour? Have I half invented it?

'There is a willow grows aslant a brook, that shows his hoar leaves in the glassy stream.' Now I'm thinking about Ophelia again. Oh, why did she call the baby that?

It was like a personal betrayal today when Justin poured the water and said 'Ophelia Rose' and the deed was done. He has a lovely voice. He had no alternative; his function is simply to give the baby a provisional ticket to heaven. He probably wouldn't know very much about *Hamlet* and so on anyway. Or would he? Is he more educated than I think he is? But in any case I don't suppose the names of babies trouble him at all. Babies just pass through his blessing hands week after week. It's more or less routine. And the second name is Rose, so that's a saint at least.

I have only ever heard of one baby named Ophelia before, and she died at birth, so that's a sad memory attached to it. Perhaps that's really why I wish Charmaine hadn't chosen the name.

It was early in 1941 and so I was five. For some reason the name of that baby has stayed with me. I used to sit quietly in the background, or even under the table, and I was always listening to the grown-up conversations. I have a clear recollection of my mother and her sister, Auntie Iris, in the garden talking about a girl called Kitty. She used to come and do the ironing. She had long pale red hair and she would play with me. I remember a jack-in-the-box made from brightly painted tin. Kitty would pretend not to understand how it worked, and then she would scream and laugh, and throw up her hands when the lid flew open and Mr Punch jumped out at us. Kitty's mother made fantastic biscuits and scones, and sometimes Kitty would bring us some of these in a basket, wrapped in a tea-towel. They smelled like heaven. Even in war time, with rations, we had butter from a neighbour's cows, and cream, and jam made from our own fruit, using the sugar rations. The pantry was always filled with jars of jam and chutney and pickles, as well as bottled fruit.

'Killian,' my mother would say to my father when he reached for a second scone, 'you can have one, do you hear, one.'

And he would always say in a singing voice – was it a song, I wonder? – 'Muriel, I hear you with my ears, but my hand can't understand.' He would pop another one into his mouth, and Mother would smack his hand and laugh.

My mother was with Auntie Iris, one of the nice fat ones. She had grey hair like steel wool, I thought, although I hated steel wool and I still do. The feel of it, and it sets my teeth on edge. She was the only member of my convert mother's Methodist family who ever visited us. They were talking in low, sad, earnest voices while they were wandering around the garden dead-heading the roses. I was walking beside them. They were wearing gloves, and would hold a branch delicately with one hand, go snippety-snip with the secateurs, and drop the dead flower into a basket on the path. They were punctuating their sentences with the snip of the stems and the soft plop of the flowers as they fell into the basket. The 'plop' is I think too loud for the sound the flowers made. Yes. There was almost no sound, more like a space in time than a sound. But the 'snip' was real. This is my memory of what I heard. I will try to write dialogue, like a play. I've just remembered the connection between the name Ophelia and a picture we had. We had a lot of pictures. We lived in Eltham. Pictures and pots.

'The poor child – snip – died within hours – plop – and yes – snip – the baby I understand lived for – snip – minutes only – plop.'

'And you say – snip – that Kitty called her – plop – Ophelia?'

Silence. 'Yes, Ophelia.'

Silence. 'Why, I wonder?'

'Oh, I have – snip – no idea – plop – I suppose she must have heard it somewhere and liked it. Well, there is the picture over the piano, Nellie Melba as Ophelia. Actually, Killian used to say Kitty looked like Melba in that picture. Perhaps she did. The hair. Sister Victoire added "Mary" I believe, to the name – snip – when the baby was baptised – plop. It was an emergency baptism, of course.'

Silence. 'Oh, I see. Ophelia Mary. Don't breathe a word to Ruffle. You know I really can't stand the way she carries on and on about the virtue of her own prayers. She would start rattling off novenas right, left and centre.'

'As if nobody else ever uttered a prayer, as if everything in the world depended on Ruffy's own conversations with God and the saints. I suppose it's hard for Catholics. Religion is so complicated for them. Do you find that, Muriel? Poor Ruffle. She should have married whatshisname – Desmond – that might have kept her sane.'

'It might have driven Desmond mad. Who did he marry?'

'Violet Snooks. They had seven boys and three girls, and made a fortune in chickens.'

The mention of Mrs Snooks gave me a shiver of disgust. She had big false teeth like a horse, and a habit of shifting the top row somehow with her tongue so that they appeared sideways on, almost vertical in her mouth. I think she did this absent-mindedly, not to be nasty or scary, but it was so ugly and it frightened me very much. It makes me quite sick now to think of it.

And so my mother and Auntie Iris went on their slow progress around the rose garden. Snip, plop, snip, as the chatter rambled on and they moved the basket along beside them on the path. As well as cutting off the dead heads of the roses, they would pinch green aphids between thumb and finger, and then flick the dead insect into the air, onto the grass. My mother would then always wipe her hand across the bodice of her apron, leaving a nasty smudge of squashed insect. Auntie Iris, for some reason, didn't bother. Life in the garden was a constant battle against insects such as the aphids, and against blight, and scale, and curly leaf, and snails and slugs, not to mention birds, such as the cockatoos that could strip a cherry tree between breakfast and afternoon tea. We had scarecrows. We had all kinds of poisons in sprays and pumps and powders. I remember we always had to wash the apples properly because they were coated in arsenic. Yes, it was a constant battle. Today is very little different, although naturally the gardens here at Bellevue are largely controlled by Rowan and his nephew whose name I can never remember. It's either Kyle. Or Karl. How rude of me. But they sound the same. I must find out what his name is and make an effort to remember.

My mother used to make Honey of Roses with the young healthy petals of her dark red roses; I now make up her recipe myself. There is a deep shelf in the pantry where I keep it in small jars, dozens of them like secret jewels. I like to give them to people for presents. For the record: Take four ounces of dried red rose petals, having removed the white heels before drying. Also three pints of boiling water and five pounds of the finest honey. Ounces, pints, pounds. This is old-fashioned magic. Pour water onto petals and stand for six hours. Strain and add honey. Boil to a thick consistency.

I see I have written 'for the record'. But now I wonder why I did that. Who is going to read my *Book of Revelation*? Perhaps in the distant future, when I am dead and gone, Ophelia Rose might discover it in a box of old things. The blue linen cover faded. Oh, I wonder what she will make of my feelings about her name.

All the memories of those times at our house in Eltham glow with sunlight. Lovely rows of washing flap about on the clothes line. Everything smells of the sun. Moments in the past seem to light up in my memory like scenes from a film. They are not always important moments – sometimes I recall tiny flashes of things that seem to have very little real significance. I will suddenly think of a place, a gutter brimming with brown water, or a thing such as a particular slice of bread and butter and blackberry jam, the deep red of the runny jam sliding over the butter and soaking into the sweet spongy white of the bread. Yes, I think I am getting poetical, as Lillian would say.

I sometimes remember with a jolt of surprise that my mother came from a family of Methodists, and that she converted when she married my father. It suddenly came to my mind as I recalled the conversation in the rose garden. I don't quite know why I thought of it. Probably because Iris was there, and she represented my mother's family. My mother had mentioned the painting of Dame Nellie Melba; I loved that picture. It resembled some of the works of Renoir, but was actually by a painter called Henri Gervex. It's a beautiful picture I think, but also sad and perhaps ominous. Hardly anybody has heard of Henri Gervex these days, but my father had a great liking for his work. I think it was the print of his coronation of Nicholas and Alexandra that first sparked my lifelong passion for the Russian royal family. My father was fascinated by Russian history, and I have some of his books. Now often I read about the Romanovs, and experience the anguish of their final months and their last moments. How can I even begin to imagine such anguish? What captivates me is the horror of a family of human beings, first of all set in a world of luxury and riches beyond belief, then reduced to trapped creatures in the dark cellar, dying by the will of the people they had promised to serve. The cellar, trapped forever in the cellar. I have a shelf of books about them, and there is a never-ending trickle of more and more books as the years go by and as different facts come to light, as different storytellers tell the tale. It's my obsession, or one of them. I have sometimes longed to travel on the Trans-Siberian railway, but I realise that it can never really take me into the romantic past, which is where I would like to go. It's just a dream. A childish fantasy. Another preoccupation I have, not unrelated to the Russian one, is the death of Princess Diana. My family by and large don't share these interests, but they humour me, giving me the latest books on the subject. I return in sorrow quite often to the thought of the nightmare moments in the Pont d'Alma tunnel. The noise of splitting metal squeals in my ears and sets my teeth on edge. But I really have no idea what it would be like. When I try to imagine it I feel my teeth clenching, and my face screws up as if I am staring into the sun or something. That's just one thing. So much vitality and loveliness so suddenly gone.

But to return to Kitty and Ophelia – when I studied *Hamlet* at school the distant conversation about Kitty and Ophelia echoed in my mind, the tragic young Ophelia in the story merging with the tragic young Kitty, everything blurring into a dreadful sadness. And in fact after listening to Mother and Iris in the rose garden, I went inside and sat for a long time studying the print of Nellie Melba above the piano. Yes, Ophelia *did* look like Kitty. Kitty singing, her dear mouth open. You could almost see the notes sailing out of her lips. She had a pretty voice. Somehow even the slightly crooked little teeth in the picture looked like Kitty's teeth. The floppy scarlet poppies in her hair and the dangerous water up to her armpits. She clutches the fragile reeds with her left hand. Nothing will save her as she is steadily pulled under into the deep and slimy water.

Round the time of that conversation I overheard in the garden, my father went to join a medical unit in Tobruk, and the picture of Melba was replaced by a photograph of Daddy, handsome in his uniform. My father was everything to me. When I was a child I truly believed he was supernatural. Now that I think of it, I have never seen our picture of Melba since, although I've occasionally seen a print, but it's vivid in my mind, hanging so brightly in its gilt frame there above the piano. I saw a rather fuzzy print of it in a book quite recently, and I had a strange thought that Melba looked as if she had a tongue piercing. Heavens, that's not possible.

Rupert and Gustav have a nanny with a tongue piercing. She's called Smith. And Charmaine's sister KayKay has a huge thing on her tongue that flashes as she talks. I try not to look at her. She also has more tattoos than any of the other young women in the family, and that's saying something. What happens when they are old and all those strange inky pictures start to shrivel up, I wonder. The nice boy who serves us at the ice-cream shop has red and black flames rising from under his collar, all up his neck, licking onto his face. He told me this is in memory of his late grandfather.

Back to memories of Father. They say girls often marry a man who reminds them of their father. In my case nothing could be further from the truth. Edmund and Daddy were complete opposites. Daddy was utterly dedicated to my mother, utterly faithful to her and to God and also to his patients. He was the very best kind of old-fashioned family doctor, the best kind of old-fashioned father. And Edmund. Well, I have written about Edmund.

The war. Father's absence and then his miraculous return from the war are also somehow mingled in my mind with what happened to Kitty and her baby Ophelia. I took the jack-in-the-box to the beach one summer and I left it in the sand dunes and never saw it again. I've forgotten many of my old toys, but the shiny tin jack-in-the-box with his cheap ugly face frequently springs up at me, for no apparent reason, and I feel again the pain of the regret and of his loss. I wonder if he lay forever rusting and silent under the sand, or whether someone found him and took him home and laughed at him over and over until his spring broke and he was tossed away or left in the garden shed or the attic for all eternity. The loss of him reminds me always of the disappearance of Kitty and of the non-existence of baby Ophelia Mary. Then I think of the picture of Nellie Melba, and then of the photo of my noble father over the piano. He looks so handsome and so good. The same picture of him hung beside the picture of Peter Pan in my bedroom. Peter Pan in Kensington Gardens with children and fairies. Above them was a Madonna and Child. I remember this odd trio of pictures so vividly – I must have looked up at it every night. Father and the Madonna and Peter Pan.

Years after I had listened to my mother and Iris talking about baby Ophelia, I wrote an essay about Ophelia and Hamlet and it won the prize for the best essay in the school. Now that I remember the essay prize, it gives me confidence to keep writing this journal. Ophelia drowned. Nellie Melba drowned. Kitty died and the baby died. The photograph of my father, the soldier, hanging in the place where Kitty as Melba used to be. The war.

Perhaps I'm being unfair if I allow these memories and prejudices to affect my feelings about the naming of my new grand-daughter. It is sometimes hard to know – but in this case I really believe I'm right, and it is simply not a good *name*. Are there good names and bad names? I think there are. Mine is a good name. St Margaret of Antioch, patron saint of childbirth. She was removed from the Roman calendar in 1969 on the grounds that she was a myth, but I don't really think that makes much difference. St Christopher and St George suffered the same fate, but people generally have taken little notice. St Philomena also. You still see travellers all over the world relying on St Christopher to keep them out of danger.

I must soon start work on a quilt for our baby Ophelia. There seems to be so much to do, and perhaps I was holding off making it because I hoped she was going to get a better name. I do a name quilt for every baby, even Frederick and Julian. I try not to leave them out of anything, ever. And I do love them.

Ophelia Rose is a very pretty baby, but she has Charmaine's idiotic drama-queen sister KayKay for a godmother. There she was at the church, KayKay, flooping around the place in her grandmother's Carrickmacross mantilla. 'Flooping' is a word I borrowed from Lillian. Oh, such exquisitely fine lace spiderwebs! Then later she was out in the garden with the precious thing flung around her shoulders rather like a football scarf. Perhaps it's just as well, since she was wearing very little else. So much bony flesh. Such long legs. Such tottering and glittering Jimmy Choos. Her proper name's Karina, not KayKay. Charmaine is often called simply Charm, but I can't really bring myself to say that. It's so silly. Should I pity Ophelia Rose for her mother's choice of godmother? Probably. But I have to say that I feel a longing, bordering on envy, for the sisterly relationship between Charmaine and KayKay. They have a deep connection that has always been denied me, and they cherish each other in a way that I can never really know. I used to beg my mother and father for a baby sister. All I had were brothers. My father promised me a sister, and I longed for her, but she never came. Daddy was so magical that he should have been able to give me a sister. I used to pray to St Margaret, but nothing ever happened.

One of my favourite books is *Sense and Sensibility*. And I think that the real reason I love it is because of the bond between the sisters. When I'm reading that novel I become lost in the feeling of that bond. It's a feeling that is so deep and wonderful. It makes me sad, but somehow it comforts me. Elinor and Marianne. I identify with Marianne. I do love Elinor too. But it's the life of sisters that I really wish for, the closeness, the intimacy, the support, the fun, the sharing. Sometimes I realise that Lillian is like a kind of sister. A gift and a treasure and a sister.

Before the afternoon of the christening was over KayKay disappeared next door to spend the evening with that silly fool of a psychiatrist Evan. It seems he is her latest paramour. We did invite him to the christening, but he was due to play cricket with a bunch of his psychiatric colleagues in Hawthorn, and he declined the christening. Rather rude perhaps, but that's Evan. Tootling over to the cricket match in his precious 1962 pink MGB. Pink! He sent the baby a most elaborate and valuable silver spoon. And also there's nothing at all wrong with the dear Famille-Rose peach bird vase KayKay gave to Ophelia Rose. It's valuable and rather rare, naturally I realise that. KayKay explained that she got it on eBay, as if that made it more interesting and exciting somehow. Well, perhaps it does. However, it's the clumsy *imitation* of the gesture of my own godmother that is so infernally irritating. 'Margaret has the Verte and now dear little Ophelia will have the

Rose. I thought that was rather fitting,' KayKay said in her barking voice that seems to come from somewhere at the back of her neck. What is 'fitting' about it I can't quite see. How is it those girls can, without fail, contrive to be so wrong when they are in fact, to all intents and purposes, in the right? It's a kind of skill, a gift in its way, I suppose. A genetic idiocy or crassness coming out. I never took to their late mother, Imogen, who shared the same ability. But how she suffered, poor soul, in the end. She simply crumpled up and crumbled away to nothing, disappearing like gelatin in boiling water, dissolved. It took years, as one treatment after another failed. She was with the Sisters at the Five Wounds, and I occasionally visited her, a truly sobering and I have to say horrifying experience. Because of my faith I don't fear death, but illness and ageing are an altogether different matter. Jim Donovan was her doctor and keeps a close eye on me. He reminds me in many ways of my father. An old-fashioned doctor. The nuns at Five Wounds are incredible women, so cheerful and patient and matter of fact. The last time I saw her, Imogen resembled, I thought, a tiny paper mouse with terror in its small black eyes. Life can be so strange and tragic, and I sometimes think in my heart that there is no comfort to be found. None at all anywhere. These thoughts are obviously heresy, as the Church offers the comfort of the life to come, but this is often very difficult to reconcile with the problems and pain of life on earth. I looked into Imogen's eyes and I saw the depth of fear in them. I was shocked and afraid. Edmund used to make up all kinds of strange sayings about death. He sent them to the staff every day. They seemed to like that. I have never had very much to do with the running of the business, although I did advise Edmund on the kinds of rides and so forth for Heavenly Days. What fun that was! That place has been a huge success.

In any case, poor Imogen in her heyday, when she was very popular and vivacious, used to display the same crassness and stupidity as her daughters. I quite vividly recall the time she turned up at a Red Cross bushfire relief centre with five Christmas hams and fancy jars of cranberry sauce when what was required were ordinary cans of baked beans and loaves of sliced bread. And now she is gone and Ignatius has rushed off and married, in unseemly haste, one of the Callie girls from South Australia. Vanessa Callie. They're wine growers, and are in fact in competition with the Italian family into which distant Tasmanian cousin Trevor married. Doria likes that kind of link, I believe. I must remember to tell her. Note to self. Tell Doria about Trevor. Vanessa is half the age of Ignatius, and exceptionally pretty in an empty-headed sort of way. She's vacuous; that's the word, vacuous. Fortunately they're on holiday in France at present, so they couldn't come to the christening. That, in any case, is a blessing. Imagine the poor child having Vanessa Callie for a grandmother; well, step-grandmother I suppose. They sent an antique Galway crystal mug. It's a rather ugly thing, I think, but perfectly acceptable.

I sometimes astonish myself as I record all these things in this book, but the recording has, in the past few days, become a kind of comfort to me. I seldom go to sleep at night before writing these thoughts, sometimes so rambling and diffuse, in these secret and very personal pages. Am I talking to myself, or talking to a non-existent reader outside myself? Who is 'Dear Diary'? Nobody has ever really established that particular identity. These are quiet reflections of my own, for my eyes only. I daresay I will never actually read them over. Should I write an instruction for the book to be burned when I die, or do I secretly wish that Charmaine and KayKay and Evan, and everybody, even Sissy, might know what I was really thinking about them? How well do I know myself and my own motives? I believe I try to do what is right and good, but do I? Do I? Silly Sissy Bagwell goes around imagining she is doing good. But am I so very different from Sissy, after all? What a truly horrible thought.

A Virtual Stranger

'Life's but a walking shadow.'
E. R. O'Day

Well, that was a lot of food for thought. We now know a fair bit about Margaret's life, in bits and pieces. She keeps letting the idea of Doria drift in, doesn't she? Yes, Doria bothers Margaret.

And how about the christening gifts, then? They are, as usual in Margaret's world, lavish and generally beautiful. Silver spoons and cups and a string of seed pearls and corals, the Heritage edition of Beatrix Potter, cloth covered, in its slipcase, one small brown rabbit wandering along the yellow pathway through the soft green woods. A lovely thing. A nineteenth-century silver medal of the Infant of Prague from Margaret's daughter Rafaela in Paris, accompanied by chewable Sophie la Girafe, something without which no respectable French baby could exist, let alone grow teeth. A shiny little suitcase containing a suite of *Very Hungry Caterpillar* games, books and toys. A Dean's bear, which is a family tradition – Margaret herself gives one at some stage to each baby, along with a rosary made from Irish horn. Someone in Charmaine's family has sent a spherical Moorcroft vase – the design is 'Ophelia's Flowers'. The opening at the top is small and black, really rather sinister. But the rarest and most astonishing object is the antique silver rattle with dark red coral handle. And who brought this precious object? The virtual stranger Doria Fogelsong. Doria arrived from Florida a week before the christening, and is living in a serviced apartment nearby. By what right is she a guest at Ophelia Rose's christening?

Dr Doria Fogelsong was born Doria Angel O'Day in San Francisco in 1965, the only child of Rita and Frank O'Day, musicians and film-makers. She married banker Phelan Fogelsong in New York in 1985, had no children, worked as an academic historian, was widowed in 2003 when Phelan was fatally stung by a bee, moved to Winter Park, Florida, in 2005 and has since been researching her family with the intention of publishing a vast and serious history of the O'Days. Phew! I didn't realise I could cover a life in so few words. In 2013 she first made contact with Margaret, and here she is, five days after arriving in Australia, in the very heart of the family under the old oak tree.

Doria is thin and sandy, with pale ginger hair, worn in a youthful ponytail, tamed by a stern gold clip. Don't you just hate that? The swinging girly hair-bounce and the devastating expensive jewellery with teeth. It's real gold, all right. Her face is narrow, her eyes bright amber and darting, with pale lashes. Tawny eyes of one kind or another run through the O'Days. Sometimes they lend a reptilian air, sometimes feline – in Doria's case, as I've already noted, they are vulpine – and can be quite alluring in their way. In Doria's case they do – well, kind of nothing. I realise I sound as if I have it in for Doria, and this could be true. She has large feet. Well, so do I, actually. She somehow radiates a terrible intelligence. She doesn't appear to wear makeup apart from pink lipstick, and her skin is dry, faintly peppered with small freckles, and alert with pale hairs. There is an aroma of patchouli about her, as if she were some kind of fossil flower-child left over from Haight-Ashbury. I said 'musicians and film-makers' – that was code for hippie, I think. Her parents were in fact hippies in their time. Margaret is wary of people whose perfume offends her, and patchouli offends her, oh yes. The white pantsuit Doria is wearing gives her a nautical air, and her neck, ears, wrists and fingers are decorated with more elaborate gold jewellery. Margaret glances at the visitor's ankles, expecting more chains and charms, but they are free of embellishment. Her toenails are painted white. Hmmm. Her toes, as it happens, are incredibly smooth and baby-like. Not what you'd expect. Her voice, which Margaret hears as something vaguely out of Hollywood, is confident and not unmusical. Her teeth are small and even and not very white, and she has a way of flashing a big American smile that does her and nobody else any favours. Her eyes don't appear to smile, or not very often. I have had a very good look at her, you see. She is tickled pink, she says, to find herself right at the heart of such a historic O'Day moment as the baptism of a brand-new member of the tribe. Tickled pink.

Watch out for this one.

For herself, Margaret is inclined to think that nothing could be less interesting, more tedious than researching family history, although she says she realises some of the things it turns up could be quite intriguing. She claims she was always more concerned with the immediate present and the future, not the past, although her own love of recollection and memory could give the lie to this claim. And her recently started journal is, as we know, full of ramblings down memory lane. Margaret is probably quite complex, really. Strangely enough, she nurtures deep in her heart a long-held secret desire to discover a link between herself and the Romanovs. Not that she is actively searching for this. She somehow hopes, vaguely, that one day the link might just become apparent. Such things have been known to happen. What she said in the journal about being interested in Russian history — well, that was true enough, but she was masking the deeper, sillier fact of her true thought, her true desire. If she knew anything about genealogy she would realise how very unlikely this relationship is, but she chooses to dream. She imagines she resembles one of the princesses, perhaps Tatiana. In fact, she doesn't.

While it's fashionable in Australia nowadays to find Indigenous people and nineteenth-century convicts on the family tree, Margaret doesn't follow the fashion at all. Secretly, since she was about eleven, she has longed to be linked to the beautiful and tragic girls in far off romantic Russia, princesses who died in the cellar with all their fabulous jewellery sewn into their clothes. A small and rather cheap modern 'icon' of the Russian royal family hangs on the wall beside Margaret's bed. The faces are the idealised images of saints. One long shelf in her tapestry room is devoted to her collection of books about the Romanovs. Whenever she takes down one of these books she becomes lost in the world of early twentieth-century Russia – not so much in the details of the hard lives of the millions of ordinary people, or the savage and desperate acts of revolutionaries, but in the intense drama and colour and poignant tragedy of the royal household. *Anna Karenina* is her favourite novel and she has read it in an almost continuous way since she was sixteen. There are maybe six different translations on her bookshelf, not that Margaret could be described, by any stretch of the imagination, as a scholar. She's a reader and a collector. Harmless enough in her way. Another book she often goes back to read is Lesley Blanch's *Journey into the Mind's Eye*. Margaret loves the idea of the Traveller in that book.

Ordinary forms of family history have become all the rage, as you would know. And even Charmaine, for whom history has hitherto been a closed book, claims to find it fascinating. Who knows what fantasies Charmaine might be harbouring about her own forbears as she trawls through ancestry.com in the early hours of the morning when feeding Ophelia Rose? Doria and her family-history project are now frequently the centre of the conversation among the O'Days of Bellevue. Margaret thinks perhaps she should send Doria off to Tasmania to get her out of the way. She could follow up on what became of Auntie Vera's Malcolm and his beehives. Maybe *he* has the periwinkle cups and saucers somewhere there in the wild woods under the willow tree. But probably he is no longer living, and the cups, the dear periwinkle cups, are no doubt piled in the back of a glass cabinet in a seaside antique shop where tourists glimpse them fleetingly and pass by. That's a sad thought, isn't it. Perhaps they are smashed into shards of periwinkle, into slivers of the lady's dress, scattered and buried in the shallow graves of ancient vegetable patches. Doria must inevitably go to Tasmania – there are O'Days and their derivatives all along the north-west coast, particularly at Woodpecker Point and the old mining town of Copperfield.

As for the baby's rattle, did Doria bring it with her in her luggage on the off chance she would be invited to a family christening? What do you think? Or did she have it sent express from her cache of such objects in Florida? Is that possible? There is a sense that with Doria many strange things are possible. Or did she perhaps find it in a Melbourne antique shop, and concoct the whole story of its history? How reliable is she? Does any of this matter? What the rattle does is lodge Doria more firmly in the heart of the family that gathers under the heritage-listed oak for Ophelia Rose's party.

Doria, ravelling and unravelling threads and fibres – forgive my metaphors – has already located the place on the family tree at which the two O'Day branches, medical and business, Eltham and Toorak, diverged in the nineteenth century. In doing so she establishes the long-lost and unexplored blood link between Margaret and Edmund. The connection had to be there, and has for years been a subject of only passing interest, and even of amusement. Nevertheless there is something irritating to Margaret about the prestidigitation with which Doria can flourish it, suddenly, just like that. A thing everyone assumed, but never bothered to investigate. Margaret is, as Lillian says, 'put out' by this.

Here they are, listening to Doria. We can listen too. This is before Margaret drifted off to the tapestry room to spy on the rest of them from her eyrie. I'm shifting all this into the present tense for your convenience.

The story is complicated – such complications are the things that bother Margaret about family history. Her mind goes round in circles and the threads tangle and she wants to throw things. Yes, really, Margaret the Virtuous would like to chuck a rock at

Doria. She listens to Doria but there is a faraway look in her eyes. Lillian smiles at her knowingly as she hands around glasses of wine. Margaret's eyes open wide, and she straightens her shoulders, pretending to pay better attention to the matter in hand.

Doria reads from her iPad, breaking off every now and again to make a comment on what she has said. They have never before sat round a party table out in the garden while somebody read to them from an iPad. The baby sleeps on – the other children have disappeared.

'In the 1880s Nicholas O'Day, a black sheep, by the way, was living in Waterford. He was one of a number of Irish entrepreneurs who spirited rubies out of Burma.'

'Rubies!' Charmaine says in excitement, her eyes snapping open, bright with the special light of greed you might expect to see in a cartoon. Doria goes on.

'Yes. Rubies. He married a noblewoman from the Ava kingdom, eventually living with her in some splendour in Paris. He left behind in Waterford another wife, Catherine, and four children.'

This is nice and colourful, racy, and now Margaret can't help but give Doria her attention.

'His less adventurous unmarried half-brother John emigrated to Sydney where he became a minor poet and painter.'

'Imagine!' Charmaine says. Margaret wishes Charmaine would shut up.

'Now your late husband, Margaret, is descended from black sheep Nicholas and his Irish wife Catherine, who was left behind in Waterford with the children, as I said.'

Doria pauses for effect and goes on. Her audience is really quite breathless. Who would have thought family history would be like this?

'You, Margaret, are descended from Nicholas's brother John and his Australian wife Mary-Ann. And who was Mary-Ann? She was the child of two rather nice, but also it appears, foolish Irish convicts from Van Diemen's Land.'

Convicts! Imagine! Fashionable!

Everybody, including Margaret, laughs with a kind of relief. Australian stories are full of such detail. It's the stuff of drama and also of a sort of quaint nostalgic comedy, the staple of television mini-series, and it has taken on the comforting quality of myth.

'The woman had stolen a length of patchwork, and the man had stolen three peacocks. It is just possible to imagine getting away with the patchwork, but surely it would be difficult to conceal three peacocks. Even if the birds were females, but supposing they were males. Did he plan to sell them or eat them? Sell them, presumably. These two worked off their sentences in Van Diemen's Land, as servants I believe, and had received pardons, their tickets of leave.'

The O'Days have always imagined there might be convicts on the family tree, and can now take a certain pleasure in being able to claim them. They generally think it's quite good now to be able to say: 'My great-grandfather's half-brother married the daughter of convicts from Van Diemen's Land. Think of that. Fascinating. So we *are* Australian royalty after all.'

'I think it's so cute,' says KayKay, 'having convicts. I wish we had some. Doria, do you think you could find some for me as well? I mean other than the O'Day ones.'

And Doria, smiling wisely with her teeth but not her eyes, says she will put her mind to it. Nobody in the family has ever realised Nicholas and John were half-brothers. The father, Michael, had one wife who died young, mother of Nicholas, and one who came after and was the mother of John. There were so many Michael O'Days in County Waterford that people can be forgiven for being unable to pinpoint the very one who fathered the two boys. But not Doria. She has the eyes of a fox and a brain like a high-speed computer. Also the determination of a guided missile. But anyone can see that all these things are really *very* complicated.

Doria flashes around on the screen of her iPad, her longish fingers somehow turning up at the tips, swiftly pointing out the lines, the branches, the names, the births, the marriages, the progeny, the deaths. Her gold bracelets go clackety-clack. The gaps, the question marks, the bastards. Margaret finds Doria herself weirdly fascinating, although also repellent, in the nature of an exotic and determined insect that invades the house, promising perhaps fine weather, but threatening also to lay eggs and produce pale grubs that will rapidly chew their way through the velvet and brocade of the soft furnishings. That's my personal take on it, you realise. Margaret doesn't exactly think like that. Clearly it's not going to be possible to exterminate this visitor, and so the only course of action, Margaret knows, will be to befriend it. Keep it well fed and within sight. Margaret is an expert in the use of this strategy. What do they say – keep your friends close but your enemies closer?

Ophelia's silver rattle, Doria says, is a family heirloom. She speaks airily, as if there might be shelves and drawers and chests of such heirlooms from whose bounty she could pluck a rattle.

'The coral is not in fact ordinary coral,' she says, as if quoting from a history text. 'It's the vivid red coral taken from the waters around Barcelona in the fifteenth century and fashioned into the teething bar on the rattle in London in 1826.' Oh, right.

To Margaret, who is interested and even impressed by the provenance of the thing, it seems to be filled with its own sinister life. The coral handle resembles, after all, a charm against the evil eye – which indeed it is. And the bunch of wrought silver bells, with a small whistle, is surely the instrument of a court jester. There is no doubt it's a pleasing object to hold, the coral soft and warm, the bumps on the bells like delicious fruits under the fingertips. The sound of the whistle is low and sweet. It's also phallic, of course. So very different from Sophie le Girafe from Paris.

'And then there is,' says Doria, 'the Spanish strain of the Waterford O'Days. So the rattle is highly significant and appropriate.'

This Spanish stuff is more news to Margaret, who has been under the impression that Irish is Irish and that's that. Unless there were a nice wistful link with imperial Russia. If only there were. Margaret's own colouring – pale skin, vivid blue eyes, dark curly hair now softly grey – is considered to be pure Irish. Edmund had the tawny eyes and long silky lashes. Another kind of Irish. All the children are more or less from the same moulds. Most of the grandchildren clearly carry O'Day characteristics. Some start off blond and then undergo a dramatic metamorphosis so that by the time they are eight or so their hair is deep brown or black against the cream of their skin.

'Is the name Ophelia a family name, in your own family I mean?' Doria asks Charmaine.

'Oh no, I just happen to think it's pretty. And it goes so well with the others.' And she firmly, with a kind of smug smile, intones: 'Oriane, Orson, Orlando…'

It's at this point that Margaret excuses herself from the party table and moves into the house for her own tea and sandwiches.

Let's look in on her now, in her tapestry room.

As she gazes down at the scene under the tree, Margaret feels the embrace of the security of her room. She is sitting now, in a deep and comfortable armchair, still close to the window, still with an eagle's view of the people in the distance around the table. She focuses the field glasses on one and then another – Charmaine, KayKay, Joseph, Justin, Paul, Isobel – but she keeps coming back to Doria. Everything seems to radiate from Doria and her iPad.

Doria is so animated, like a leaping spark of electricity zapping around the table. She has announced before that since the death of her husband she has never eaten meat. Margaret has wondered what that could possibly mean, how it could possibly matter, but has declined to ask for further information. There seems to be something unpleasant about the connection between the dead husband and the consumption of flesh. A couple of Edmund's uglier daily epitaphs were about meat. She always hated those. Margaret enjoys not asking questions, letting people unfold their stories at their own pace. Letting them uncover small pieces of the truth for the listener, perhaps inadvertently. Sometimes it takes a long time, Lillian being a case in point, but it's usually worth the wait. Margaret would say *always* worth the wait. Lillian's personal story moves and jumps and doubles back and thickens as the years go by. It reaches back into the distant past, sails along into the present, flips back again to the day before yesterday.

It seems that, almost every day, over the years, in the leisurely course of the day's work about the house, Lillian will offer some fresh detail of her distant or recent past that will further colour in the fabric of her life. Her four grandchildren are now the most frequent source of interest, although she doesn't dwell on them in her conversation. She gives just passing happy references. As for her past – that she wore a blue dress to be married was one thing; that she was married in the sacristy because Ralph was not Catholic was a detail that didn't emerge until much later. Margaret's own mother, Muriel, wisely converted when she married Killian O'Day, and the wedding was a splendid affair at the high altar, with frothing cream lace, arum lilies and trailing orange blossom, almost as much a celebration of Muriel's entrance into the Church as of the nuptials themselves. Muriel brought with her a great deal of Methodist wisdom, as well as all the hymns that she would play on the tiny blue and gold pipe organ in the Eltham parlour. Such conversions are less important now, but in those days there were very rigid rules about such things; rules that frequently had the effect of tearing families apart. Muriel's family cut her off. The only aunt on her mother's side that Margaret knew was Iris, who occasionally visited the family in Eltham. The others might as well not have existed. Most of them, as far as Margaret could tell, lived in various towns in New South Wales. Margaret was an O'Day twice over, her maternal ancestry having long since faded into shadows and nothingness. Iris had no children. Lillian had lost two babies – sadness and tragedy in the past, mourned, but life must go on. One daughter refuses to speak to her, although the reason is not entirely clear to Margaret. Probably one day this will be explained. The other daughter is the mother of the four grandchildren, and lives not far from Lillian herself, across the river from Bellevue, in Richmond. I should tell you about Richmond, and how it relates to and differs from Toorak. You see, Toorak has always been the home of wealth and privilege; Richmond began as a crowded and busy working-class suburb close to the city. But times change, places change, and now Lillian's little Victorian cottage, where she has lived for fifty years, is worth millions. The houses on either side of her have been glamorised and glorified and gentrified, but Lillian's house remains as it always was. Such strange humility among the gorgeousness. Some of the cast-off toys and clothes of the Ooops O'Daisies are discreetly passed on to Lillian's daughter's children. And when Charmaine sends over a parcel of almost new – some in fact never worn – designer labels for the Toorak church jumble sale, Margaret chooses the best things for Lillian's grandchildren before sending the rest on to the church. One of Lillian's sons is a very successful golfer who owns a chain of sport shops; the other lives as a homeless person under a bridge somewhere in Brisbane with his dog. Lillian's husband, Ralph, died from emphysema in 1990. Emphysema. Lillian always says this word in a hushed and drawn-out manner. Her voice, in fact, is always soft, with a lovely kind of dignity, a resignation to the fact of the awesome will and power of God, and a rather old-fashioned acceptance of her own place in the scheme of things.

'Things are as they are,' says Lillian, 'and only faith and prayer will see you through. Rain falls on the just and the unjust.'

Sometimes Margaret feels that there is an almost medieval flavour to Lillian's attitude to life. Perhaps she is a saint. Perhaps this is what saints look like. Lillian's origins remain more or less shrouded in mystery, but one day she reveals the fact that two of her younger brothers died in a polio epidemic, adding to the sadness in her background, but not disturbing her unwavering belief in the mystery of the fabric of existence, in the power and majesty of the love of God, the rain, the just, the unjust.

Although Margaret doesn't quite realise it, Lillian is her only friend. It's perfectly clear to me. The rest are, as I said before, acquaintances. It's Lillian who is keeping the party going down there under the oak; Lillian who moves quietly to and from the house in her modest skirt and cardigan, monitoring the ribbon sandwiches and the petits fours, bringing and taking and offering and generally doing. Unobtrusive. Reliable. Margaret plans to make Lillian the gift of a final resting place in the Melbourne Cemetery – in the glamorous new Saint Mary of the Cross Mausoleum. Lillian doesn't know this; it's to be a surprise. Would that be a surprise after death, do you suppose? Or will Margaret reveal it before the event? I can't say.

To an outsider looking in on Margaret as she sits or stands at a wise and careful distance from the window, with her field glasses, she might resemble a large, slender, quiet, spying, elegant moth. For her gown is of an iridescent silk, flowing from the shoulders, shades of blue and gold, and faintly sinister. Margaret is conscious of all this, is theatrical, and she half realises she might be at this moment a character in an obscure Celtic opera. Her only jewellery is a pair of luscious pearl earrings, and her rings, which are remarkably small and almost discreet. In the jewel cases in her dressing room there are several brilliant treasures, not least a pigeon's blood ruby handed down through Edmund's side of the family. Did it originate with the wicked Nicholas of whom we have recently heard? And there's an enormous diamond pendant that could be mistaken for circus jewellery. Margaret believes in keeping her treasures nearby, refusing to send them to the bank. She likes to take them out from time to time and admire them in a rather childlike way. When Edmund was alive she used to wear them in public – to receptions and the theatre – but all that is in the past. To old-fashioned Margaret the display of jewels is somehow unseemly in a woman of her years. In her will she has divided them between her daughters Rafaela and Isobel – forget about Charmaine. And of course Paul will never marry, will he?

A few feet behind her in the tapestry room stands a tall folding screen, known as the Zephyr screen, framing her mothy presence with its own eerie beauty. This screen has been in Edmund's family for many years, brought back from an uncle's visit to somewhere in South America. It is in five folding sections, eight feet high, made from a deep golden wood voluptuously carved, framing great panels of glass. Between the two pieces of glass are trapped the bodies of dozens of iridescent blue Zephritis butterflies from Peru, their giant wings spread and stilled. Each specimen is matched, underside to underside, with another, so that both sides of the screen are virtually identical. The screen is sumptuous against the pale apple-green walls of the room. For a long time the screen stood in the foyer of O'Day Funerals. But when Margaret and Edmund married, because Margaret was so entranced by it, they brought the screen, in her honour, to the house where Edmund and Margaret lived. What a grand gesture, what a statement of confidence in the new bride. The foyer of the funeral home has never really been the same since the big screen went off with Margaret. The truth is that the place needed modernising, and the screen was never going to be a part of that. The butterfly screen was, everyone said, a symbol of the family itself, although exactly what it signified was never really defined. Edmund used to laugh about it and call it the Blue Vagina screen – teasing Margaret because she liked it so much. Margaret was embarrassed, but she couldn't help loving the screen. It was just a great and rather mysterious heirloom, a haunting reminder of past moments in the history of the family. The history of the family – ah, yes. Margaret became its curator; it went with her from the first medium-sized house to a bigger house, and finally into the tapestry room of Bellevue where it was at last at home in the luxury and grandeur of Margaret's personal world. Doria hasn't seen it yet, not having been invited into the sanctum of the tapestry room, but I expect she'll surely enjoy tracing it back to its origins in due course.

The patterns formed by the wings on the screen are mesmerising, the shimmer and unearthly glow of the colours, the sense of arrested flight. But the truth is that the insects are the stiff little bodies of dead things, creatures captured at the height of their beauty and bloom, trapped now between glass for the pleasure of their killers and admirers. And their complex undersides are concealed from view. Margaret sometimes formulates these thoughts as her gaze settles on the screen each day, but still she is drawn to the beauty. She delights in it, loves it, her eyes following the designs and patterns made by the insects under the glass. But they are, as I say, dead things.

Butterflies, Margaret knows, are commonly taken to signify the soul, and there are myths about them in many cultures. Margaret herself even has a personal belief that they are somehow a thread in the fabric of her life, as the image of them seems to run like a recurring pattern through her memories. At times she thinks all this is meaningless poetic nonsense, and yet at others she thinks she can discern a significance of some kind. She is strongly attracted to the screen in the tapestry room, almost unconscious of the fact that her intense pleasure in it is partly composed of a deep horror at this shining collage of fine dead things. She loves it and she fears it, it disturbs her, she is drawn to contemplate it often, her mind moving into a strange mood of arrested consciousness, suspended in a kind of breathless ecstasy. Is it too much to say that she finds the screen weirdly erotic? Looking at it is like meditation. Is it an intimation of mortality? Death is the real source of the O'Day fortune, so perhaps the screen is after all just the pretty face of death, and that's all there is to it. Evan Keene, the psychiatrist with the pink sports car, sometimes likes to banter with Margaret on the subject of the screen, its meaning, and the meaning of butterflies in general. Do I have to tell you that Margaret, who claims to despise Evan, enjoys these conversations? Evan has a nice gift for a kind of harmless flirtation that can feel, to a respectable widow, like pleasure.

I do have to go into some detail here, as I seem to be checking out Margaret's character generally, and the butterfly *is* a significant element, strange as that may seem. And you remember that Margaret has died and had a funeral with butterflies.

In Margaret's own life the image of the butterfly goes back a long way, long before she ever encountered the funeral O'Days. There was the time when her family moved from one house in Eltham to another, and Margaret ran into the empty house after all the furniture had gone. Lying in the corner of her old bedroom was a toy butterfly made from tissue paper. She picked it up and put it in her pocket. Then the odd thing was that, when the family moved in to the new house, and the empty furniture truck was driving off, there on the front path just inside the gate was another toy butterfly, this one made from painted feathers. Margaret put both creatures in a box and in fact she kept them, forever and for no clear reason. Their coincidence, the punctuation marks of the two houses, was beyond understanding, if indeed it had any real meaning at all. Who can say? Coincidence. Serendipity. Synchronicity. Big words. That box of old toy butterflies is still in her possession at this point in the story, in a drawer in the tapestry room where the scene is more or less dominated by the screen from Peru.

When she writes at night in her *Book of Revelation* – sometimes in bed, sometimes in the chair in the tapestry room – the screen embraces her. The yellow light from her lamp falls in a cone onto the book, and she writes swiftly in a firm hand, with a fountain pen that once belonged to her father. The pen is green and the ink is blue, the nib is fourteen-carat gold. Margaret's handwriting has scarcely changed since she was a girl; it is still the fat regular copperplate she learned at school. It is in fact almost indistinguishable from the writing of the dreaded Sissy Bagwell. She writes swiftly, she scrawls, and yet the letters form themselves as if by some higher power into the girlish shapes made by well-trained convent schoolgirls.

After a while, having had her tea and sandwiches, Margaret has become more composed and she leaves the tapestry room to stroll out across the lawn and take up her place again at the party table. She can hear the children shouting in the distance – it's a comforting sound. Doria has scarcely drawn breath; everyone seems to be enthralled by the stories she can attach to the O'Days of yesteryear. Margaret wishes she would just put the iPad away. What on earth has become of ordinary manners? Baby Ophelia Rose sleeps on. In the perfect little baptised package that she is,

Ophelia Rose must surely contain somehow – this is me being a bit mystical – all the things that have ever happened to Margaret, as well as to all the other people mingling there in her sweet little bloodstream and psyche. Psyche. Did I say that? For now, let's see how Margaret is going with her rambling journal-writing.

I Imagined Her Falling Slowly:

The Book of Revelation

'The afterlife is our true home. It needs good furniture.'
E. R. O'Day

How was my life changed by meeting Edmund? Was he my defining moment? I suppose he was. He's gone now, but life goes on. As Lillian often says. Life goes on. How did my life change when we met, Edmund and I? Was it fate, destiny, grace – I wonder what governs such things. God? Yes. But that's such a simple answer. Was our marriage made in heaven? What does that really mean? We met at a dance in this very house. That certainly gives me pause for reflection. Our paths had crossed sometimes at family events, but this was really the first time I took any notice of him. Or, for that matter, he took any notice of me. His sister Frances, the closest to Edmund in age – he was the youngest, the beloved only son with five older sisters – was celebrating the end of her schooldays. I came to the party as the partner of my brother Michael, who used to play tennis with Frances. Michael and I were very close in age, and had been, as my father used to say, partners in crime since early childhood. Dear Michael, how I adored him when I was little.

By the standards of today, the party was a most dignified gathering. That was to begin with. The dancing was in the front hall, which is still paved in the same black and white marble tiles, not ideal for dancing, but it's a lovely big space, and from above couples in party clothes appear like flowers and insects on a chess board. When our children were little, in fact, we sometimes played mad chess games there using all kinds of teddy bears and dolls for pieces. Rather silly but rather fun. The staircase divides at the top and sweeps down either wall. Everyone had gone into the long dining room for supper; the band was playing softly. What was it playing? I can't recall. I came out of the dining room to get my silk stole, which I had left on a chair in the corner of the hall. Just as I picked it up there was a strange commotion on the upper landing. One of Edmund's sisters, Marina, the next one up from Frances, erupted from the powder room, shouting something. Suddenly, with no warning at all, Marina took a great athletic leap over the banister and landed on the tiles below.

I froze in the act of picking up my stole and then I couldn't move. It had all happened suddenly, and yet it also happened very slowly. Then people came from everywhere. Edmund's father pushed forward, and Dr Glashen, one of the guests, took charge. Before I knew what was going on the ambulance was out the front and Marina and her mother and father were gone. I was standing in shock in the corner, the only witness, or so it seemed, to what had taken place. Dr Glashen came over to me and took me into the small downstairs reception room. We sat together on a sofa. The room, I remember, smelled of vervain, which is a perfume I love. I remember we were told that it was used on Christ's wounds. I have also heard that it is a charm against vampires. Funny, the things one knows.

'Now Margaret, dear,' said Dr Glashen in a very kind voice, 'you must sip this.' He gave me a small glass of brandy. I was not used to brandy, but to tell the truth I hardly noticed it as I did what he said, and sipped. He was kind but somehow intimidating, and even godlike. Or to tell the truth, he was, as the children say nowadays, creepy. My brother was standing behind him, looking helpless. Then suddenly, on the chair opposite us, Edmund appeared. He looked incredibly handsome and – I have to say – sweet and gentle. And in command. That was a thing Edmund always did; he had this air of being in charge. His hair was ruffled and his white bow tie was askew. There was a smudge of blood on his white shirt cuff. He did not touch my hand but let his own hand hover over it, and it felt as if a field of powerful energy was beaming warmly down on me. His breath was perfumed with gin – even I knew that smell. It had previously always sickened me, but on Edmund's breath it was very attractive and intoxicating. I wanted to keep breathing it in. He was mesmerising. I looked into his eyes.

'Marina will be all right,' he said – I could almost believe him – 'but, Margaret, you must be very shaken. Would you like me to drive you home? Or maybe you would like me to call your father?' He had never really spoken to me before, other than to say hello in passing. I think he had never properly noticed me. Michael stood behind us, like a guardian, but he said nothing and did nothing, receding into a shadow. He also was in shock – but Edmund was composed. Looking back on it now, I see we were so very young. Oh, so very, very young.

I didn't know the answer to Edmund's question. Should he call my father? Probably he should. These days, I know, a girl in my position would be a candidate for intensive counselling, but this was long before such things had been even thought of. It was 1952. The party was dissolving out in the hall, supper forgotten, one of the uncles had taken charge. Then when everyone had gone, including the band and the caterers, the police came and a policeman asked me what I had seen. I didn't really know what I had seen.

'Just tell him, Margaret, dear, anything you remember,' said Dr Glashen.

It was then that I burst into tears. I had never been so close to a policeman in my life. Edmund moved over to the couch, and he sat on the side of it and put his arm around me, pulling my head towards his body. For a few moments I sobbed great tears onto his jacket. He gave me his handkerchief and it smelled of something wonderful. Perhaps it was Essence of Edmund? My mind was spinning – the shock, the brandy, Edmund, the police. The relief of giving in to my own tears. The handkerchief.

I had a vivid recollection of the shouting and the slamming of a door seconds before Marina jumped. Did I imagine the slamming? Who was shouting? Was it just Marina? Who else? Who was she shouting at? It was all a blur and a jangle, and had almost immediately become unreal. So I said I had heard some shouting, and the next thing I knew Marina was on the floor of the hall. I could see the crumpled splat of her, her frosty-pink taffeta frock concealing much of the blood on the floor. A dizzy blur on the dazzle of the tiled floor. But I didn't say any of that. And I didn't describe her descent, her swift falling flight, because I think I really only imagined seeing it. Did I see it or did I imagine it? Earlier in the evening I had stared in amazement at her strapless pink taffeta that was constructed like a bell from the waist down. Her lovely tiny waist. My mother used to talk about 'wasp waists' – perhaps Marina's was a wasp waist. All over the surface the taffeta was pinched into large diamond shapes, and on the corners of every diamond there was a teardrop milky pearl. Several of these pearls ended up in the blood on the tiles, resembling the eggs of an insect. I imagined her falling slowly, air filling the skirt, like a fairy floating down to earth, her long dark hair playing out above her, straight up in its own airstream. But I had not seen that. That had not happened. There was the violent shouting and slamming of doors high above me; there was the still and crumpled body on the floor. Did I hear a thud, a splat? A crunch maybe? I don't think I did. Reality had somehow stopped and only certain bits were available to me, like sections of a film, like single photos, fragments of photos, separated in time. My imagination could fill in the gaps, but most of the event was not there.

'I heard shouting,' I said, 'and then she just seemed to be on the floor.' My voice was soft, almost a whisper, and my head was bowed. Was I lying? I didn't even know the answer to that, and I don't know the answer now.

Later I heard that there had been an almost empty bottle of Gilbey's gin, and evidence of a struggle, in the upstairs powder room. Someone told me there was a lipstick smudge across the wall, and blood on the floor. That little room still exists, a leftover from the past. But who had been in there with Marina? In the powder room? Who was she shouting at? To this day I don't really know, although I have over the years formed a theory which is almost too dreadful to think about. I believe that other person could have been Edmund. Why? How? The blood on his cuff – what did that mean? And possibly the only person who knew the truth was Marina's companion who was sharing the bottle of gin. Was that person Edmund? In fact it was possibly the gin that saved Marina's life, for she did not injure her spine, although many of her bones were broken, and the incident, as it was called, probably shortened her life. She died in her fifties, never having fully recovered any real equilibrium. They said she had always been emotionally unstable anyway. If she hadn't had all that gin in the first place, I suppose the incident would not have taken place. Edmund always loved his sisters, but what did *that* mean? Did he think I knew more than I did? I really didn't know anything about anything much. I used to observe how tenderly he cared for Marina throughout her life, how he spared no expense, gave so much of his time to her. But I could never ever consider questioning him on his part in the accident. Marina herself would never speak of any of it, and she took the truth to her grave.

My story of the night was very thin. I could tell them virtually nothing. My father came to get me and take me and Michael home. Safe, I was safe. Edmund helped me into the white velvet cloak I had borrowed from my mother, and he squeezed my shoulders, warm and comforting, and then he kissed me lightly on the hair. I still marvel at his composure on that night. There was something unnatural about it, I think now. And I even thought it then. In the car I huddled silently on the seat beside Daddy, clutching tightly the evening bag I had borrowed from a neighbour – silver beads with a pattern of orange beads that produced the image of a fire-breathing dragon. My eyes were fixed on the darkness through the window to my left. Michael sat still and silent and shocked in the back seat. In the dark mirror surface of the side window I could see a ghostly image of myself, a pale tragic figure embedded in the thick folds of the white velvet collar, drifting on an unfamiliar cocktail of horror and romance. And brandy, I suppose. My pearl earring was a bright gleaming berry reflected in the glass. I was breathless. The memory of Edmund's fingers was singing on my shoulder; the sight of his dazzling smile, his crooked white bow tie, the blood smudge on his cuff; the false memory of Marina sailing down in her pink frosty bell hovering before me, an illusion I longed to brush away with my hand. And yet my thoughts kept coming back to it, the girl sailing slowly down, thin as a reed in the parachute of her frock, and this image would move into the memory of myself, my own body, my shoulder under Edmund's electric fingers. Suddenly I called out: 'Daddy, Daddy – stop, stop the car, I'm going to be sick!'

And then the car was still and I was among the weeds at the side of the road, and my father was holding me as sickly vomit gushed out of me and I began to sob in my father's arms. The night was cold and starry, and I was warm and safe. In my mouth was a sour and bitter taste.

The next day Edmund telephoned. First he spoke to my mother and asked after my wellbeing. I was in bed and had to run downstairs to the phone. He said he wanted to come and see me because he was very worried about me, and his mother had said he should come. So he did. I recall putting on a green dress and some soft brown leather slippers, and quickly brushing my hair. My face looked terrible. I met him in the sitting room and I just remember how handsome and kind he was. I was still in shock from the events of the night before. He brought me a posy of tight little Cécile Brünners – did he know they were my favourites? How did he know? It was always typical of Edmund that he would hit upon the perfect gesture, the very thing that would touch the other person. It seemed magical and mysterious on that day after Marina's accident. We sat on the sofa, and Edmund handed me the posy almost casually, and gently placed his hand on the head of my little terrier Mimi curled up between us. To this day I feel a rush of sweetness at the memory of Edmund's hand on Mimi's brown head. She gazed at him with the huge black-eyed trust she had, and he spoke to her in a kind of silly voice that I thought was funny. He made me laugh. Oh, Edmund could always make me laugh.

I knew Edmund's reputation as one of the fast set at Loyola; I had heard the stories about how he had a love nest in the old underground bombshelter at the back of house, deep below the wine cellar at Bellevue. A love nest! There, besides making love to girls, he conducted experiments – mostly failed experiments – growing mushrooms and raising silkworms, making poisonous imitation 'champagne'. He used to go to dances driving a hearse, wearing a long raccoon coat that had belonged to his uncle. His greatest claim to fame was being centre-forward on the Loyola football team, and he was known as Naughty Ned. He was two years older than me, and incredibly worldly and sophisticated. I have always called him Edmund, never Ned. Other people called him Eddy. Edmund is a dignified name, and refers in his case to a distant ancestral connection, the Blessed Edmund Rice. I expect Doria knows all about that.

My Edmund had perfect manners, completely beguiling my mother and father on this first occasion. He stole my heart. I was sixteen and in love. The shocking unreality of Marina's accident moved into the haze of an overwhelming infatuation – my mind was numbed as my heart skipped and my whole body seemed to hum with pleasure and anticipation.

After a while we went for a walk together that day across the garden and out under the fruit trees to where we could see the wooded hills in dark distant silhouette, Mimi pattering along beside us. The trees seemed luminous, outlined in fine haloes of soft gold, as we talked of nothing very much – our friends, our families and our hopes for the future. He was going to university and then into the family business – about which he was quite amusing. He called the funeral parlour the 'box office'. I didn't find this shocking at the time, making fun of dead bodies, although afterwards I thought it was probably not a nice thing to do. I was really quite prim and proper, but I had laughed. Yes, as I said, Edmund could always make me laugh.

We went back indoors and my mother brought us a tray of lemonade and coconut cookies. Edmund nibbled politely at first and then he laughed, threw a cookie in the air and caught it in his mouth. He smelled of cigarette smoke, which I found highly intoxicating at the time; it disgusts me now. It seemed that Edmund could breathe anything onto me and I would succumb to the aroma. 'Breathe on Me Breath of God' – a hymn from my mother's old Methodist hymn book – 'Fill me with life anew'. We used to play it on the parlour organ. Obviously Edmund was like a god to me then. No, not a god, a prince; my father was the god. And beyond all this, beyond logic and reason, I felt in my heart that I had always known Edmund. I am, after all, a romantic. Definitely.

When Edmund had gone that first day, I went back to the sofa and fell asleep in a new glow of bliss, my heart overflowing with brightness. The world was spinning on a different axis. For a few days afterwards the stars and the moon were brilliant jewels pasted in the deep velvet heaven of all the romantic stories I had read, and I confess I had read my fair share. As I walked, my feet didn't touch the ground. My skin was alert, tingling, waiting to be caressed. I was adrift in the bubble and hum of a young girl in love. I am getting really poetical now that I am putting these things down on paper.

I put thoughts of Marina's accident to the back of my mind. But sometimes I have imagined that the violence of that night still possibly hovers in this house, in the air above the balustrade. I am a believer in the power of supernatural forces, for both good and evil, but I do prefer to concentrate on the good, and to let past evils fade and rest. And yet, and yet, I occasionally shudder and imagine I see a falling figure, sometimes at twilight, in the front hall. Do houses contain imprints of the lives of the people who have gone before? I suspect perhaps they do. Well, I give myself a little shake and look to the practicalities of life today. Heaven knows there is enough to be getting on with, both good and bad. Although sometimes my thoughts roam back into the past, my real energies are concentrated on the present, on the everyday.

Thus, as a girl infatuated with her beau, I began a whirl of teenage courtship which lasted, not without some heartache, for nearly five years before we were married, six months after my twenty-first birthday. I would wait at home for Edmund to ring. How different it must be for girls now, with their mobiles always in their bags or under their pillows. Like most good Australian Catholic girls in 1957, I was a virgin bride, even though I did nursing, and life in the nurses' home was quite wild at times. Girls used to tell me, and whisper behind my back, during those years, that Edmund was still pursuing his romantic adventures in all kinds of other directions. I call them 'romantic adventures' but they were really pretty hot affairs. Rosemary Cotsford had a baby that she gave up for adoption, and people said Edmund was almost certainly the father. She killed herself not long after. I chose not to listen to the gossip, but I was not stupid enough to think the story was not based in fact. I said nothing. It now amazes me that I could preserve the strange fiction of our relationship without ever questioning its validity. I think I accepted the notion that a man would have a principal girlfriend, even a fiancée, and be free to pursue his sex life elsewhere, giving the fiancée the chance to maintain her virtue, which would later carry them into the serious business of marriage. These ideas were fashionable at the time, if you can believe that. It was just before the sexual revolution in the sixties, when these roles of men and women began to change. I used to read a lot of history and historical fiction, and was quite familiar with the idea of the royal mistresses. Throughout his life Edmund always came back to me, and my loyalty to him never wavered. I like to think I understood Edmund, and in my heart of hearts, I believe I felt a higher pride in that he simply always returned, that he never found, in his dalliances, anyone he could trust the way he could trust me. I believed – or perhaps I imagined – that my role was to love him and nurture him, and pray for him and somehow save him. Do I believe that, or is it a story I just wish to believe? There's a kind of spiritual arrogance in the thought that *my* prayers could somehow save *his* soul. Am I so much more virtuous than him that my prayers could cancel out his misdemeanours? I just can't think all this through properly. I now pray for his soul. It's easier to do that than not to do it, and they comfort me, the forms of the words, the echoes of the old truths. I sometimes think that prayers help the one who prays more than they help anyone else. These are private thoughts. I would never talk about them. Specially not to, say, Father Justin.

Did that first night when Marina went sailing over the balustrade bind us together forever? Edmund and me. Sometimes I think it did. Because my secret theory is that Marina's companion upstairs that night really *was* Edmund, and I still dread to think what they were arguing about that could so upset her and send her flying over the railing. I think he imagined I knew that truth. The lipstick and the blood. We never discussed the matter. Never ever. I have always known when to keep my own counsel.

By the time, later in our marriage, that Edmund met Fiona Ashley, he had formed the habit of confiding his transgressions in me. To a degree. In spite of these transgressions, or perhaps it was even because of them, Edmund and I shared much happiness, and many moments of great sweetness and grace over the years. I suppose I knew Edmund, knew his good side and his not so good, as I could never know another human being, apart from myself. We shared and still share the passage of time. I feel that our marriage continues to this day, even after his death. Can it be that Fiona and the boys are part of this continuing life? It's strange, but I actually think they are.

These are unorthodox ideas, but they are part of my understanding of myself. I've never shared these thoughts with anyone, not even with Lillian. Lillian and I are close but distant. Parts of our lives, our thoughts, remain unshared, other parts are open. That's the way it is. I think if I had had a sister I would have been able to confide in her. I always longed to have a sister, but it was not to be. Lillian is the closest I have come. Is that sad? The housekeeper is my next-best thing to a sister. Well, I suppose I must count my blessings. And I don't really think of her as the housekeeper, anyway.

I was aware of the significance of Fiona from the beginning. I decided to accept her and the two sons she had with Edmund as a kind of branch of the family. They were often included in family events, and I made sure the boys, Frederick and Julian, were given the best of everything. Fiona insisted on sending them to a curious school where she herself was educated. She and her friends there breastfed their children until they were about five, and wouldn't let them associate with other children, even in parks and playgrounds. They didn't receive immunisations against such diseases as whooping cough. There was no sport at the school and, as far as I could tell, very little reading and writing, but a lot of music and dance and painting and sculpture and climbing trees and building strange nests and cubby houses. All this was something I was not used to, but I more or less embraced it – as I embraced Fiona herself. I did eventually step in when it came to the question of the immunisations, however, and finally saw to it that the boys got the usual shots. How Edmund coped with the breastfeeding business I have no idea. Heavens above! It was not the kind of thing we ever discussed. He always had other less serious romantic interests anyway – strange young women in the outer suburbs, sometimes even in depressed rural towns. I never understood that; I did understand Fiona. Although it went against the grain, I agreed that we should fund the educational folly of Frederick and Julian, with the proviso that the boys' secondary education should be somewhere more orthodox. Not necessarily

Loyola, but somewhere that might train them for life in the real world where people die from measles and whooping cough if they're not immunised. The poverty of their vocabularies today I put down to Fiona's own failure to grasp the English language, although I realise that their education has not helped, either. As it turned out, we did send them to Loyola eventually, and they seem to be doing quite well, particularly in art and music and, strangely, science. Clive Bushby, Justin's partner, seems to have taken Julian under his wing. I am pleased about that. In any case children generally are able to surmount and survive all manner of parental peculiarities and educational eccentricities, given the chance.

On the day of Ophelia's baptism, they were there, Fiona and the boys, under the oak tree with all the others. I must say Fiona was looking quite elegant in oyster silk. If I'm honest and generous, she actually looked beautiful there in the shade of the oak. Now, if Julian and Frederick are the half-brothers of my children, what is their relationship to Ophelia Rose? And to all the other Ooopsies for that matter. Is there such a thing as a half-uncle? Well, I can't imagine. Perhaps I should ask Doria. Then again, perhaps not. I find I tune out when she is going on and on about this cousin and that cousin and all the removeds. She goes to great lengths and into the finest details, and her amazing American voice grates after a while. There was some distant O'Day cousin in California who was killed in a car crash with his wife, and Doria arranged for their child, Angelina, to be adopted by another branch of the family somewhere in Canada. Doria had never known the couple, but she stepped in to help Angelina when she heard about the tragedy. I was very impressed by that. Although it's not always evident to me, there is a degree of goodness in Doria, and I need to be more charitable towards her. Yet so much about her irritates me – her truly dreadful focus on her family history project so that every single thing relates back to it; this drives me crazy, although I attempt not to show it. I must try to be more kind and charitable. I probably won't succeed.

Whenever I consider my own practices of charity, my mind naturally flies back to my father who was, I think, a saint. He was a family doctor; I idolised him from the beginning, and I always will. It's a strange thing – but I have always felt that my father was more a part of me than my mother was; he was my genesis, without him I would not exist; he was completely bound up in my identity, in my core. My idea of my mother wrapped me round like a soft red blanket, enfolded me, but my father was the spark that set me going. He was very handsome, dark and maybe vaguely Spanish. Doria insists we have Spanish blood, and after all she would *know*.

I have always loved Spanish things. I remember a strange shop somewhere in the vicinity of the Mercy Hospital when I was a child. My mother used to visit the mothers and babies in the hospital every so often, and sometimes she took me with her. Charitable works were very important in my family, and I've continued this tradition myself. The shop I am thinking of was low and dark, with old-fashioned diamond lattice windows. There was a jumble of things such as Spanish mantillas and paper knives from Toledo and rosary beads from Avila, made from rose petals from St Teresa's garden. The things I really loved and longed for were soaps and talcum powder and perfume wrapped in exotic black and red paper with a Spanish lady on it. It was called Maja. Actually my mother bought me a large round box of the talcum powder, and I still have the box with its wonderful lady in her soft red dress and black mantilla, with her slender left arm exposed, her deep dark eyes and her glorious open fan, its dusky ochre flower on pearly cream silk. Loving Maja packaging doesn't signify a Spanish heritage, although when I first visited Spain I kept thinking I glimpsed Daddy's face and bearing in men passing by. So perhaps there really was Spanish blood in the Waterford O'Days. Ireland is close to Spain, and there was plenty of coming and going in days gone by.

My memories of my handsome father – I recall the time when we were all at a picnic somewhere beside a creek near Eltham.

Me and my brothers, my father and mother, and several cousins, uncles and aunts. I was four, so it's a very early memory, but vivid. There are photos, hence memory is mingled with these images and so memory is blurred. My hair was in two bunches of sausage curls, with huge silk bows over my ears. I imagine the bows were pink. In the summer I wore floral dresses elaborately smocked by Aunt Iris, and lacy cardigans knitted by my great-aunt Minnie in Tasmania. I had a new pair of blue suede sandals, and my brother Philip was pushing me higher and higher on a long swing that hung from the branch of a gum tree, and flew out over the murky waters of the creek. I was screaming with delight. In memory and imagination the swing seems to hit the sky, the ropes twist, I kick in alarm, and I let go of the ropes. For a long moment I hang suspended on the narrow wooden seat, midway between the sky and the water, and then in the slow motion of the mind I float down to the muddy surface of the creek, outside myself, observing myself from above. Does the imprint of this fall, this sailing, this flying, somehow influence my perception of Marina as she drifts over the balustrade and down onto the chequered tiles, pink party dress forming a silken bell? Or has the memory of Marina infected the memory of the swing? Oh, memory!

Almost instantly my father dived into the water. In a few swift strokes he reached me, and swam back with me to the bank where Uncle Jack reached for me. As I lay on the grass Daddy gave me the kiss of life, and muddy water dribbled down my skin and clothes. I was wrapped in the tartan picnic rug and bundled into the car and taken home to bed, my mother rubbing my hands briskly as my father drove at speed. My cardigan and one of my new sandals remained in the creek forever. So I was told.

Memory is such a curious thing. I believe I remember observing myself as I floated down to the water, and I think the other details are also part of my recollections. However, I heard the story quite often when I was young, and realise that perhaps the tartan rug and the muddy runnels of water were just part of the tale I was told. They certainly *seem* to be lodged in my memory. But I do recall the sensation of my mother rubbing my hands. In the fading black and white photos of the picnic I have seen the floral dress and the cardigan and the ribbons and the sandals many times. Mother is sitting on a large cushion with me on her knee. We both seem to have a faraway look in our eyes as we smile and squint into the camera. The sausage curls in bunches over my ears are shiny and immaculate. My brothers are grinning like imps behind us. Daddy isn't in any of the pictures because he was holding the camera. Of course it's not unusual for the photographer, often the father, to be missing from family photos. These fathers are invisible gods of the camera – such was my father. Pictures of him that did (and do) exist took on, at least for me, a rare and special power.

No image survives of me as the soggy, bedraggled, half-drowned figure who was saved from the river that day. In the faces of my brothers I can see the adults they became, and in my mother's face I can see the mother I knew, but in my own child-face I can't really see myself. I believe that this brush with death has lodged in my heart and soul, and I also believe that it in some way coloured my understanding of the value of all life. That sounds incredibly grand and philosophical, but that's the way I did and do see the things that happened that day of the picnic.

My father is the hero of the story, as he was the hero of my life. Every single thing he did always seemed to me to be an example of his goodness. I wonder did he have to struggle with uncharitable feelings as I do? How would he have coped with Doria, for instance? But then would she have irritated him the way she irritates me? Probably not. It was a source of jokes in the practice that my father's first name was Killian, a terrible name for a doctor. Our local dentist was called Dr Blood, by the way. He was very sweet and funny and always gave us purple elephant stamps on our hands for being brave in the dentist's chair. The silvery black amalgam fillings Dr Blood put in my molars are still going strong.

One of the biggest efforts I ever made – to come back to the matter of me and Edmund – was in my attitude to Fiona Ashley and her place in Edmund's life, and in mine. Eventually I came to the point where I really did accept her, and now Fiona and the boys are in fact very dear to me, and curiously I am pleased about this. The boys treat me as a grandmother, although they call me Margaret. Doria says it's quite easy to 'organise' them on the family tree. There I go again, revealing my irritation with Doria and her project. I am happy for anybody to know who Frederick and Julian are, but somehow having it all set out in black and white in Doria's elaborate documents worries me. Yes, the black and white reality of all this family history is something that unsettles me deeply. I wonder why that is. There's something about facts – and lies for that matter – when they are written down, something real and permanent. The boys have their mother's surname, Ashley, and when Orson was in Prep last year, his half-brother Frederick was assigned by sheer chance to be his Grade-Six buddy, which was quite nice all round. Frederick is a very clever boy, and has such a look of Edmund; he is handsome and elegant and, yes, rougish. But he has not inherited the gene for sport. It is curious that he seems to have developed a fascination for Doria's research into our family. Perhaps he has a deep need for connection with Edmund. That would make sense, I suppose.

An Advertisement for Border Collie Puppies

'For in that sleep of death what dreams may come?'
                                                    E. R. O'Day

It was in the blue sitting room, actually a few days before the christening of Ophelia Rose, during one of Margaret's regular Sunday afternoon teas, that Doria first encountered the full force of the Bellevue O'Days. We go backwards and forwards here, don't we? But you can keep up, I know. Members of the family would gather on these old-fashioned ritual afternoons, being sure to put in an appearance at least once every few weeks. It was expected. Friends and visitors were also welcome. On this occasion Fiona and the two boys were there, and Frederick showed an immediate interest in Doria's project.

'How far back can you go, then?' Frederick asked.

'So far I have traced parts of the family back to the thirteen hundreds. The time of Richard the Second.'

Margaret was astonished. In fact, she didn't believe Doria.

'Really? Richard the Second? You amaze me, Doria.'

'Oh, I don't mean there's a royal connection. Not so far as I can see. But, yes, the thirteen hundreds.'

Ooops O'Daisies, no royal connection then! Nothing about Russia? No mention.

This is what Doria sees:

The blue sitting room is one of the rooms off the central entrance hall, the hall where long ago Marina landed splat on the black and white tiles. A painting of Edmund's parents, framed in discreet gilt, hangs on the wall above the marble fireplace. Colonial grand is really so sweet and storybook, isn't it? Larisa and Wilfrid O'Day are young, and are sitting under the oak tree where Ophelia Rose will have her christening party. Wilfrid is standing, Larisa sitting, wearing a pale blue dress and pearls. They each gaze softly at the viewer: Wilfrid with the tawny eyes, Larisa with pale green. There is a dreamy, milky light.

Larisa's Bösendorfer Imperial graces one corner of this blue room, and sometimes on a Sunday one or other of the family will play. Margaret's son Paul is by far the best pianist among them, having inherited his paternal grandmother's talent. Margaret's two border collies, Venus and Jupiter, sit on the floor, one either side of the pianist, and appear to enjoy the music, occasionally thumping the floor with their tails. Venus sometimes sings a few notes. She could be on television or something.

Backing up a bit – when Edmund's funeral notice appeared in the newspaper, there was, on the reverse side of the page, an advertisement for border collie puppies. Margaret, who had always had these dogs throughout the marriage, drew a strange little comfort from this. In fanciful moments she imagined that Venus and Jupiter were watching over Edmund's spirit – for in spite of, or because of, his faults she retained her affection for him, and wished him well in the life to come. Margaret had always had her own idiosyncratic interpretations of things. She had a habit of reading the reverse side of funeral notices. It was an aspect of dying that nobody could control, and it often revealed sad or funny coincidences, such as border collies.

I can fill you in here: Edmund's mother, Larisa, grew up in Lviv, learning music there before going to Vienna for more study. It was in Vienna that she met Wilfrid when he was on his grand tour. Larisa abruptly abandoned her musical career to marry

Wilfrid in the Bavarian basilica of the Fourteen Holy Helpers. She then spent the rest of her life in Toorak. There is no record of how she really felt about this dramatic dislocation, but she appears to have adjusted quite well to what she called 'the Australian mode of doing'. Her Ukrainian features mark some of her descendants, in particular Oriane and Frederick, both of whom have her blonde hair and high broad cheekbones. Doria has little interest in such genetic matters, confining herself to names and dates and places. She's practical. But she knows who has been where and when they were there and who they married and who they produced. That's her thing.

You are, and I am, interested in fuller detail. Here goes.

The house itself, Bellevue, was built in George Avenue by Wilfrid in 1933, when he and Larisa already had four daughters and before Edmund was born. It's a smaller version of a house named Bellevue, an Irish house with some family connections to Wilfrid's mother, that Wilfrid visited in Waterford, and of which he had many happy memories. Warm brick, two storeys, rectangular, with long Georgian windows, and a classical portico at the front, facing the circular gravel drive. Quite grand, but also comforting and familiar, like a house in a storybook. Over the years the surfaces of the Toorak house have been softened by the weather, and by a Virginia creeper that cloaks some parts of the walls, as well as festooning the roof-edge of the portico. Since the beginning, children have liked to clamber out onto the paved roof of the portico to look down upon the world. The view stretches across the patchwork of other rooftops, and also the gardens, pools and tennis courts of other houses, and shows glimpses of the river which moves, slow and brown, between its scrubby banks. The back of the Bellevue garden, in fact, reaches down to the water, and there is a rickety jetty and a boatshed. In the past, summer parties would set off from the jetty in small boats to row up the river for picnics – a tradition that died out when Margaret's children grew up and left home. That seems a bit of a pity, doesn't it? Do people still have family picnics? Some do, I suppose. The boatshed was, and probably always will be, the perfect place for youthful drinking, smoking and sex. Margaret might have been in some of the boating parties long ago, girls in flowery dresses and boys wearing straw boaters, but she never visited the boathouse for any of its lower, more exciting purposes. She never added her name or even her initials to any of those cut crudely into the timbers with pocket knives. She remembers herself as being prim and proper, and she was. Oh, believe me, she was. Part of her propriety originated in a fear of the unknown, the great big unknown labyrinth of sex and pregnancy and sin and – oh, you know – death of one kind and another. And she was blighted and spooked for years by the experience of being in the hall when Marina came flying over the balustrade. Splat! I like saying that. Splat! Poor Margaret, she did miss out on a lot of fun. Edmund made up for that in his own life – he had enough fun for several human beings.

'So, Margaret, this house has been your home since Edmund's parents died, then?' Doria said. 'Your parents' home in Eltham' – how the names of the places and suburbs of Melbourne seemed to roll off her American tongue – 'what has become of that? Is it still in the family?' Doria had rather a formal, direct way of speaking.

'Alas, no,' said Margaret. 'When my mother passed away it was sold to an artist who has lived there ever since. He's quite well known, and the house appears from time to time in the arts pages of the weekend papers. I feel a certain nostalgia. In a way I would like to live there myself.' Margaret's eyes took on their faraway, dreamy stare. Doria waited politely for her to get herself together. Then Margaret suddenly snapped into focus as she said: 'In fact, we lived in three different houses in Eltham – and I would actually like to go and live in the first house. Yes, the first one. It was white with high gables and a blue door. But it's gone – there's nothing there now, nothing left but the old chimneys and the ruin of the orchard. However, the last house is still there and, yes, sometimes I imagine living in the last one. It's a pretty house, too, mud brick and set back in the bush, like something in a fairytale. Designed by Alistair Knox – you probably haven't heard of him, but he's a famous Australian architect of the time. Every house we lived in had a lovely garden, and fruit trees, always fruit trees. My father loved his fruit trees, and he was really very gifted with grafting. I can imagine living there, in the last house.'

Did Doria wrinkle her little fox nose, just a bit?

'What, and leave this beautiful place behind? Surely not.'

'You're right, I wouldn't want to leave here, really. But, you know, the memories of my childhood in Eltham are very dear and quite vivid, and sometimes I really do think about living there again. Or spending weekends there, or something. Of course it would be so different, wouldn't it? Time changes everything, including people, even me.'

Margaret laughed, and Doria laughed with her. I think her laugh was a kind of hollow one, but it was a laugh. Doria became, in a way, if not one of the inner circle, at least one of the family, a person who would come and go at Bellevue with some ease. She would often walk to Bellevue to talk to Margaret and have coffee. Margaret, superficially, and even perhaps beneath the surface, polite and welcoming, would sit in the garden or the conservatory – or even the tapestry room – and listen to Doria's latest observations on the state of the family tree. Doria constantly looked things up on her phone, and sometimes brought her iPad too. Margaret found the devices – well – stressful. Why couldn't the woman have a conversation without having to consult whatever it was she consulted?

Margaret later reflected on those thoughts about the houses in Eltham. She remembered the stark dead gum tree on the hill behind the first house, heard again the screech of flocks of white cockatoos, saw the vision of them as they perched like blossoms or washing all over the branches of the tree. Everyone called it the ghost tree, and it sometimes appeared in the pictures local people painted, a huge, stark and lonely open hand etched across the skyline, sometimes empty, sometimes blooming with the fat bodies of the white cockatoos. Or the cartoonish balloon heads of politicians. Would that tree still be there? Probably not. Something held Margaret back from ever going to look. Her connections with her past were often confined to memory, undisturbed by the realities of the present day, undisturbed perhaps by the realities of the past.

As a child Margaret sketched the tree herself, carefully outlining it on the grey pages of her pastel book. 'Look,' she said to the girl Kitty who was hanging out the washing, 'I've done the birds in the tree.' And Kitty said how clever she was, and said it was like the partridge in a pear tree, only better because there were more birds.

Dweller at the Sign of the Bird:

The Book of Revelation

'Take your time. Sleep on it. If you wake up in the morning you can order a family plot.'

E. R. O'Day

The appearance of Doria that Sunday afternoon in the blue room was striking. She was really quite different from anyone I, at least, had ever met. She was a surprise. Was it her air of confidence? Her strange, seductive accent? An accent that grates on my ear after a while. Was it her bland grey suit? Her small Victorian gold lapel pin? Her perfume with its hint of patchouli and something weird and unidentified? I suppose it was a combination of all of those things, and something else, some Essence of Doria that gave her a dramatic force, a force somehow stressed by her apparent colourlessness. She is mysterious and disturbing. I don't believe I'm over-dramatising. I do over-dramatise, of course. Edmund always said that.

Clive, who was not with us on this particular Sunday, later said to me that Doria's looks remind him somewhat of Andy Warhol. Perhaps he has a point. I looked up photos of Warhol in Steiglitz and, yes, I think he's right. Or a fox, maybe.

Doria had been in touch before, explaining her project, but I never really imagined she would turn up here. Then she wrote to me from Florida, saying she was coming, and before I had time to reply she rang me from the airport. She was here! She had taken an apartment near Bellevue. This all seemed odd enough to me. Is that how things are done these days? I invited her for our Sunday afternoon get-together. KayKay was coming, and Evan, and Isobel and Hugh and the children, Charmaine and Joseph and the Ooopsies, as well as Fiona and the boys. Old friends sometimes drop in unexpectedly. I thought it was an opportunity for Doria to get some idea of how things are at Bellevue, always supposing this is relevant to her work.

I've never actually met anyone doing serious family research before. A few of our old friends are taking it up in their retirement, when they're not travelling the world. But that's different, I think; with them, it's more of a hobby. Doria is so deadly serious, she unsettles me. What is it about her? Is it me? Am I the only one who finds her a bit, as my mother often said, fishy?

Frederick was at once captivated by Doria. He is a very frank and outgoing boy, and has charming manners. He often takes to new people, as if he hopes to find something different and valuable. Perhaps he'll become a diplomat or a politician. He says he's going to be a pianist like Paul. Well, he could do that. He graciously saw to it that Doria was comfortable, handing her plates of sandwiches and so forth. Being a child, he was able to ask her questions that I, for one, would not have asked. Such as, where did her first and second names come from. It seems her surname, which is her married name, is Dutch, and has the delightful and mysterious meaning of 'dweller at the sign of the bird'. I don't really understand what that means. Her first name is quite different, coming from the fact that in 1956 her mother was one of the passengers rescued when the *Andrea Doria* sank off Nantucket. Why you would name your own baby after a shipwreck, I fail to see. I suppose it could have been a perception of good luck. In any case Frederick was fascinated by the story. By coincidence, it seems that one branch of the Fogelsong family has a funeral home in West Virginia, but it isn't her late husband's immediate family.

My mind was blurring and buzzing with her voice and her stories. I think I drifted off. She drones on a lot.

At some point she told us the story of a patchwork quilt she had brought with her. I listened to this bit. She plans to take it to Hobart because she's going to donate it to the heritage museum. She was more excited and animated as she talked about this. Being an amateur quilter myself, I was keen to hear about it; and anxious to see it eventually and to handle it. This aspect of family history, this appearance of an artefact which has been made and used over time, really interests me. Doria told the story more or less without emotion. Whereas I tend to get almost overwhelmed with sadness. Tearful. Feeling the fabric between my fingers, thinking of the hands that made it, all those years ago.

I might have some of the dates and other details wrong, but I recall the story starting in 1843. Two sisters, Catherine and Rosetta Hart, who worked as seamstresses, were convicted in Bristol of stealing two petticoats from their employer. I could weep when I hear these things. Two petticoats! They tried to sell the petticoats and were caught out. Stories like this are so terribly sad, full of such desperation and tragic hope. The girls were only sixteen and fourteen at the time, so young. Transported on a ship called the *Emma Eugenia*, they each had a seven-year sentence – seven years! – and were put into service in Van Diemen's Land. At least, once they got off the hideous convict ship, they weren't put in prison. But I think of the loneliness, the strangeness, the bitterness they must have suffered. Catherine, the elder, worked for a family called Drake at Bothwell, and Rosetta worked for the Lynch family at Richmond. During the voyage the women on the ship were provided with the materials to make patchwork. The quilts that were made on these ships were often sold in ports along the way, or were simply lost. In any event they mostly disappeared. There's a famous one at the art gallery in Canberra, the Rajah quilt, but most of them have gone, partly because they carried awful memories for the women who made them, and partly because they would have been completely worn out from use. So this one that Doria has is really a rare treasure. The story goes that Rosetta took it with her when she went to live with the Lynches, and she continued to work on it, using extra bits of fabric given to her by Emilia Lynch and other ladies of the colony. It is called the Rosetta Quilt. When Rosetta got her ticket of leave in about 1850 she married our family connection James O'Day, originally from Waterford, a ticket-of-leave man himself. Before long Rosetta and James — and I am always amazed at the courage and strength these people seemed to have — set sail for America with their young family. They settled in Detroit, James going to work on the docks. Somehow the quilt survived.

When Doria visited the O'Days in Detroit she persuaded them to hand over the quilt so that it could go to the museum in Hobart.

'I can't imagine how they could bring themselves to part with it. Why they would hand it over?' I said.

Doria did not, in fact, meet my eye. Oh, surely she didn't *steal* it?

'Why wouldn't they?' she said with a kind of frosty impatience. We were on this occasion in the tapestry room, as it happens, among my treasures, and Doria was sitting by the window. She was looking past me, past the *Lady with the Unicorn*, out at the sky.

'You must be gifted with great powers of persuasion,' I said. 'I just can't think that I would ever have surrendered it, if it had been mine. But then, I am a quilter. Perhaps the people in Detroit were not quilters.'

'Oh, but I believe they were. I think that was more or less the point, you see. They wanted to share it with the world and they wanted it to go where it really belonged.'

She still wasn't looking at me, but was speaking softly and staring at the clouds. I imagine I knew what she was thinking. Her unspoken words were condemning me for being over-privileged, mean, insular and selfish. She knew I would probably never consider donating such a family treasure to a foreign museum.

I always like to think the best of people, but I felt suddenly cold. And now that I reflect on it, I can sort of imagine Doria, with her eyes concealed by a black mask, and her hands in black gloves, the epitome of a masked robber, stuffing my Famille-Verte into a big brown sack. So it could go where it belonged, wherever that might be. Edmund paid a fortune for it, of course. I think that means I own it. And all this was only in my imagination anyway. And I shouldn't have let her into my private rooms – bedroom, tapestry room – no place for the likes of Doria, I feel. I wonder if she senses how much she irritates me. Well, to be honest, she enrages me. The following week she brought the quilt over for me to look at. She was carrying it, carefully folded and wrapped in tissue paper, in a dark red cloth bag. She knows what she's doing. We went into my bedroom and spread it out on the bed. I found the sight of the quilt affecting, most moving. In fact, it brought tears to my eyes. It's soft and it's small, just large enough to cover a narrow old-fashioned single bed, or a child's bed really. The tiny size of it was so deeply, deeply sad. And it was thin and worn. Poor Catherine, poor Rosetta.

The Rosetta Quilt

'My secret is safe with me.'

E. R. O'Day

The truth is that Margaret almost wept as she caressed the quilt. Doria did not see her emotion, She carried the bag into her bedroom, Doria following, and she spread it out on the bed. It lay there, a softly faded creature, naïve, alive, vigorous. It was worked on milky calico, with a central medallion, a basket of flowers cut from a piece of chintz. This was sewn onto the calico with a heavy brick-red thread. Margaret ran her fingers softly back and forth along the stitches, which were sometimes crude and uneven, sometimes fine and delicate. Precious scraps showing pictures of the hunt, of insects, of children in a village, were sewn on in a geometric pattern, and around the edge was a strip made from pieces of washed-out orange and pink and Turkey red. The precision, the mathematics of it were so poignant. The names – Catherine and Rosetta – were embroidered on opposite corners, a dusty blue star above each name. These stars, Margaret felt, were the strangest and somehow the saddest things of all. On their lonely and comfortless journey to Van Diemen's Land, the sisters stitched two sweet and sorrowful stars, so soft, so unshining. So sad.

The miracle was that the thing had survived at all. A few rust stains, a rough rip, some grey smutty marks. Catherine died of a fever while still in service in Van Diemen's Land. She and Rosetta never saw each other after they got off the boat in Hobart, and were parted. Parted forever. Well, that was yesteryear. Not always a pretty place. I can become almost as tearful as Margaret when I think of that. But I have plenty of sisters to be getting on with, and so maybe I'm not as deeply affected. And I'm not in the story anyway. I know and I tell, but I don't act, being the skeleton in the wardrobe, you understand.

We need to be getting on to see how Doria fitted into everyday life at Bellevue, how she went about adding grist to her family-history mill – if that's what she was doing. Silly expression, isn't it – grist to her mill. But the English language is like that.

At the Tomb of the Unknown Zombie

> *'The past is a ghost, the future a dream,
> all we have is now – and the funeral industry.'*
>
> E. R. O'Day

Doria has stirred all this up. So what else is she doing, then?

As it happened, she became sort of friendly with Evan Keene, the psychiatrist in the house next door to Bellevue. The O'Days had very little to do with their neighbours, but Evan was different. He was, in fact, a significant part of their lives. He took Doria shopping in the city and also in Carlton. She seemed to buy nothing at all – while Evan stocked up on cheeses, wines and exotic sausage. One afternoon he drove her, in the pink MGB, out, out to what she called the boondocks – to Heavenly Days. They roamed the pathways under the spreading trees where lifelike birds warbled sweetly, and lifelike blooms nestled permanently among the leaves. This was nothing new to Doria, America being well stocked with much bigger, wilder, better, stranger death parks than this. They read a few clean, expensive headstones, and Evan became very quickly bored. Doria would have kept going – this was an area closely related to her life's work, after all. But in the end they gave up and lunched on death-watch beetle wraps and Blue Bat merlot in the Catacomb Café. Things had begun to look up! They went on the rides in the theme park. Yes! Evan was like an ecstatic child on the ferris wheel, while Doria took everything in a strangely solemn mood, scarcely batting an eyelid, never uttering a sound, let alone a squeal. Inside the sepulchre that housed the tomb of the unknown zombie, Evan grabbed Doria's hand in alarm when two zombies, accompanied by threatening music, came slowly tottering towards them, and Doria said, 'Woah, Evan, it isn't real!' But of course it was; the undead lurched up against Evan's arm and almost knocked him over. Doria was unmoved. Evan went to jelly, rushed from the place and had to sit down on a pile of coffins at the entrance. Still Doria didn't even crack a smile. Remember she looks like Andy Warhol – that's something to think about. Doria had wanted to take the option of being locked up for five minutes in the dark with the zombies, but Evan drew the line. Daylight, daylight! He was almost hysterical. With some relief he went for a ride on the Spooky-Kooky, and had a grave-robber's sundae with wiggly worms. And this man, Doria said to herself, is an eminent psychiatrist. Yes, Doria, he is. A loony-doctor. What are you to make of that?

On the drive home – in the pink convertible, remember – Doria started talking about Margaret. She said she was finding her cold and difficult to know. Evan was surprised to hear her say that; not because it wasn't true, but because it was disloyal. 'Oh no, not at all,' he said, 'Margaret is the kindest, warmest woman you could ever meet.' He sounded as if meant it. Well, that's how conversation works. And Margaret had a reputation for high generosity. She was a philanthropist, after all, patron of this, that and the other ballet and orchestra and gallery, not to mention a dogs' home and a shelter for homeless people.

When Evan told Margaret about the zombies in the sepulchre she said perhaps Doria felt at home because she was part zombie herself. They both laughed. Well, a woman's generosity can only go so far. After that Evan confined their excursions to shopping in Toorak and the odd cricket match, at which Doria remained bewildered and unmoved. The other thing Evan reported – for Margaret and the family almost never visited Heavenly Days – was the fact that the Hungarians who had bought one of the largest family plots were giving regular concerts there, selling tickets, and making a little fortune. It seemed there was no law against what they were doing. And Evan said it was very jolly. I happen to know that one of the little violinists was the son of Eddy O'Day and a gorgeous Hungarian dress-designer. Evan didn't realise that, not that it makes any difference to anything, although it is a nice detail for a family tree. Doria missed out there.

Will any of Margaret's sharp remarks make their way into her jolly journal? Hmmm, well, she's actually a bit careful of what she writes sometimes. I think she has an idea that she is going to die one day and that people such as Doria might have a read. Sometimes she tries to go all self-analytical and revelatory. Such as now in the journal. I find it interesting.

Dancing with the Dog:

The Book Of Revelation

'We who are alive will be caught up together with them in the clouds.'
E. R. O'Day

I feel drawn to the closeness between the sisters who made the Rosetta Quilt. I've always longed for a sister, having only brothers. Families of sisters at school always seemed so magical and fortunate, as if supported by a private world. Not least Cecilia Feeney and all her many sisters. Rosetta and Catherine are therefore very dear to me, and the quilt they mostly made together on their dreadful journey to Van Diemen's Land arouses in me profound pangs of sorrow and of sisterly feeling. I can almost imagine I was Rosetta – but that's fanciful. We're not even related, really. It occurred to me that I might make a smaller facsimile of this Rosetta for Ophelia Rose, so I took some photos.

It's thinly filled with wool that must have come from Tasmanian sheep. And it's backed with plain calico, quite worn and soft. I think perhaps the calico was second-hand when they used it. It's quilted with white thread and red thread in a rudimentary way. I held it in my hands, and its graceful, fragile beauty seemed to bring into existence for a moment the tender hearts of Catherine and Rosetta. I couldn't help weeping. So many tears must have been shed in its making; I join my tears with those of the sisters. It is some kind of miracle not only that it survived, but that the girls survived the journey themselves.

Doria was very matter-of-fact about it all. She tells the heart-rending stories of people in her research with a scientific tone in her voice. I don't like that. I suppose she thinks of us a bit like that too. We are names on the vast family tree she is constructing, and all our stories are in some way equal, and without very much emotion involved. I've heard plenty of people getting enraptured about the exciting events and lives on their family trees – well, Doria is the complete opposite. She is quite weirdly cool, precise and scientific. I suppose that's how she can get her vast research under control.

But how the stories do spin off into other stories. We sat around Larisa's piano listening to Paul playing Satie, and Venus and Jupiter softly beat their tails on the rug. I thought about the link between poor lost Catherine Hart and all of us. Strange. When Justin is here, Venus sometimes gets up and dances with him to the music. It's sweet and funny. And today, she went over to Doria! She wants to dance with you, I said, and to her credit Doria got to her feet and did a little turn around the floor with Venus. She seemed to relax at last, dancing with the dog.

I keep thinking that if I'm not careful Doria might draw me in to all this family history and family tree business.

The Freud House

'Four things can not be hidden: death, the sun, the moon, the truth.'
E. R. O'Day

So it's not the Four Last Things of theology in Eddy's book. The truth's an interesting one, isn't it? Following the christening of Ophelia Rose, the next big event was Christmas, but the weeks leading up to this were naturally marked by minor celebrations. One of these was a great big mad party at Evan Keene's house. By the way, Evan was known among his colleagues – they had a boyish fondness for nicknames – as 'Heaven'.

It was a hot bright night, and Evan's house was lit up like a cruise ship in the Pacific. Margaret didn't go in for Evan's type of party, but she was a polite and loyal neighbour. So she made a brief appearance in pink and grey – Evan compared her to an elegant flamingo – and returned home early to work on Ophelia's quilt, which was slowly taking shape.

Evan entreated her to stay longer, but she was firm in her decision to retire. She felt out of place in the loud, brash world that Evan created around himself.

She sat in the tapestry room with Lillian, who was knitting, as always, for some baby or other. Picture it. There she was, Lillian, a relic of the nineteen fifties, skinny and straight in her thin brown tweed skirt and pink cotton blouse, her grey hair in a bun at the nape of her neck. She wore small gold sleepers in her ears and a Miraculous Medal in nine-carat gold on a chain around her neck. Margaret had abandoned her flamingo look and changed into lilac silk pyjamas and a lilac floral house coat. This get-up looked like stuff Edmund's mother used to wear – kind of Edwardian, or thirties movie star – fitted at the waist, flowing to the ankle. I wonder where she got those things? Her feet were shod in white velvet slippers. Her grey hair, dyed a gentle brown, fell in soft waves on her collar. At first glance she didn't look as old as she was, yet at second glance she looked even older. They sat, Margaret and Lillian, like characters in a scene from black and white Hollywood. Looked at from one angle, the movie might be some old-fashioned domestic drama; from another, it could be the beginning of a Beckett or a Stoppard play, or, for that matter, a TV comedy sketch. I'm inclined towards the comedy sketch. They could hear the music from next door, but it was distant enough, since the grounds surrounding each house were broad and deep. Things would happen at Evan's house that night, but Margaret was nicely sealed off from them all. I'll get to that in a minute.

While they worked Margaret and Lillian were watching a comforting DVD about the life of Audrey Hepburn. As well as having the large home theatre, Margaret had put small flat screens in several rooms throughout the house. Lillian often stayed with Margaret until bedtime, pleased to take on the role of companion as well as housekeeper. She would make a pot of camomile tea for both of them, and then she would pack her bag and return home in a cab, to come back in time to make breakfast. There was an unspoken understanding between them that, whereas it would make perfect sense in many ways for Lillian to move in to Bellevue, there was a necessary distance between the two women, a distance preserved by Lillian's disappearance every night. There was something magical about it. She disappears into the darkness and comes back with the dawn. How Lillian would have scoffed to hear such an idea.

Charmaine's sister KayKay (well-known slut, remember) was next door at Evan's house in the role of hostess, resplendent in the minimum coverage of silvery bugle beads on purple silk. She shimmered under the lights that were lavishly strung across the garden, leading through orange and lemon trees down to the pool. There were life-size statues of mythical women – Diana, Venus, Athena, Mnemosyne. The grounds of this house were strangely out of keeping with the house itself, which was a curious replica of the house where Sigmund Freud spent his last years, in Maresfield Gardens. Evan had inherited a solid imitation of an antebellum mansion on the property in 1999, but had proceeded to demolish it and erect this copy of the English house, which was always known in the neighbourhood as 'the Freud House'. The external structure certainly resembled the place in Maresfield Gardens, but Evan's idea of interior decoration was very far from the darkness, austerity, rich oriental rugs, and painted Viennese cupboards of Freud's old home. However, those things were to be found, along with a replica of Freud's famous couch, in Evan's city consulting rooms. Evan was considered by the profession to be out of line in doing this, but he was generally tolerated like an eccentric uncle or even a fanciful child. In his house, however, he had all the glass and stainless steel and marble and sandstone and Victorian ash you could ever imagine. Floors were pale timber, rugs slate grey, soft furnishings were shades of bone. The pictures were mostly large and brilliant dot paintings by Indigenous Australian artists. His china, somewhat like the paintings, was a collection of intensely coloured and patterned pieces from every corner of the globe, so that it emerged like jewels from the bland and unforgiving texture of the house. There were no flowers, no potted plants, no dogs, no cats. No dust. Two men from Keepem Kleen came in each morning to see to things. To walk from Freud's front door into Evan's interior was to move from one world into another. 'Welcome to my unconscious mind!' Evan would say grandly as a guest arrived on his doorstep. When the inside of the house was filled with the swirling, glittering confetti of Evan's friends and acquaintances, and you stood upstairs looking down, the place resembled an exotic and overcrowded fishbowl. Teeming with species.

KayKay loved it. She felt at home when she was in Evan's house. There was for KayKay something about the trick of entering the Freudian front doorway with its big circular porthole of a window, and slipping suddenly into the stark white world of granite and stainless steel with its sudden accents of crazed colour that lifted her spirits and stirred her heart, brightened her eye. It was sexy, just walking into Evan's house was sexy. 'Heaven's Heaven!' she would say, and just saying it always made her laugh. KayKay had a very engaging laugh. Heads would turn when she laughed her laugh, and conversations would pause. Evan adored her, his eyes following her wherever she went.

At the party on that sparkling summer night, as waiters carrying trays tinkling with glasses of champagne wove their way among the guests, as the seductive rhythms of a jazz quartet sang into hearts and minds, as asparagus began to wilt on beds of melting ice and the shells of a large catch of lobsters lay cracked and abandoned on dozens of gleaming bright blue plates, Evan in his crumpled white linen suit and smooth pink silk shirt scampered halfway up the glass staircase and blew a long note on a trumpet. A sudden silence fell. Somebody dropped a glass, which shattered on a stone table. Silently a roving waiter appeared from nowhere with a cloth and whisked the fragments off the surface and away.

'Goo' friends,' shouted Evan, his eyes bright and his cheeks glowing rosy under the lights from a beaten copper chandelier. His speech, often marred by a stutter, was flawed and slightly affected by drink, 'goof friends, I thank you for joining me tonight, and I wish you all a very h-happy festive season. I would like to make an – ah – important announcement which I know mar-many of you might have been expecting. Please, KayKay my dear, will you join me up here for a moment?'

KayKay sidled up the glass stairs, a vision glistening in purple and silver, and took her place beside him. There was a little gasp that went around the company below. One of Evan's ex-wives, now married to the architect who had designed the Freud House, tittered. Evan went on: 'I have asked KayKay to b-buy my wife and she has done me the honour of ackspecting – accepting me, with all my fer-faults and foibles.' As he produced a ring from his pocket, a roar of approval and great rush and clatter of applause came from the crowd below him. KayKay held out her hand and the ring slid onto her finger. The waiters zipped expertly round refilling glasses and somebody yelled, 'To KayKay and Heaven!' and the cry went up, 'KayKay and Heaven!' as phones recorded the joyful picture and people rushed up the stairs to kiss and hug the couple. The band went wild with saxophone, cymbals and bass. Women examined the huge diamond with shrieks and even tears, and the couple were physically swept down the staircase to the dance floor where the dancing broke out in a frenzy of drunken hysteria.

Why didn't you tell us, KayKay, people cried. But I didn't think he was serious, said KayKay, herself breathless and almost overcome with surprise and delight. Charmaine was pleased enough by the news, although she felt also that KayKay could have done better than Evan Keene who was already twice divorced and, Charmaine privately considered, frankly nuts. He was established and prosperous, although supporting two children from the other marriages. That can't be good, can it? KayKay had been such a wanderer for so long, it was probably quite fortunate that she had caught Evan's eye at all. Or perhaps it was inevitable. And it had helped that the Freud House was next door to Bellevue, where she was a frequent enough visitor. He was fifty and KayKay was thirty-nine. Maybe it wasn't too bad. It was a pity, Charmaine would say, that a church wedding was out of the question. But already her swift imagination had gone to work on some alternatives. Religion had never meant anything to KayKay. Little enough to Charmaine, actually, but she followed the form set out by the O'Days, at least on the surface. We mustn't forget the little matter of the probable paternity of Oriane.

As the night shrieked on, people threw off their clothing and jumped into the pool, which, by the next day, was something of a mess. Keep'em Kleen came in at nine. They were used to this kind of thing. At the bottom of the pool were a scarlet sandal and a string of turquoise beads, on the surface floated and bobbed a horrible old sneaker of unknown origin, while around the periphery, among the lounges and low tables, were bottles and glasses, squashed strawberries, the empty skins of oranges, and what must have been the contents of a bucket of maraschino cherries. Pieces of clothing, condoms and a few towels lay damp and forlorn about the place. Like a bunch of undergraduates, guests had draped the statues in lacy underwear. The garden below the pool stretched away towards the river. It was in the willows along the riverbank that a kayaker discovered, the following afternoon, the body of Clement McGrath.

Clement had been at the party, but nobody remembered when or where they had last seen him. The police interviewed Evan and KayKay and a few other strays who had passed out about the place and stayed the night, but nothing useful came of this. Other witnesses were invited to come forward, but none had anything much to say. Clement had imbibed freely at the party, but seemed to have dissolved into the shadows. After an autopsy and inquest it was concluded that he had wandered alone down to the water's edge, had slipped, hit his head, and drowned. If he had cried out, nobody would have heard him. A widower with no children, he was a poet and novelist, known for announcing drunkenly at smart literary gatherings: 'I am writing itself!' Nobody really knew what he meant by that, but he was tolerated, people smiled and indulged him. There were a few academics who kept predicting that he was the next big thing, but nothing seemed to come of it. He was briefly mourned by the literary world. His books would slip for a while into obscurity before enjoying a new lease of life as ebooks. In fact, they were to become quite the thing in new printings on cheap heavy paper and very small print. Doria, who had been at the party, got two of his novels called *More or Less* and *Time Out of Mind* on her Kindle, but she found them too mysteriously Australian, and failed to finish them. The novel he had been writing, a satire on the legal profession, was set, as it happened, in the heart of Toorak where he had met his end. A book closely resembling this work in progress was eventually published by a barrister-novelist and became the basis of a popular television series called *Value for Money*. Stories went around that Clement had been silenced by his Toorak and legal enemies that night at Evan's party but, like many an entertaining conspiracy theory, they came to nothing. Death by misadventure. Drowned while under the influence. No suspicious circumstances, but a few colourful suspicions.

Margaret, cosy and comfortable in her study with her sewing and Lillian and Audrey Hepburn, had missed two momentous events – the engagement of KayKay and Evan, and the drowning of Clement McGrath. These days, particularly after the death of Edmund, Bellevue was a bastion of respectability; bad things happened elsewhere, in the west, or maybe down the road, across the river. Occasionally right next door. But not in Margaret's house. No, not at Bellevue. Nothing bad ever happened at Bellevue these days.

I trust you are alert enough to hear a faint bell ringing?

Doria had had a brief conversation with Clement before he disappeared, recalling later that they had discussed horse racing. Clement had said to her, quite suddenly, 'Youwannafuck?' At first Doria had been unsure of his meaning, and by the time she had caught on Clement had returned the conversation to horses. It was difficult to be near him because his clothes, an old brown tweedy suit from long ago, gave off an odour of mingled sweat and dust and fish and tobacco, and his breath was that of a man in urgent need of dental work. It was a hot night. Clement smiled a lot, grunted sometimes, and leaned in close to Doria. He had a great desire to go to the Virginia Gold Cup, something Doria was happy enough to discuss. He also said he longed to attend the Kentucky Derby. Doria remembered later that Clement had seemed to be sad, but not really *very* sad. Hardly sad enough, she would have thought, to drown himself. In the river. Drunk as a skunk was what Evan said, and always a maudlin drunk, always trying to race off some woman or other, sometimes with success, often not.

'Was Mr McGrath a patient of yours, Dr Keene?' asked the detective.

Evan's answer was too detailed. All it needed really was a yes or a no. He was shocked and nervous and suffering from a hangover. He was appalled that his latest engagement party had ended up like this. Appalled and shaking, actually.

'He was not. As a general rule I never invite patients to my parties. Sometimes it's unavoidable – social circles overlap. Clem was an old friend, we go back a long way, and we would occasionally meet for a Friday afternoon drink at the Cricketer's Arms. Um, yes. C-catch up on old times. Although we were of different gen-generations we had a fair bit in common. Once we shared a girlfriend for a short time, but that's all in the past. He worked on the principle that if you put the h-hard word on enough women, sooner or later you'll strike it lucky. Not a bad principle, when all's said and done. But none of this is relevant. Forgive me. I am not myself.'

'So the deceased was not a patient of yours, Dr Keene?'

'No, he was not.'

For someone who offered his patients the talking cure, Evan was a man who practised what he preached. Once you started him talking it was hard to get him to stop. He would run his fingers through his hair at the end of a sentence, take a breath, throw back his head and begin again, running on and on as his busy mind took him hither and thither. Some of what he said was true, and some of it was not. Artistic licence was one of Evan's character traits. However, in the matter of the death of Clement McGrath, he in fact knew virtually nothing, and was utterly wretched to think that the thing had happened at his party. That was the problem. At his *party*. He occasionally held his head and moaned: 'On my watch!' as if his party had been a ship, and he the captain.

Nobody knew anything. There was little to know.

Eventually Clement's funeral took place at the Toorak Church of the Assumption, which featured briefly on the evening news with images of celebrities from all corners of the arts mourning the passing of one of their own. Only the week before, a longer news item had featured the same stone porch as the family, friends and enemies of a local member of the criminal underworld wept over the casket of their beloved. A vast blanket of deep-red roses had swathed that casket, while Clement's was decorated simply with a bunch of purple irises. These flowers would wilt and not last the afternoon, yet a young woman poet had insisted on them. They were his favourite flowers, she declared, and quoted a line of her own work on the subject as evidence or confirmation of the fact. It was she who read at the service Clement's celebrated 'Atlantic Salmon' poem.

You can see that O'Day Funerals was doing a brisk trade. Well, for that matter they always did, being very good at the job, and having business hand in business glove with the Grim Reaper himself. I said that nothing bad ever happened at Bellevue, and that's a fact, but plenty of gruesome stuff went on at the rooms of O'Day Funerals. Well, of course it did. That was the point.

The death of Clement McGrath cast its shadow over the engagement of KayKay and Evan. The couple decided to bring forward the wedding and celebrate it early at the end of January. For the purpose, KayKay said, of dispelling any lingering cobwebs of sorrow that might be clinging to the rafters – there were no rafters – of the Freud House. It would be an exorcism, exorcising poor old Clem; he would have liked that, Evan said, and then he hooted with laughter. I don't care for Evan.

'It will have to be in Evan's garden, with a celebrant,' Charmaine announced, having given the matter her careful, domineering, sisterly attention. And so it was.

The Trappists of Kentucky

'The price of caskets is rising. We blame it on the cost of living.'
                                                     E. R. O'Day

Doria was dazzled when she arrived at Bellevue on Christmas Day. The front door stood open, and on the broad chequer of the tiles stood a tall Christmas tree perfectly decorated with frosty white baubles and crimson ribbon. Tin and wooden trinkets – tiny gingerbread men, little horses, dolls and teddy bears hung from the tips of branches. There were many bright miniature feathered birds nestled throughout the tree. And some of them, I have to report, would actually twitter at the slightest vibration so that unless the place was empty, there was a more or less constant little cacophony. The Austrian angel high on the apex was also small, pale blue, with worn and weathered wooden wings. She, like all the ornaments, with the exception of the twitterers, which were added by Charmaine, was from a collection handed down over the years in both Margaret's and Edmund's families.

Doria brought with her two parcels wrapped in thick orange paper – Bourbon fruitcake and red raspberry fudge from Gethsemani, the Trappist monastery in Kentucky. Amazing! She placed the parcels among the pile of gifts under the tree. Always alert for curious detail, Doria noticed, half concealed, a small brown suitcase that was ancient, battered, forlorn, mysterious. Wait and see, she thought, just wait and see. Meanwhile she was one of a joyful group that, besides the immediate family, included Evan and KayKay, Evan's children and his guests (an Italian psychiatrist and his wife and children), as well as Paul's friend Gerard who had arrived from Milan. Gerard Laval was an opera singer, tall, blond, a perfect Seigfried. When he heard about Doria's work he explained that he was descended from the original Bluebeard, and this gave him an extra special cachet of terror with the children, who in fact adored him. He had brought with him a large box of marzipan mice in coloured jackets, which he scattered among the gifts under the Christmas tree. His laugh was boisterous, and rang through the garden during the afternoon, when people had dispersed to swim or play tennis or sleep. The children played games indoors on their various new devices.

Christmas dinner was in the dining room, utterly English and traditional with turkey and a flaming plum pudding and crackers. Everything gleamed white and silver, glittered with Waterford crystal, shimmered in the light of the chandeliers and the candles. Lillian had been busy, enlisting the aid of her two nieces and also a professional waiter. But first the Toorak O'Days and their guests gathered around the tree, seated, while Joseph, handsome in grey linen trousers and blue silk shirt, handed out the presents. Doria had been right about the suitcase. It was the first thing to be given. When Joseph picked it up, there was a hush in the hall.

'This year the suitcase is for Ophelia Rose!' he said, and Charmaine came forward to claim it for the baby.

Frederick, who was sitting beside Doria, leaned over and whispered: 'The youngest always gets the little case.'

'Oh, why is that?'

'It's a tradition from Grandmother's family.'

'What tradition?'

'It means there are sad children somewhere. Children who won't get anything for Christmas. It's empty.'

Doria found this quite touching, but also rather sinister. But the gift-giving had moved on, and the children were duly receiving parcels of electronic devices as well as the usual dolls and scooters. Because Frederick was about to turn twelve, Margaret gave him a handsome copy of the *Shorter Oxford Dictionary*. An optimistic gesture in the case of Frederick. But it was another family tradition. When, after a great length of rowdy and joyful time, the hall was littered with wrapping paper, and the children were running up and down the stairs in glee, they went to the dining room. Doria was seated next to Margaret, and she asked about the suitcase.

'Oh yes,' Margaret said, 'when my father came back from the war he started the tradition. Every year we remember sad and lonely children who won't be celebrating Christmas, won't be getting any presents. I think it's good for our children to see that, in a graphic way. Don't you? It's so typical of Daddy.'

Doria agreed. The suitcase had disturbed her somehow. But her fruitcake and fudge were a great success.

'You must have packed an Aladdin's cave in your suitcase, Doria,' said Margaret, and Doria laughed, showing her little teeth.

Thank God for the Trappists of Kentucky.

Wedding Bells

'With mirth in funeral and with dirge in marriage.'
E. R. O'Day

That's one of Edmund's more telling headstones. If you give people the chance they will reveal their true thoughts eventually.

The afternoon was hot and sticky. KayKay had taken the possibility of this into account when she prepared a PowerPoint presentation for Irina the makeup artist. KayKay went to the salon with her laptop and dramatically gave her presentation. Believe me. There were pictures of sections of KayKay's face that were annotated by text boxes in different colours. KayKay would then address the text boxes, pointing with a laser. There were twenty-seven non-negotiable points to be attended to, and an astonishing eighty-three things to be avoided. There was cold hysteria, even madness, in KayKay's eyes. Irina, who had never, in her many years of preparing the faces of nervous brides, encountered such neurosis, wondered about giving the whole thing a miss, but she persevered. This was the daughter of the millionaire dry-cleaner, after all. She solemnly took notes as KayKay gave her PowerPoint, and then she presented KayKay with a detailed list of her own observations. Finally they agreed on how things were to be done, and how KayKay was going to look. In essence, the eyes were to be dewy, the skin was to be matt. You'd think they could have decided that without the PowerPoint. Dewy eyes, matt skin.

And so, on the day, they were.

Margaret was a woman who liked to take control, but in comparison to KayKay, it turns out she was an amateur.

On the wedding day, KayKay was in an almost catatonic state, and everything was managed brilliantly by Charmaine who had engaged a large team of busy workers. The celebrant was Victoria Bone-Smyth, the fashionable choice, a middle-aged woman who resembled in appearance and dress a benign and portly sweating priest of some unknown and artistic sect. There was even a vaguely purple hue to her face. Evan's garden was at its carnival best, resplendent with ethereal swags of ivory silk held in place with bunches of fresh orange blossom. You can get anything flown in. The jazz band was there again in full force, glorious in pale linen shirts, the instruments gleaming in the sunlight. At the appropriate moment, they burst into the wedding march from *Lohengrin*. In the shining snowy marquee the central table was exquisite with lace and crystal and silver, the cake a small and perfect tower of milky marzipan, intricately sculpted with rosebuds and topped with two white chocolate hearts that merged, melted into each other. KayKay had designed all this in deadly earnest, not being given to irony. Finally she, in a simple confection of coldest white, faintly tinged with pistachio, demurely veiled with a vast Honiton lace mantilla, by some trick of happiness and slightly melting cosmetics, appeared youthful and strangely innocent. It was one of those lovely optical illusions. Evan wore a suit of pale straw linen which crumpled a little, but which showed him to great advantage as almost handsome, his hair paper white, his pink scalp glowing, his Freudish whiskers short and silvery, his skin as smooth as a balloon. There was something touching and even graceful about Evan Keene on his third wedding day. Third time lucky, people said out loud. They did, they said this *out loud*. His two teenage sons George and Isaac from other marriages were there, looking very handsome but somewhat scruffy. There were no bridesmaids, but Charmaine was elegant and regal in pale greenish satin, acting as the matron of honour.

'Oh, green, such bad luck at a wedding,' Margaret said. 'And I hadn't imagined KayKay would be taking Evan's name. Does she realise she will be KKK? Perhaps she doesn't care. Or realise.'

Charmaine, after talking to Doria about weddings in Florida, devised the magical event that accompanied the vows. When KayKay and Evan promised to love and honour each other until death, a flock of Migrant White butterflies was released from a large green basket. Oh no, not more butterflies. Oh yes. Butterflies.

'It's an old Peruvian saying,' Charmaine said, passing on information gleaned from Doria. 'The butterfly is the messenger of love. They say it in Peru.' Doria had suggested she get in touch with Spineless Wonders in California, since she believed they were the people who had supplied the weddings in Florida. Spineless Wonders suggested Winged Victory in Tasmania, and sure enough Winged Victory were able to source the Migrant Whites from Queensland, and get them to the Freud House in time for them to be let loose, an ivory tumult, at the wedding. They were a complete surprise to most of the guests who had expected, if they had expected anything, a flock of doves. The whole thing was also a surprise to the Migrant Whites. They disappeared in a flurry of lepidopteral befuddlement, if I can say that.

'Spirits, melted into air, into thin air,' Justin Rhys said aloud, heavy on the irony. And KayKay thought this was a beautiful sentiment. She wasn't at all well read in Shakespeare, or anything much.

The Migrant Whites at KayKay's wedding were, as things turned out, a rehearsal for the bright blue butterflies Charmaine would bring to Margaret's funeral. Remember those? Of course you do. Like the blue ones, the whites were bewildered and hesitant in their movements, and one or two of the slower ones ended up being crushed underfoot, leaving a mustard yellow smudge on path or lawn. Much that is profound is visited on the fragile wings of butterflies these days; they are meant to bring to mind the soul, and to be messengers, as Doria said, of love. It's a lot to ask. They are also common symbols, Eddy would have told you, of the female sex, but maybe that doesn't come into it here. Leave that for the gates of Heavenly Days.

They Had Slits Where Their Eyes Had Been:

The Book Of Revelation

'Everything's coming up daisies.'

E. R. O'Day

When I see white butterflies — and I've never before seen a flock like the one at KayKay's wedding — I am transported back to my grandmother's garden in Mont Albert. It was the night before she died, and so I think my memory is sharpened by the fact that the day is marked by death. I was four, and Grandmother Ellie had recently finished for me the pale yellow dress I was wearing as I ran about among the flower beds and vegetable plots. I was chasing the white cabbage moths. I was always chasing things — butterflies or birds — running along the wet beach after the seagulls. I recall the thrill of hope in my heart, the expectation that one day I would catch one, a butterfly or maybe even a bird. I was so sure I was going to catch a seagull.

There seems to be a desire people have to arrest bright flying things, to capture them and curtail their freedom, to subdue them to the human will. My brother Michael had rainbow finches in a cage in the garden. I loved those. On one occasion I did get a cabbage moth, but the poor thing had been damaged by a bird before I got to it and, as it lay fluttering helplessly on the palm of my hand, and as I touched it tentatively with my finger, it dawned on me that now I didn't know what to do with it. After a few minutes of indecision I dropped it in the grass and left it there. I felt bewildered and sad.

Beautiful, ephemeral, endangered, fluttering things – but why do I have the urge to chase after them? It isn't just me; everybody loves chasing flying things, I think.

There was nothing special about that summer afternoon, yet everything is etched on my memory, or at least on what I think of as my memory. I am probably filling in a lot of the details from my imagination. Even from photos. Great-aunt Phyllis was there. She lived with Ellie – they were half-sisters, Phyllis the unmarried one who was a companion and virtual servant. She was a darling and I adored her. I learned many years later that she was the daughter of Ellie's father and an Aboriginal woman on their property in the Hunter Valley. That was a shock. But it made sense of her looks; she resembled a much paler version of the Thomas Bock portrait of Tasmanian Mathinna in her red dress. I never met the Aboriginal woman, her mother; all I knew were a few old photos. If I decide to co-operate with Doria I'll tell her about Phyllis, but she can probably work it out for herself. Since Phyllis had no children, she may not count. And then again, since she wasn't even an O'Day, I realise she *is* beside the point, being on Edmund's mother's side of the family. It would have been different if she had been his mother, but of course she wasn't. So I don't have to tell. That's a relief.

I remember playing tea parties with Phyllis under the lych gate in the garden. There's a painting of the lych gate here on the wall of the tapestry room, so I see it every day. Not that I particularly notice the picture. Written on the wall above the seat are the words: *Beauty without Virtue is like a Flower without Scent*. In gold letters that have faded with time. It recalls the foxgloves, the hollyhocks, the lobelia, the lavender, the calendulas, the silverbeet, the parsley, the mint, the cabbages. The two cherry trees down by the fence, their fruit so vivid and shiny, the low brick walls beside the gravel paths, walls for sitting on in the sun. The goldfish pond, fat fish gliding beneath the waterlilies. The clothes line that was just a piece of rope between two tall poles. The smell of the copper when it was boiling up the washing. Frisky the rabbit in his cage. All this is etched by the sadness, the well of hurt and wash of sorrow that came to me for the first time when my grandmother disappeared forever. It's a long time ago now.

I don't remember anything at all about her funeral, or anything much else about her except some details of the house, maybe the smell of baking bread, and her china dolls, and the delicious soft comfort of the bed where I sometimes slept, but the last afternoon in the garden is lit in my mind by a glow, a supernatural glow. It's the last blaze of sunlight before the fall of night. I run and dart and pounce but I never catch anything, so I pick a bunch of mint and rush indoors with it crushed between my palms like a small wet green bird. Grandmother Ellie went from being the sweet warm presence in her apron in the dark kitchen, in her pale dress in the formal sitting-room where the wallpaper was covered with peacocks, to being an object of our prayers, a dreamy spirit, an additional name, Eleanor, on the list.

I didn't need to ask if she was in heaven; I knew she was in heaven. She didn't need my prayers; I needed hers, and I was confident that I had them. She was beyond the sky, working on my behalf. I had no real idea of what this meant; and in fact I still don't. If I'm honest I must say here that my understanding of my own religion is pretty much what it was when I was four. Perhaps that is not such a bad thing; perhaps it's the same for everyone. Except maybe saints and poets and musicians.

Much of this came back to me with a rush – it was, in any case, forever present in my memory – when they released the Migrant Whites at KayKay's wedding. Like when people release white doves at weddings and funerals and probably football matches, I felt this cloud of butterflies was an act of cruelty. Surely balloons would do? Does the RSPCA actually allow these things to happen? I suppose insects don't count as animals. A gasp of surprise and delight went up as the poor creatures came fluttering out of the basket, seeming to blink in the light. I don't suppose they blink. The sun was shining; they appeared to be blinded. They hovered, tentative, and took flight in all directions until they had swiftly disappeared into the trees, into the distance, presumably to be eaten by birds. Some were trampled. Some stuck to people's clothing. It was easy enough to catch one, but then what? It's somehow so like Charmaine to introduce this kind of thing into the proceedings. She's a fool. I kept my counsel, but I will not forget. Naturally I described it to Lillian, who was appalled.

'I once saw them let a whole lot of doves go, at a very fancy wedding,' she said, 'in the Botanical Gardens – we were having a picnic. I think doing it to doves is bad enough, really, but poor butterflies – well, that seems really awful to me. You said they were from Queensland? What would they do with themselves in Melbourne, then? But I suppose they would soon get eaten. Oh, it does seem so unnecessary, doesn't it? Such a waste.' And she shook her head, looking down at the floor in a way she has when she is bothered and puzzled.

'Was it pretty, though?' she asked in a quiet way. I realised that there had been a moment of beautiful surprise when they had come stuttering out into the hot air, fluttered, suspended between darkness and light, and then dispersed slowly in their various ways and then were gone. The air became empty, as if they had never even been there at all; empty, yet occupied by their absence. I do think I am developing a poetic way of saying things. I didn't know I had it in me. It must be all this writing I'm doing.

'Yes,' I said to Lillian, 'yes, they were very pretty.'

'But sad.'

Yes, they were sad – well, to tell the truth, I was sad. And they were meant to make us all happy, weren't they? Some people seemed pleased, happy enough. Evan was beside himself with glee, beaming and sweating away next to KayKay. He kept eagerly squeezing her. It was rather embarrassing really, the way Evan went on. And one of his other wives was there. And his sons as well.

'She looked lovely, didn't she?' the generous Lillian said. 'What a beautiful veil. I suppose it was an heirloom?'

'Oh yes, it was.'

'Green for a bride is bad luck.'

'Bad luck, I know.'

KayKay and Charmaine's family is well endowed with heirlooms. Lace things from all over the world, collected by their grandmother when their grandfather was in the French diplomatic service. It's quite funny to think that Charmaine and KayKay spring from a diplomatic family that has turned into a family of wealthy dry-cleaners. They're the most undiplomatic young women you could ever hope to meet. But very clean, I suppose.

On my bookshelf there's a travel book; it's called *Mariposa Road* and is about crossing the United States looking for butterflies – there are about eight hundred species, I think. Scientists, lepidopterists like the author, catch them in nets and preserve them for science, but that's miles away from trapping them in boxes and flinging them out to live or die. I sometimes wonder about the ones in my screen, placed between the glass panels for the purpose of design. I suppose they were caught and killed instantly in the name of art. That makes me uncomfortable, too, but I still love to look at the screen. My feelings about butterflies are obviously quite conflicted. No doubt Evan would have things to say about it.

I should try to be more charitable about KayKay's wedding, but it did seem to me to be a wild and silly business. His third marriage and her first, although she has had more boyfriends and affairs than anyone can count. Several of her love affairs, I understand, have been with married men, including her personal trainer and a peculiar young man she met in a youth shelter. Promiscuity hardly begins to cover it. I understand they plan to have children, KayKay and Evan. She talks about it a lot, and Charmaine encourages her. Nothing wrong with that. And it will be nice to have babies again in the house next door – I remember when Evan himself was little, an only child in the Keene house; the house he demolished to make way for his weird Freud monstrosity. The thought of KayKay as a mother gives me pause, but perhaps she will change for the better, people sometimes do. I really wish she would give up smoking, for one thing. Perhaps when she's pregnant she will. She and Evan are both heavy smokers. I have never allowed smoking in the house, except in Edmund's study, where he made his own rules. People said he died from living too well, which is code for overdoing everything. As far as smoking was concerned I was absolutely firm with him about the rest of the house. Perhaps for him his study was a bit like the old bombshelter of his boyhood: a haven, a refuge, somewhere to have forbidden fun. If he and his company wished to smoke in other parts of the house they had to go into the garden. Edmund liked to obey my rules, I think, and the men were often out under the trees. I would sometimes watch them. Edmund knew that. Personally I have never taken much to either tobacco or alcohol, with the exception of my glass of whiskey on retiring. I'd be lost without that. I have a bottle of Powers Gold Label with me wherever I am. It's ironic, I suppose, that I have one of the best wine cellars in Toorak, but seldom touch more than half a glass. When we were at school we all experimented with drinking and smoking, but I never liked either. Quite a few of the girls I was at school with have died from lung cancer, and I realise that several of the living are alcoholics. I became a wowser for a while – a word I recently had to explain to Doria, who had never heard of it. Perhaps I inherited this from my mother's Methodist family, who never touched a drop, ever, with the exception of Uncle Vernon – an uncle I never met. He was a bachelor who sang in the Royal Opera but drank himself to death at an early age. I was quite amused to hear myself describing myself to Doria as a fanatically puritanical person. That's not me at all, really, but it's a reasonable perception. People sometimes wondered how Edmund could stand that about me, my wowserism, but he used to laugh and say I was his shining example, and that he could indulge for both of us. He did. His death was sudden, one night over at Fiona's. By the time the ambulance came he was gone. I like to think he was happy, being there with Fiona. She imagined at the time that I would never forgive her, but of course I did forgive her. There's no point in harbouring the feelings she imagined I had – I didn't have them, and I'm not entirely sure what they are.

Doria seems to be something of a smoker, too. That surprised me. She looks so pristine and she is perfumed with her frightful patchouli, which might disguise the tobacco. I'm always wary of people who smell odd. She commented to me at the wedding that it was fascinating how families link up and how family trees spread before your eyes. She pointed out that because Joey and Charmaine are now related by marriage to Evan, his boys George and Isaac move into the picture. I didn't think family histories went as far as that! But she said one of the fascinating parts of her work happens when she goes off on a tangent and follows, for instance, someone such as Isaac's mother's family. In fact she said that the idea of the family tree, while useful, is very limited and restricting, and that human beings are linked by incredibly complicated threads which form an amazing web, more like a vast and unimaginable lace cloth than a huge forest of oak trees. Her eyes were very bright when she was telling me this, and her voice seemed to take on a different and rather eerie tone, as if she were speaking to the stars in the heavens. Well, that's an exaggeration, but she was speaking to something beyond me, certainly. It occurred to me afterwards that the idea of the *tree* is upside-down. If I start with me and build a 'tree' up the page, I go to my parents and my brothers, back up to my grandparents and great-grandparents, with branches out for uncles and aunts and so forth, but the beginnings are way up in the sky, lost in the clouds. I'm not the root. It seems to me that, whichever way you look at the thing, the image of a tree is inadequate. So the idea of the lacy web of fantastic cloth appeals to me more than a tree. But the whole thing makes my mind spin. I don't know how Doria does it. Her fingers almost never leave her iPad, and so I suppose her mind works like a computer, too. It's as if she is an extension of the iPad, not the other way around. Sometimes, with her pale tawny features and sharp and knowing nose, she really does remind me of a fox. And now my thoughts leap backwards. To foxes.

When we were children in Eltham we had a great big wicker dressing-up box. It was like something at the theatre, and children from all around used to come over to dress up. We did plays in Dr Blood's garage. Among the old dresses and shoes and pieces of lace and ribbon there were two battered fox-fur necklets with dangling paws and bushy tails, one darker than the other, and more sinister. They had sweet clattering tortoise-shell chains that joined the two ends so that the tail was virtually dangling from the jaws. The bright black glittering eyes. Oh, the eyes. But as well as the necklets we had several raw fox pelts. They had slits where their eyes had been, and some had slits for ears while others still had ears. The boys and I would slip the fox heads over our foreheads and grip the front legs under our chins, letting the tail flow down our backs, and we would run and leap and hide. We were the Fox Family. I was Mrs Fox the matriarch, and my brothers formed a gang of marauders. The nastiest part of the skins was the strong black whiskers that stood out from the sides of the jaws. I could not resist stroking them, repulsed yet attracted by the gloss and spring as they slid between my fingers. Kitty would sometimes hide sweets and cakes in the long grass under the fruit trees and we, the Fox Family, would hunt them down and fight over them. They were lovely, those fights I had with my brothers.

Some days we put on our fox skins and took a picnic down to the ancient cemetery on the side of the hill, where I was posted as the lookout. The gang spread out among the tombs and headstones, while I lurked behind the gates of a large tomb that was dug into the clay of the hill. I peered through the iron bars, watching for the imaginary farmer who was lying in wait for us with his rifle. My brothers, fox tails flying from their shoulders, pelted down the hill, in and out of the crumbling graves. On the signal of my low cooee they would freeze on the spot, duck behind a headstone or into a tomb, waiting for my second call, a soft whoo-oo, which was the all-clear. Then they came dashing back up to my hidey-hole where, on one of the flat gravestones, we set out our picnic of sweet rock cakes and apples. We were then the Fox Family at rest after a hard night in the field. I was carefree about cemeteries in those days, they were exciting places to play; now I find them too horrible for words, even though they are the foundation of the family fortune. Heavenly Days is – well – something else again. I rather like the idea of the Hungarians and their concerts. One day I might go and hear one.

When I remember all that about the fox pelts, tears spring to my eyes. The scene in my mind's eye is so vivid, so filled with vigour and happiness. My brothers have all died. Columb, Michael, Augustin. Columb's wife, Mary, came to Ophelia's christening. Her garden round the corner in Glamis Court is vast and incredible, mostly roses. She has several Ophelias, which she says are fragile and troublesome. The indefatigable Doria plans to interview Mary, although I don't imagine Mary has much documentation of interest. But you never know. I suppose that's one of the things about Doria's kind of research: you follow every possible lead in the hope of discovering – what – the equivalent of a speck of gold or something. What if Mary has that speck of gold? I hate the thought of Doria *finding out* things, things that should stay forgotten, where they can do no harm. They say that every family has dark secrets. What is the good in stirring them up?

There is Little That is Private in the World Today

'Bring out the coffin, let the mourners come.'
E. R. O'Day

In the garden at Bellevue one day, Doria discovered one of these specks of gold, not from the past but from the present day. It happened when she was playing cricket with Margaret's grandsons Rupert and Gustav, the sons of Isobel and Hugh. The boys' nanny, the girl named Smith, was with them, too. They lost the ball in a dense patch of ornamental ivy. As they all pushed their way through the tangle of tough branches and shiny leaves, Doria said she hated ivy.

'Our baby is an ivyeff baby,' Rupert said.

There was Doria's speck of gold.

'Oh, I didn't know you had a baby.'

'She isn't born yet. She's ivyeff.'

'He's not supposed to say,' Smith added.

Gustav found the ball and the boys ran off, accompanied by the dogs.

'Really?' said Doria. 'Does the family – I mean, Margaret – know?'

'Oh no. I think she disapproves of IVF. She's old-fashioned, you see. No, it's a deep, dark secret.'

'I won't tell.'

'Rupert would be in awful trouble if you did. I don't know if they plan to tell when the baby's born. Maybe not. My sister had IVF and everybody knew from the start. I reckon that's better, don't you?'

Smith lit a cigarette and offered one to Doria.

They stood, knee deep in the ivy, peacefully smoking, watching the boys as they ran into the distance, tossing the ball to each other as they went.

'Well, secrets have a way of coming out,' Doria said, and Smith laughed.

'This one just did,' she said.

'I won't tell,' said Doria, thinking, I won't tell until I need to. Gossip was not, after all, her thing. She wasn't about to unsettle Margaret, to stir up unnecessary trouble. She could save the story of IVF for some distant future use.

'Oh. OK. Whatever,' Smith said, flicking the stub of her cigarette into the ivy. One of these days she'll set something on fire.

The idea of IVF set Doria off on a whole new train of thought. Is the genetic material of Isobel's ivyeff baby even O'Day material? What if it isn't? Where does that put bloodlines? Doria's mind was occupied with such puzzles as she sat down with Smith and the boys to watch afternoon children's television in the luxury and comfort of the home theatre at Bellevue. Venus and Jupiter were there, too. The scene is set for nothing to happen. But children can get meaning out of the most unpromising material.

They watched *Romeo and Juliet* performed by garden gnomes. Then they saw a cartoon about Henry VIII. Gustav watched patiently, chewing on a blanket and laughing out loud in appropriate places. But Rupert watched with close concentration and fascination, wide-eyed with his wide O'Day eyes. Doria told them the king was a real person from history.

'It's a story though, isn't it?' Rupert said.

'Well, yes, it's a story, a true story.'

'But it's just like a story.'

Doria had no way of dealing with this faintly disturbing piece of paradox and philosophy.

Afterwards, when the screen had moved on to a lot of teenagers in a spaceship, Rupert turned to Doria and said thoughtfully:

'If he didn't like his wives, he didn't have to chop off their heads.' And then he added, rather wistfully: 'He could have given them to another family.'

Smith snorted. Doria, virtually useless with children, said nothing. She couldn't formulate a response to this amazing piece of thinking. Gustav scoffed and said Rupert was so stupid, you couldn't just give your wife away to some other family like a cat or a dog or a horse. Again Doria had to keep her own counsel. She just said mmm in a way she had, and they all continued to watch the teenagers in outer space without much interest or comment. Smith roamed in and out with dishes of chips and glasses of apple juice, pausing sometimes to watch the TV, but really moving in a world of her own, going outside every so often to smoke. Doria decided to change places with her, and left her with the boys watching TV and playing a board game called *Skeleton in the Closet*. They liked to do two or even three things at once, attending also to games on their various electronic devices. Of course the board game appealed to me.

It was still hot out of doors. Doria strolled down to the table beneath the oak tree, and felt herself relax as the light began to fade, and the thin smoke from her cigarette drifted into the shadows. She sat for a long time gazing back at the house where here and there the surfaces of the upper windows were brightly lit by the last rays of the sun.

Her imagination was piqued, since the story of Henry VIII is really a story about heirs and inheritance, and that was her field. It's nice, isn't it, to think of fox-faced Doria enjoying a smoke under the trees, pondering the problems of history and fertility.

What if Henry had had recourse to IVF? If the royal sperm had been able to meet the Queen's egg in a laboratory prior to being nurtured in her womb? The history of the world would have taken a whole different turn. Supposing there had been no Elizabeth I. Do current royal families resort to IVF, I wonder, and will they ever confess to doing so? Probably yes in the first instance and no in the second, but *no* secret is safe in the world of blogs and hackers and the tabloids and the World Wide Web in general. But you know that, don't you? There *was* the interesting story about the Queen Mother who was supposed to be the daughter of the head of the family and the cook, Marguerite. No secret is safe when there are children like Rupert around. So Isobel was being very private and secretive about her IVF and I think there was something rather sweet about the story being leaked by the boy as they searched for the ball in the ivy.

Smith was right: Margaret was unaware of her daughter's fertility problems, and of the pregnancy, which would soon be announced. Lillian, as it happened, had an inkling of what was afoot, because her own daughter was in the IVF program and had several times seen Isobel in the clinic car park. But Lillian also knew when to keep things to herself. Margaret had no real prejudice against IVF; it didn't necessarily conflict with her religious beliefs. Yet she had a kind of reserve and distaste about such clinical interference in the process of having a child. Why, she wondered, do so many women these days find it difficult to conceive a child? Is it the pill that's to blame, as some people said? That and all the stress of careers and leaving conception too late? Then there were all the toxic things in the air, in the water, in the food, in the clothes and the houses. Perhaps, Margaret thought, the popes were right when they condemned the pill. Perhaps, for one thing, it ravages the woman's body, causing all these fertility problems. Margaret was, as Smith said, old-fashioned, and had always shied away from the gory details surrounding conception and birth. She liked it when daughters or daughters-in-law simply announced they were pregnant and then went ahead and produced babies. That was how things ought to be. Anything else she didn't really want to hear about. Celebrities of various kinds kept thrusting their pregnant bodies (Margaret didn't really say 'bellies') at the world – and of course pregnancy was big business, very very big business, so it was everywhere. And the idea of paid (or even unpaid) surrogacy made poor Margaret feel ill.

Doria was different, of course. She was longing to know whether the work in progress was using exclusively O'Day materials or not. Bits of Hugh and bits of Isobel – or perhaps bits of two entirely other people. Family trees have always been subject to the danger of illegitimacy, which is often concealed, but the fertility techniques of the twenty-first century, not to mention the social media, pose a whole new set of questions. And how much, for instance, did Smith know? Might not *Smithereen herself* be a source of further vital information? Think of that. It was possibly not the kind of thing to interest Smith, really, since she was absorbed in the care of her own hair and nails and outfits, and was welded to her phone. She was good with the children. She was saving money to go to visit her relatives in Ireland and Greece. Hugh provided Smith with a car and fuel, a bonus that went with the job. He also flirted with her. Was that another bonus, or a liability, and how far did it go? Smith obviously enjoyed it, took it as a kind of given, by right of her gleaming youthful looks and her position in the household.

I rather like Smithereen.

Doria found herself being drawn, and willingly, into the lives of the family and those around them – such as KayKay and Evan. Occasionally the memory of Clement's clumsy request at the party would cross her mind and she would wonder – if she had agreed to what he asked she might perhaps have, in a sense, saved his life. But it was a bit horrible to think about, disappearing into the bushes with Clement McGrath. To save him from drowning himself in the river. She always imagined her role among family members and their friends was sort of at a remove – she was the listener, the observer, but not the player. This attitude was partly what got on Margaret's nerves. Doria would record the information and construct the narratives, but would not really enter into the game. She could bring gifts such as the christening rattle, and fancy foods from the Trappists of Kentucky, but would never in any way make a gift of herself; she was above and apart. So to have been perhaps the last person to speak to the dead man at the party in the house next door was a novel role for her.

Doria told nobody about her conversation with the scruffy, drunken Clement. Well, after all, nothing had happened. For that matter she didn't ever say much about herself to the people around her, apart from simple facts. Her personal story was not relevant to the pursuit of family history; she was the detective, the recorder. Should she have offered Clement at least friendship? He wanted sex, not friendship, after all. Or perhaps both? Too late now, in any case. Doria shook off all thoughts of Clement McGrath; he was gone, it was sad and horrible, but she had her own serious work to do. She also tossed the stub of her cigarette into the carpet of ivy and re-entered the house through the tradesman's door, said goodbye to Margaret and the children, who were about to have dinner, and walked back to her apartment, accompanied by the dense harsh chorus of cicadas in the hot air of the evening.

She carried with her the lovely speck of gold that Rupert had given her as they pushed their way through the ornamental ivy. Our new baby is ivyeff!

The Letter:

The Book Of Revelation

'Death is the supreme festival on the way to freedom.'
                                                    E. R. O'Day

My father always used to say you just never know what will come up with the sun. You have to be ready for anything, but you must also hope for the best. I love the dawn. I love the way the light breaks over the garden at Bellevue, the soft colourless glow as it filters through the old trees, the carolling of the magpies. I really love this house. I am at home. It is, somehow, me. I was having a cup of tea when the letter came.

This is What it Costs

'Enjoy a lifetime guarantee in a dead-end street.'
E. R. O'Day

The day was already heating up, it was early February, when Margaret was having tea in the morning room at about ten thirty. Everything beyond the window was tinged with rich gold, and the light fell on one of the curtains, washing out a swag of the deep carmine and ochre pattern. A white tablecloth, some butter yellow tulips in a fat white jug, their stems bending over, their petals beginning to spread open, the soft green spears of their leaves. The china was the floral pattern called 'Bellevue' that had belonged to Edmund's mother. It carries long memories, and Margaret has grown very fond of it. The beautiful tang of strong Irish Breakfast tea. One teaspoon of sugar, no milk. Butter on the silver dish that's lined with green Depression glass cut into the rays of a star. Someone gave this dish to Margaret's mother for a wedding present. So it has great sentimental value. How objects can outlive us, and survive, and carry meaning along with themselves down the years. Margaret was feeling happy, feeling comfortable, pleased with the morning, ready for the day.

Lillian brought in the post. As she placed three ordinary envelopes on the cloth beside the cup, Margaret felt a sudden jolt of alarm. There was something out of the ordinary, some special and dangerous thing in one of those envelopes. Margaret does sometimes have these feelings, and they're often right. Lillian left her, as she always does, to return to the kitchen, and Margaret slit open the first, then the second, then the third. She held the paper knife lightly in her right hand, slitting, one, two, three. It was the third one that contained the thing.

It was a letter from a Charles Clark-Finn, a solicitor with Colley, Morton and White of King Street. Margaret had never heard of these people before. In the family they have always dealt with Malony and Malony from the Paris end of Collins Street. They are practically part of the family. Mr Clark-Finn wished Margaret to call his office and make a time to meet with him. He was writing to inform her that her half-sister had passed away at the Convent of the Holy Child in Greensborough.

Margaret stared at the name of the convent for a long time in breathless silence. It was where her mother had spent her final weeks. The letter said that the Sisters were desirous of handing over to Margaret, the closest living relative of the deceased, her personal effects. She had been buried as per instructions in the convent graveyard in December. Her name was Ophelia Mary O'Day. Margaret stared at the name. She couldn't make any sense of it. It seemed like a curse.

Then her mind went completely blank and she sat at the table staring down at the letter with its nasty legal letterhead in dense shiny burgundy ink, staring down for a long time. The paper was thick and faintly cream coloured, the lettering shimmering before her eyes. It shone up at her like poisonous red slime. Mr Clark-Finn's signature was neat, done with a fountain pen in blue. He seemed to have put two dots over the 'i' in Finn. A mistake? The letter must be some absurd mix-up, some insane and ghastly error. Yes, surely the whole thing was some kind of terrible mistake. It was like a letter that floats down in a movie dream sequence, opens itself up and falls on the table with a little 'ting', the words dancing in mockery. Mr Clark-Finn was so sure of himself, with his two dots, so matter-of-fact, so legal, so blunt, so lacking in all emotion. In its bluntness the letter was like a bill for electricity – here are the units you have used to bathe and shower and wash your sheets and knickers, to iron your blouses, to heat your rooms, to freeze your ice cubes, to cook your meals, to clean your floors, to light your rooms and run your televisions – and here is the sum of money owing to us as a result of your activities. Electricity use is mysterious but almost explicable. This letter was mysterious and inexplicable. It was saying: here is how the past looks, and *this is what it costs*. This is what it costs.

But no, he must have it wrong. Wrong. Half-sister? What half-sister?

And yet, this was all so incomprehensible that it could only be expressing the truth. Was that possible? It was a truth that would not begin to fix itself in her brain. Everything about it cried out that it was true; everything in her heart, yes, everything in her heart cried out against it. And yet, and yet, here was a document that was telling her she had a sister. Had *had* a sister, the sister she had always longed for. But what does it mean, a *half*-sister? And the name? This was the third Ophelia in her life. Or was it a chilly possiblity that she was the same one as the first? The baby, Kitty's baby, who died? *Could* that be possible? No, not possible. Her mind, although stunned, was beginning to work fast. She was overwhelmed by shock, but the brain went into overdrive.

Gradually the pieces began to fall into place as she sat staring down at the paper, occasionally looking up to stare out at the golden garden, now strangely unfamiliar, strangely sharp and vivid. Ophelia Mary O'Day. Was this true? *How* could it be true? Kitty, dear Kitty, who did the ironing, who ran in and out of the apple trees with us, poor Kitty who had a baby and died. And the baby died. Surely her mother and Auntie Iris said the baby *died*? Of course the baby died. Ophelia Mary died. Margaret could not reconcile the information in the letter from Charles Clark-Finn with the conversation she had overheard about Kitty, so long ago. And yet she *could*. Suddenly her brain refused to recover the memory of the conversation. Then it came back to her in hollow snatches.

Died within hours. Plop. Called her Ophelia. Snip. Emergency baptism. Plop. Ophelia Mary. Snip.

They did say the baby died. They did. The more she tried to hear their voices, the more distant and empty they became. Their words, the tones, the rise and fall of sadness, of a kind of relief too, relief that the death that had reached out and claimed Kitty and Ophelia had passed by her mother and aunt and their own babies. Something vast and terrible had nodded at them and had passed on by. When Kitty was taken, Margaret's mother and aunt were safe, in the frightening magical game of life and death. And her mother's babies were safe. The little O'Day family had been spared; Kitty and Ophelia Mary had not.

A dreadful fog began to creep into her head – while her heart cried out for some help, and for some understanding.

The past is not the past – it can rise up in the present and take new shapes, like a creature that sleeps as if it is dead, and gradually or suddenly, with the flick of a paper knife in a smooth white deadly envelope, with the flash of the letterhead as the page is unfolded, gradually or suddenly the creature raises its scaly head and smiles with dreadful teeth and opens its scarlet mouth and licks its shining lips and says: 'Ophelia Mary was your sister and she is dead. You missed her. She walked the earth in Greensborough and your paths never crossed.' Or was there some mistake? Yes, that was it, Mr Charles Clark-Finn and his letterhead were mistaken. There are so many O'Days – Doria could tell him that in a moment.

Ophelia Mary? Kitty and Killian? It is impossible, utterly impossible.

Doria. Doria was suddenly the face of all the danger. Here was the secret she had come to uncover. This was what Margaret had dreaded. Yes, it was this. Doria and the lawyer's letter.

Margaret knew at once – oh yes, she did, she knew *right then* – if Doria ever hears of this she will 'incorporate' it into her vast spreading story of the family and there will stand Killian, beloved and spotless father, kind and darling father, with Kitty in his arms, Margaret's tiny unborn sister rocking sweetly pink inside her. Impossible.

Margaret whispers, staring out at the sky, 'My father has lied to me. He has betrayed me.'

He has given her half a sister and he has hidden her away from everyone forever, and now she is dead. Margaret never saw her, never knew her, she never knew Margaret was there, waiting to love her. How she would love her! When Margaret was ten her father asked her what she would like for her birthday and she said, I want a sister, and he smiled, tenderly, and said: 'Now Margaret, what you would really like is a lovely gold watch.' And they gave her the watch, and it *was* lovely, with a thin brown band made from crocodile skin. But she remembers feeling sad and tricked. Oh yes, she was tricked all right. Her sister Ophelia Mary was there all the time. There, close by at the convent in Greensborough. Or is it all a dream? Untrue. Clark-Finn fabrication, error, glitch. Half-sister. Did Margaret's mother know?

And Doria will write all this into her charts, her cold charts covered with lines and dates and births and deaths and marriages and half-marriages. Doria can kill Margaret's past, and killing the past she can kill Margaret herself, and everyone she loves, everything she loves, everyone who loves her, everyone.

To the sky Margaret whispers: 'I do not know my father; I do not know myself.'

She was becoming silently hysterical as she sat there at the table like a statue.

From the moment Margaret set eyes on Doria, she knew she was somehow an infection; now she knows she is the angel of death. 'Doria is here to kill my father.' Oh, she masquerades as simple history, as wholesomeness and goodness as she opens up the story of the family's past, this vast and sprawling O'Day family that moved out of Waterford in skips and steps, sailing to America, fleeing the potato famine, was forced to sail to Australia, sent in chains. Doria can track them all down, a hunting dog will chase every rabbit down every rabbit hole. Doria can find Ophelia Mary. Doria can destroy Margaret with one word, one gesture.

Ophelia Mary did not exist. Ophelia Mary lived a long life and died in Greensborough.

Margaret's head was a whirl of fact and fantasy, and she could feel a bright zigzag just behind her eyes. She breathed deeply. Better.

Lillian came in to see if she needed more tea.

'Oh,' she said in alarm, 'is something the matter, Margaret? What is it?'

As she spoke Margaret jerked around to look at her and knocked the green butter dish to the wooden floor where it landed with a clunk. Lillian rushed forward to pick it up, and by some miracle it was unharmed.

How could Margaret ever begin to express what was the matter, even to Lillian? Supposing there were no mistake? The letter that lay on the white cloth, beside the jug of yellow tulips, carried a vast message that was beyond her comprehension, and beyond the simple words of a reply. For what the letter had done was destroy the glorious beauty of the father. That's *some* destruction. For if Margaret had a sister, a half-sister, born when Margaret was five, and living until she was seventy-eight, until the sister was seventy-three, her father knew, and he had lied. He was a lie. This is not possible. If Margaret had a sister, then she never knew her own father, he was a duplicitous stranger, a play-acting stranger who sang to her the songs from a lying songbook.

Seventy-three years old, my sister, my little sister. All my life I have longed for a sister to love, and here she was, and was not. She had been and I had never known her. Living – why? – in some convent in Greensborough. Was she a nun? What of Kitty's family? Where did they come into this? Surely Ophelia Mary died at birth?

In the long minutes Margaret spent sitting in bewildered horror, she was not really forming coherent thoughts. As she sat at the table she was a heart filled with a swirling cloud of feelings, of conflict and of the impending collapse of her whole construction of the past.

'No, no,' she said to Lillian in an even voice, but a voice that still betrayed her state of mind, 'there is nothing the matter. Nothing at all the matter.' And she was then able to fold the letter up and return it to its envelope. But Lillian knew, of course she knew, that Margaret had had a shock. A deep and terrible shock. Lillian could not begin to imagine what that shock had been, and how far it could carry Margaret away from the bright sunlight that streamed into the morning room.

Lillian took the three envelopes, Margaret saw them disappear, and she put them on the desk in the tapestry room as usual. Yes, Margaret was somehow capable of pretending that all three pieces of mail were equal. And the letter lay all day in the tapestry room, like a dark and black and brooding warty toad. In her heart it was breeding a terrible dread that reached forward into a fragile future, while spreading back into a past where everything was deformed and utterly spoiled.

White cloth. Yellow tulips. White jug. Later, Margaret went into the kitchen and watched Lillian as she chopped up rhubarb. Thud, the green ends fell away as the knife came down.

The image of Nellie Melba as Ophelia kept swimming into Margaret's mind, the sad eyes, the wild golden hair, the small open mouth, singing as she drowns.

You never know what will come up with the sun.

What Will Come Up with the Sun

'Death is the cure of all disease.'

E. R. O'Day

In the picture-perfect office of Mr Charles Clark-Finn, solicitor.

It is on the second floor of a breathless handsome grey Victorian building in the city. Stone griffins decorate the columns at the silent entrance hall. The lawyer's desk is broad and deep, mahogany, showing signs of the wear and tear of many years, but glowing as if with knowledge and confidence. One of those pieces of furniture about which you might say – *if this desk could talk, such stories it could tell. Ha-ha!* Mr Clark-Finn's law books are sternly ranked behind the glass doors of the bookcases. Mr Clark-Finn himself is forty-five years old, fit and tanned and well draped in his charcoal Zegna suit and vermilion Dior tie. Handmade shirt from his man in Milan; hand-made shoes from his other man, in London. The socks by Paul Smith are his only little joke, but so comfortable. And handsome, too. Yes, he is a hand-tooled mahogany and fine wool and silk and linen kind of man. He exudes a dry confidence to match his desk, and exudes also a Hermès fragrance that mingles leather, lemon, herbs and sandalwood. He is coiffed and manicured, his hands large and capable, and his smile reveals the care of a most skilful and expensive dentist. His wife, whose name is Sally, smiles winsomely from the frame of a single photograph that stands beside the green desk lamp. She has one lovely arm around a boy of about ten, and the other around a girl of fifteen.

By coincidence or something, the Clark-Finns live in a house at the other end of George Avenue from Bellevue, a vast newish house made from glass and slate and granite and steel. Charles remarks on the fact that they are neighbours, but Margaret can not recall ever having heard of him before. There are strange newcomers, many of them Chinese, mysterious and beautiful in long gleaming cars. She half smiles politely and says nothing. The Clark-Finn house is the kind of building that works like a fortress – I suppose you could say it *is* a fortress – the family entering and leaving in large dark SUVs, with tinted windows, cruising in and out via vast electronic garage doors. For that matter Margaret enters and leaves her own property by car, sweeping through the ornate iron gates that are also electronically operated. Some neighbours Margaret has known for many years, although she seldom sees them. The Clark-Finns she has never known, never seen, never heard of. Neighbour Evan Keene is in a category of his own, having been there since he was born, and having recently become part of the family.

But the matter in hand in Charles's office, where there is a prevailing aroma of beeswax, that honeyed ambiance of convent hallways long ago, is far removed from the trivialities and fortresses of the neighbourhood of George Avenue. It concerns the life and death of Ophelia Mary O'Day, late of the Convent of the Holy Child, Greensborough. Although Charles is almost aware that the words he has to say, the papers he has to refer to, are as a shower of long needles, swift darts aimed at Margaret's heart, he knows he must deliver, he must refer. It's not for Charles to listen for the echoes of grief, a grief that is probably beyond his understanding. Of course you never really know what depths there are to other people, but I can hazard a guess that Charles's imagination wouldn't follow where Margaret's distress is located. I could be wrong.

'And are you able to tell me, Mr Clark-Finn, what the child was suffering from, what – syndrome, what...' Margaret's language fails her, she flounders, spreading her hand palm down on the handbag that is lying flat on her lap like a small grey shark. She leans her head forward slightly.

'In fact, no, Mrs O'Day, there is no real documentation of the case, I am afraid. It was a long time ago, you understand. All I can determine m-yes is that the child did not thrive from the very beginning, and was not expected to reach her first birthday, was in fact expected to – yes – die within the first few weeks of life. But with the medical care of the time, and with the loving ministrations, and I daresay the m-prayers of the Sisters, she managed to outlive expectations by – m-yes – seventy-three years. I believe the Sisters considered her life, from beginning to end, to be a miracle. A quiet and miraculous example of the – yes – grace of – m-yes – God.'

The grace of God does not come quite as easily to the lips of Charles Clark-Finn as the language of the law, but he is as familiar as he needs to be with the rhetoric required for the conversation. He sounds like someone quite a bit older than himself. It's a persona he has adopted for these cases.

Suddenly they are in the realm of the miraculous, a recognisable realm for Margaret. Charles presses on, returning as soon as possible to the safer territory of the language of the law.

'...and any funds remaining after the death of the Ward shall become the property of the Guardian. The residuals are, as it happens, minimal.'

It comes down, in the end, to funds. Yes.

But we are not yet done. It's not quite *only* funds. Someone at the convent has made a small parcel to be delivered to whomsoever it may concern. It concerns Margaret. Charles hands it to her across his desk.

It is tiny, Margaret's name written in felt pen on the outside. It is the size of a small thin paperback book, strictly and carefully wrapped in thick brown paper, tied with white string. Strangely, it resembles packages as they used to be wrapped by Killian O'Day, who was noted, within the family and the practice, for his meticulous making of parcels. He would prepare things for the post, and he would wrap gifts, always in brown paper, with a variety of strings, red string for Christmas, white for birthdays. Margaret holds the parcel for a moment, her finger softly stroking the centre of the string knot. She looks Charles steadily in the eye, thanks him, signs a document, and then she puts the parcel in her handbag and clips the handbag shut. Something mysterious is now trapped inside her grey handbag, held in by the amber clasp. You wonder if there is a fly or something in the amber? There is. Funny thing, metaphor, don't you think? They stand, Margaret and Charles, shake hands, walk side by side across the dense and comforting green surface of the carpet to the door. Exit Margaret. Through the reception area and through the high ornate Victorian doorway into the sudden assault of the crowded street. Hither and thither, eyes on many a distant goal, people furrow forward this way and that, creating a buzzing jungle, a tangle of worries and woes. And no doubt joys.

But Margaret is a still and isolated single beating heart as she stands on the pavement's edge to hail a cab. The cab, yellow as a dangerous insect, slides in to the kerb, and Margaret, her handbag with its unknown contents clutched to her abdomen, gets in the back. As the cab moves out into the traffic, Margaret relaxes on the seat, gazes out the window, almost in a trance, her handbag resting in her lap. Suddenly she sits up. As they pass the intersection near the elephant-coloured Town Hall she sees, there at the traffic lights, waiting to cross, a frown of concentration on her brow, Doria Fogelsong, urban fox! She is probably on her way up to the State Library of Victoria to look at files, documents, whatever she does.

Oh, there it is again – coincidence, synchronicity, serendipity, fate, etc. Doria and Margaret crossing paths at the traffic lights.

As if Margaret needed to be reminded of the dangers of Doria. With an involuntary gesture Margaret clutches her handbag tightly, conscious of its mysterious and precious contents, which must never, never be revealed to the prying eyes of Doria. Or anyone, but most of all Doria. Hurry, hurry, taxi, hurry home to Bellevue. Margaret is feeling faint with anxiety. She is conscious of the beating of her heart, and has a sensation that every now and again something seems to slip, ever so slightly sideways, in her brain, just behind her eyes. She takes deep breaths, in, out, and stretches back against the seat, pushing her feet forward as far as they will go. The cars and the people blur past the windows of the cab. She closes her eyes, breathes deeply, and holds fast to her handbag.

Every now and again her mind moves back to what Charles has said about Ophelia's life being considered a miracle within the convent. It dawns on her quite quickly that this is deeply dangerous territory. If the Sisters believe Ophelia Mary's life to have been miraculous, then it is possible, even likely, that they will not only be praying for her, in a routine way, but will be addressing her as an intermediary in their prayers. If she answers these prayers, and she almost certainly *will*, then she will become the object of great and terrible interest. She could progress to become the Blessed Ophelia Mary, a celebrated public figure to be venerated, someone who might, eventually, join the company of canonised saints. Such things can happen. God forbid! Oh, Heaven help us! Holy Mother of God! Holy Michael Archangel!

Margaret's imagination is going berserk. She can't even identify the nature of any sins she is falling into. Is it the sin of pride to imagine her sister is a saint? Then what is the sin that tells her to conceal from the world all knowledge of this saint? Is she planning to silence the Sisters – with what – money? Can they ever be silenced? She knows they can't. Deep down in every convent is the desire for a saint, no matter how often this fact is denied. Is she hoping to silence God? Yes – that is, in fact, her real project.

Margaret O'Day must silence God.

She must ask God to hush the matter up. She must go into a flurry of prayers. It's the only way. She has at last arrived at the solution to her dilemma. But how close is she, really, to God? She realises that there is no human being with whom she can discuss the problem; she must rely on her own relationship to God. The thought of sharing all this with Justin Rhys is almost laughable. Well, it is in fact laughable. Perhaps there is somewhere a wise priest who would listen and advise. This is unlikely. And anyway, such is Margaret's pride — for she was right when she identified pride as the stumbling block — it so often is — that she will not consider the possibility of finding a wise and patient priest to hear her case. After all, what *is* her case?

These thoughts are carried along in the cab to the accompaniment of a radio station talk-back which for some of the time happens to be about the rights and wrongs of abortion. A group called Right to Live sings a strident number called 'Foetal Blood'. Margaret, deaf to all but her own thoughts, doesn't even register what they are saying, relevant as it is to her story.

At last the cab begins to wind through the quiet streets of Toorak. If there are people in the houses behind the high walls, behind the tall trees, at the end of the long drives, they must be resting quietly. Or perhaps they are whispering into telephones, or murmuring in each other's ears as they lie on the slightly rumpled beds of love affairs, amid the tumble of lovely lace underwear and perhaps a used condom. Perhaps they are smiling down at their keyboards, sending off swift messages of illicit love, or deep details of financial optimism. They would be tweeting. There is not a soul in sight, scarcely a car parked at the kerb. Finally there is a young Chinese man walking a brown dog, then suddenly he disappears, and the street is empty again. The only thing that disturbs the air is the insistent yellow of the cab as it slides along towards Bellevue and home and safety, far, far away from the trap of Charles Clark-Finn's immaculate room, far from his horrifying bookcases, his long clean fingers, his firm and shining smile of reassurance. He *knows*. Charles Clark-Finn knows that Ophelia Mary lived and died, and out in Greensborough there are nuns cleaning floors and washing dishes and praying for Ophelia Mary. Are they also praying *to* Ophelia Mary? What will the miracle be?

To Charles it was a small matter. Every day of the week people come in to collect envelopes and parcels of effects – a gold watch here, a bundle of letters there, a whole canteen of solid silver cutlery of a design that will not in any way enhance the dinner table of the recipient, the deeds to the run-down estate in County Down, the shares in Singapore Airlines. A small suitcase filled with unused baby clothes. A train of thought. Margaret thinks of the little empty suitcase under the Christmas tree, and in a flash she understands what it was really for. It was Ophelia Mary's suitcase. *Ophelia Mary's suitcase.* And tears come again to Margaret's eyes. Every Christmas since the 1940s Ophelia Mary had been with the family at Christmas.

With his routine smiling gestures Charles Clark-Finn changes people's lives, sometimes for the better, sometimes for the worse. What he has handed Margaret is a parcel of truth, and a black and monstrous burden of anxiety, an anxiety composed of things she has never before imagined possible.

If only Doria had not appeared on the scene, the turbulence of all these things would be simpler. Margaret can now begin to hate Doria with the energy of her own betrayed love. Perhaps she should ask God's forgiveness for this hatred. She does not.

For better or for worse? Would it be better if Margaret had never known about the existence of Ophelia Mary? Is it better to carry forever the unblemished saintly father, the doctor, the soldier, the faithful husband, the man who could wrap up anything and make the parcel beautiful? He was, back in those days of general medical practice, known also for the perfection of his sutures, the straight and narrow line of the scar that obediently faded over time. Killian was an artist with his scalpel and his thread. Or is it really best that Margaret now knows, at the expense of her father's character, that she had the sister she always longed for? Well, this knowledge is not perfect, since the sister, to whom she could have offered her love and care and affection in her extreme need, has passed through life never knowing what Margaret was holding in reserve for her. What difference would it have made to life if Ophelia Mary had been brought home to the doctor's house in Eltham, cared for by Muriel, cared for by Margaret? How remote, in fact, *was* Ophelia Mary from the norm? Would it have been possible to have her at home with the family? In Margaret's imagination she is like a strange doll in a room full of other toys, a doll with bright rolling eyes, a doll who is at least a fact of ordinary life. She is not a secret saint about to be revealed by nuns in Greensborough. You can relax – this isn't the way the story is going. We can leave the few nuns who remain in Greensborough to their own good works. And we can note that Margaret plans to send them a very large donation in due course.

How Margaret's imagination races ahead. What she realises, what has dawned on her during the strange drive from the city to Bellevue, is that she is now a different person from the woman who left home this morning to visit Charles Clark-Finn. The father she knew is now nothing but a myth, and so in some horrible sympathetic gesture she herself is beginning to feel she does maybe not quite exist. One of the key building blocks of who Margaret is has been quietly removed in the lawyer's office, and a sense of unreality has enshrouded her whole being. Later she will attempt to recover scraps of ancient conversations, images of almost forgotten days when Kitty skipped in and out of the laundry, the kitchen, the playroom, the orchard.

The orchard. Does Margaret remember Kitty in a pink dress and old brown sandals running away into the leafy embrace of the apple trees, trees with squeaky green and yellow and red fruit hanging like decorations on a Christmas tree? Granny Smith, Golden Delicious, Ladies in the Snow. Or is Margaret's imagination subtly constructing old scenarios, old games, old transgressions, old serpents, old Bible stories from Muriel's Protestant past? Who to blame for the sudden collapse of everything? Margaret's thoughts try to be focused on Charles Clark-Finn, he who held the document, but naturally her mind and heart keep swinging back to her father, who is now a stranger, who gave her a sister in the worst possible way, and then hid that sister forever from view. Margaret's eyes are dry, and her back teeth are clenched in the bewildered sadness of grief.

She opens the gates for the cab with the small remote that she carries in her handbag, steps out of the cab at the front door of Bellevue and stands for a short time as the cab drives away. She draws a great deep breath and feels faint as the light around her takes on a greenish tinge. But she goes in and then she stands in the hallway, her sunglasses in her hand, for a long moment, there on the black and white tiles. One lone chess piece. A faint zigzag behind her eyes. She tries to breathe deeply. Weak at the knees. Then she passes out. Her sunglasses skitter across the marble floor.

Lillian has heard the cab leaving. She watches it disappear up the drive and closes the gates when it's gone. And after a few moments she comes into the hall and discovers Margaret face down on the floor, her sunglasses lying some distance away, her handbag squashed underneath her. She calls Jim Donovan, Margaret's doctor, who says to call an ambulance. But by now Margaret is coming round, and says all she needs to do is go to bed. No ambulance. She asks for camomile tea. So Lillian helps her upstairs and into bed, and late in the afternoon Jim arrives to see how she is. Everything seems to be normal, but he says she must stay in bed for at least a day, and he ups the dose on her heart medication. She needs to have a test for cholesterol levels as soon as possible. And needs to see the heart specialist. Perhaps he realises she has a broken heart. He wonders about a brain scan. Has she perhaps had a tiny stroke? Something that will never even show up on a scan?

The room is filled with light, and is fragrant with bowls of yellow roses. A tall Famille-Verte, Margaret's favourite piece, stands on a table in the corner.

'So what took you into town, Margaret?' asks Jim.

'Oh, I needed some new gloves.'

'Well, that doesn't sound very stressful. Did you find what you wanted?'

'Actually, no. Not what I wanted at all.'

Jim Donovan laughs and says: 'Well, that *is* stressful, isn't it? Susan would probably just order them online.' He's smiling.

Did women really go into town in cabs to buy gloves these days, he wondered briefly. Maybe they did. Women like Margaret O'Day had little enough to do with their time, after all.

'Next time I probably will.'

'Good work. Now you promise me you will rest for at least a day. No buzzing about. Lillian will see to you, won't you, Lillian? I'll drop in again in a day or two. Or maybe Bing could come over after surgery.'

Margaret's eyes widen, and she sits up in alarm.

'Ah – no need. I wouldn't wish to trouble Bing.'

'No trouble, Margaret. He's very handy, just across the street.'

'Oh, I know. But he doesn't have to worry about me. I'm fine you know. Just fine. Really.'

One of Jim Donovan's partners in the practice, Bing Honey, does indeed live in the forbidding black box of a new mansion across the street. Unlike Jim, who reminds Margaret of her father in his grace and understanding extended to all his patients, Bing is a vain and handsome man of fifty-five who has no time for anyone over sixty. He makes this clear in subtle and not so subtle ways.

'Oh, Bing,' Evan the cheery psychiatrist once said to Margaret, 'Bing's so terrified of age and death he can't bear to look old folks in the eye, you know. That's why he keeps marrying younger and younger women. Retreat from death. It's a wonder he can tolerate living across the street from the family home of O'Day Funerals. I think he refuses to have a garden because flowers only remind him of mortality. They bloom and then they die on you. Take Bing Honey on a picnic and he'll just be listening for the rumble of thunder in the distance. For sure.'

Dr Honey has a policy or a habit of reminding people over sixty that *seventy* is the lifespan appointed by the Old Testament – the idea being that there is not much point in treating their symptoms, which are only the symptoms of the approach of death. So why bother? Margaret imagines that she is particularly repulsive to Dr Honey because she also reminds him of the funeral industry. She always gets the feeling that he wishes old patients would simply go home and take an overdose and stop clogging up the waiting room. He's very active in the movement to legalise euthanasia, something with which Margaret herself is, as it happens, sympathetic. Edmund never met Dr Honey, but he would have had many a laugh at his expense.

Jim Donovan can tell that Margaret doesn't want to see Dr Honey, and so promises to come back and check on her personally. Lillian shows him out.

Lillian realises that Margaret's story of the quest for gloves is a fabrication, but naturally keeps her counsel. She has put Margaret's clothes away, placing the grey handbag on the dressing table where it stands up, as if waiting to be addressed.

So now Margaret is alone with the parcel.

She sits propped up on pillows and, breathless, gently pulls the string apart and folds back the brown paper. There is an envelope in which there are some old photographs, a Miraculous Medal which appears to be solid gold, and a tiny pair of scissors. That's all.

Margaret smoothes the medal between thumb and forefinger. This medal hung around Ophelia Mary's neck. Margaret herself has not worn a medal since she was a girl. Sissy Bagwell wears one, and that's no surprise. Lillian wears one. But most of the Catholics of Margaret's acquaintance do not. Old Italian grandmothers wear medals, and young Spanish girls. So Margaret thinks. Greek men perhaps. Oh – probably pious Irish women; yes, probably. Margaret feels a long way from jewellery like this. What is she to do with it? Keep it safe. Put it with her own childhood trinkets, which are in the old Maja powder box. Her mother used to wear several medals – it was the fashion then in those days of greater superstition. Some of Muriel's medals are in the Maja box. Most of them are cheap. Only one of them is gold. They are wrapped in a piece of white silk and labelled: *The medals Mother was wearing when she died.*

Is this all that remains of Ophelia Mary's possessions? One medal, a pair of scissors, and five photographs? No birth certificate? No baptismal certificate, no death certificate? Perhaps convents don't hand such things on. But Margaret wishes she had them. Why? So she could destroy them? Well, at least she could conceal them. Or she could fondle them and love them. But can anything really be concealed forever? Would not the day come when Doria or her equivalent (her equivalent!) would ferret out the birth certificate, the death certificate, the record of Baptism? First Communion, Confirmation? Did Ophelia Mary pass these milestones? She must have, no matter how incapable she might have been to comprehend them. It's something, at least, that the convent has seen fit to send Margaret the medal and the photos – but the lack of the documents suggests to her the nuns just might be planning to take the matter of Ophelia Mary to a higher level. Margaret tosses herself back against her pillows. She will have to look at the photographs.

Five pictures. Four black and white, one colour.

One: A baby, wrapped in a lace shawl, lying in somebody's arms. The person holding her is obscured, but is clearly a nun. The baby looks perfect, if very, very tiny. On the back, handwritten in ink: *Ophelia Mary, three months.*

Two: A large pram in which lies a small thin girl with sparse hair, over-large teeth and rolling eyes. She is surrounded by soft toys. On the back: *Ophelia, fifteenth birthday.* (Fifteenth! She's so very small.)

Three: The same girl, now in a more conventional wheelchair, in a dining room, older, still extremely small, squinting at the camera. Nothing on the back.

Four: This is the coloured one. In a garden. Two nuns either side of the wheelchair in which is a wizened figure in pale blue. On the back it says: *Happy sixtieth birthday, Ophelia.*

Five: A battered picture, fading, criss-crossed with cracks, feathered and furry at the edges. A very pretty young woman sitting under an apple tree in bloom. She is smiling confidently and Margaret recognises Kitty. It is Kitty Sullivan. There are no words on the back. No words.

By the time she has stared over and over into the photos, Margaret is in tears. She feels completely exhausted and depleted. Sad beyond any sadness she has ever known. She slips the pictures back into their envelope, along with the medal and the scissors. Later, she will think about all this later. Where to put the envelope? For the time being it is probably safest in her handbag. She even keeps the paper and the string. This is all she has left of the sister she never knew.

And her father?

She never knew her father either.

Margaret feels now very lonely, adrift in a new world, a world that has been remade, re-ordered, distorted beyond recognition.

The tiny scissors lie in the palm of her hand. They have a faintly art deco look to them, elegant smooth oval holes for the fingers, a slight kick to the base of the arms. How to analyse the parts of a pair of scissors? One tiny battered screw holding them together, the blades short and sharp, the points incredibly pointy, like needles. The metal is something dull, discoloured – steel resembling pewter. And the mark says *C. Johnston, Sheffield*. Tied to one of the finger holes is a faded pink silk tassel, so soft and aged it seems to whisper as it slips between Margaret's fingers.

Why the scissors?

As Margaret looks at them, turning them over and over in her hand and in her mind, they spring into life in her memory. These scissors are identical to the scissors her mother used to cut her children's fingernails. Were they a very common type of thing in the forties? Or is it possible that these scissors are the *self same scissors* used by Muriel O'Day? The tassel? Was that a clue? Margaret doesn't recall the tassel. She remembers her mother's fingers in the holes, the firm grip Muriel kept on Margaret's small hand as she worked her way across the fingernails. It occurs to her to snip at her fingernails as she sits there, but then she doesn't. She tells herself she mustn't wreck her manicure. Even in panic and distress

Margaret is capable of being practical and vain. Then she spreads out her fingers, these fingers that once lay in her mother's hands as the soft little nails were deftly cut with the scissors. Now they are such old and wrinkled hands. And Margaret is in tears again, the scissors flashing in and out of the fabric of the remade world where Killian has a new face, and where nothing is any longer what it seemed.

The revelations, in all their glaring simplicity, have now silenced *The Book of Revelations*. Margaret lacks the heart, let alone the skill, to get any of this down in words. The day will come when she takes up her fountain pen again, when she offers the journal and tells her story. Be patient.

Charles the Handsome

'Anyone's death is yesterday's news.'
E. R. O'Day

Some weeks after the events in Charles Clark-Finn's room, Margaret had occasion to meet Charmaine for a late afternoon tea at the Windsor Hotel. Even when one's world has been turned upside-down by a lawyer's letter life must go on, and there is shopping to be done, and not online. There are afternoon teas to be had.

Great bowls of flowers, soft shaded lamps, broad mirrors, the hush and rustle of luxury, tinkle of glasses, chink of china. Waiting for Charmaine, who has never been on time in her life, Margaret was seated, as she always liked to be, at a table in the farthest corner of the room. She had a nice view of all who came and all who went. And one who came was Charles Clark-Finn, in the company of a glamorous, a very glamorous young Indian woman. If Margaret was not mistaken, and she surely would not be in such a matter, the two were very close indeed, casting around them at their table a glow that placed them in a joyous world of their own. It was love not business that brought them here. So they didn't really care if they were seen? This elegant man, who had delivered to Margaret the grenade that scattered her heart, was dallying at the Windsor in the late afternoon with his love. And why not? And although the facts of the matter of the Ward and the Guardian were lodged in his memory, those facts were but minute elements in the long and complex trivia of his vast professional life. What mattered to Charles now was this moment at the Windsor, this tryst, this congress of Charles the Handsome and his Love.

Suddenly, to Margaret, this seemed only right, only what might be expected. The Charles who had handed her the photographs and the medal and the scissors, who had stated his credentials as a solid family man by displaying the picture of his wife and the children on his lovely old mahogany desk, was also the Charles who felt and loved and dallied. Margaret didn't think all this through, but you and I can imagine that Mrs Clark-Finn would be driving the children home from tennis, swimming, violin or – no – pretty Mrs Clark-Finn would be in the arms of her Spanish tutor in a hacienda in Cockatoo. Perhaps there were no real secrets between Charles and his wife. Or perhaps there were, and perhaps these secrets kept the family together. That had more or less been the state of affairs in Margaret's own marriage, after all. Open secrets. Well, on one side at least. Margaret's virtue in the matter of marital fidelity has never, believe me, ever been in doubt. Ever.

The children, tired and happy, and their driver, friendly but discreet, enter the silent electronic doorway of their fortress home on George Avenue as the sun sets over the city.

But it was in fact a shock to see Charles outside the closed world of his office, functioning independently of the mahogany desk, being in love in the late afternoon, gazing into the eyes of his companion, so relaxed, so serene, so unconcerned about anything but the lovely circle of their moments together. So public. Oh well, what did it matter?

Then Charmaine swept in, bunches of large and glossy paper shopping bags in her left hand. She brought with her a bright whiff of lively glamour as she strode across the handsome room, beaming at Margaret, and seated herself at the table. One or two heads turned, registering the ruffle of her entrance.

'Ouf!' she let out a puff of fake exhaustion as she descended into the chair held out by the waiter. She put the large paper bags on the floor beside her, effectively blocking the way.

Little in the room had escaped her notice as she made her progress.

'Did you see Charles Clark-Finn over there with his latest?' she said to Margaret.

Margaret felt herself freeze. Her face showed nothing, but there was a stillness in her body, and a blankness in her eyes.

'Who?' she said.

'You know. Charles Clark-Finn. He lives down the street from Bellevue. In the big black fortress place. The bat-cave. Those teenage drug-dealers used to live there. His wife's the tennis player. You know. Sally Clark-Finn. He's with some law firm in the city.'

'Well, no, I'm afraid I don't know them. What did you say the name was?'

'Oh, honestly, Margaret, you are impossible sometimes.' Charmaine was smiling indulgently. 'You think the O'Days are the only people in the street who matter. The only people in the world, for all I know. I should introduce you to him some time. Not now, of course. That would be out of line. Lillian will know all about him.'

'Really? I rather doubt that.'

'Oh, believe me, Lillian will know. Nothing much escapes Lillian.'

'You make her sound quite sinister.'

'Hardly. She's just practical. And of course she's very discreet. If I ever want to know something I go straight to Lillian.'

'Straight to Lillian? Really? How extraordinary.' Straight to Lillian? That's the good news and the bad news all at once, isn't it?

Charmaine laughed. Her laugh was softer and even more attractive than that of her sister KayKay, who was inclined to bark.

Margaret was by now tense and troubled. She could feel that a net was closing in, trapping her and the sorrowful story of Killian and Kitty and Ophelia Mary. How far had that story spread, down the years? Who knew? How quickly was it spreading now? Were the nuns and the lawyers the only ones who knew the full story, the story that could end up as an entry in Doria's vast family file? How her mind had lately taken to spinning and then freezing up. Lillian? What did Lillian know? But Margaret's heart made a little leap of comfort and confidence when she came to Lillian, for Lillian was her utterly faithful friend and companion. Whatever Lillian knew, she would never betray Margaret. Not ever.

'Oh, I got the silk scarf KayKay wanted. I think it matches that parasol she bought in Rome. Wasn't that lucky?' Charmaine patted one of the bags.

'Lucky, oh yes, very lucky,' Margaret said in a wooden voice.

Margaret, are you feeling quite well?' Charmaine said. 'You look a bit strange.'

'I am rather tired. I think I had better call the cab quite soon.'

'Here's the tea then. And oooh, scones. This'll revive you.'

And it did, to a degree. Then Margaret and Charmaine made their way across the lounge to the front lobby, thence to the cab door.

Charles Clark-Finn did not look up as they passed, and they did not look down.

The Block of Chocolate, Extremely Dark

'Once you're dead, you're made for life.'

E. R. O'Day

Margaret liked to take the dogs for walks along the river, starting at the bottom of the garden, passing the old boatshed, heading east. She also sometimes took them in the car for a good run in the dog park. 'Venus! Jupiter!' The call could have been an exclamation of immense surprise, or else an invoking of the gods, or at the very least the planets. Other dog people were blithely calling to Amadeus, Lamborghini and Bollinger – one gorgeous golden labrador answered to the name of Misery, don't ask me why. There was a Kryptonite, but mostly they were Max or Fang. It was on the river walk, one afternoon as dusk was falling, that Margaret had the first of what she came to think of as her Charles Clark-Finn apparitions – disappointing, as well as alarming, for a religious woman. Were they apparitions, or was Charles really there? I think sometimes he was and sometimes he wasn't, but don't necessarily take my word. I'm only the skeleton in the wardrobe.

Like a shadowy figure in an early twentieth-century watercolour, there he would be, in the corner of her eye, swiftly disappearing between the twisted papery trunks and branches of the melaleucas. Pale yellow and silver green and grey trees, favourites of the

Australian landscape. Venus and Jupiter appeared to be oblivious, marching cheerfully forward, shifting blotches of black and white in the gathering gloom. Wouldn't they sense a ghostly presence; wouldn't they warn her of the corporeal? But Margaret knew that Charles was somehow there, perhaps a figment of her troubled thoughts, for what else could he be? What would lead the suave creature in his immaculate suit and thin cloud of perfume to lurk behind the ti-trees spying on her? It was ridiculous. It had to be ridiculous. And yet.

Just beneath the surface of her mind lay always the reality of the message he had delivered to her, whispered in his steady voice: your father, your idol, had feet of clay; he betrayed you, he betrayed your mother, he betrayed Ophelia Mary, he lied, he lived a lie, he didn't love you, didn't love you at all. He killed Kitty Sullivan. Murderer.

In the mauve and dove-grey light of the late late afternoons, the shape of Charles Clark-Finn flitted, swift and purposeful, across the gaps between the mysterious scrubby trees. The flash of his vermilion tie, the glint of his Italian spectacles.

Venus and Jupiter, happy dogs, trotted noiselessly along in the twilight.

Each time Margaret set out on the river walk, she told herself the figure would not be there. She took to formulating a clear slow prayer to the Little Flower – a prayer for a walk that was free of apparitions, a prayer for strength, for common sense. Imagine that – a prayer for common sense. Part of the problem was that, if you believe in the reality of the saints, you are quite close to believing in the reality of ghosts. And what if Charles really *was* there? But of course he wasn't. Would it be better not to go on the river walk, to give up, to stay in the dog park for an extra half an hour? What if he turned up in the park? And while these thoughts bubbled and darted about beneath the surface, life went on, and Margaret smiled and organised, just as she always did.

Then one afternoon Margaret made one of her little excursions down to the local supermarket. Groceries were regularly ordered by phone and delivered by van, but occasionally Margaret would walk into the village and visit the shops herself. She was not a great shopper, but occasionally liked to feel the bustle of life around her, noting the changes in the shop windows, noting the things that always stayed the same and were therefore comfortable, like an old melody that runs through your head, or an old game of *Happy Families* – Oliver Lovering the optometrist, Randall Greene the florist, Hopetoun and Eberhard real estate agents, Lilly Pilly children's wear, Scoops the ice-cream parlour, Henry's Café. The object of her visit this day was to get some of her favourite chocolate at the supermarket, Swiss, extremely dark. She liked to eat a square or two with coffee, she liked to share it with Lillian.

So there she was in her fine caramel Ferragamos, sensible tweed skirt, ivory silk blouse and Prada blazer in Sahara sand, blending and not blending into the glass wall of the imported chocolate display, carrying her own woven basket on one arm. The only thing going into this basket was the block of chocolate, extremely dark. The wrapping paper was so velvety brown it was almost black. And as she stood there, her eyes moving slowly across hazelnut, fudge and coffee bean, a too-familiar shape drifted eerily behind the wall of glass. The apparition of Charles Clark-Finn formed momentarily, and was gone. Margaret stood very still, her teeth clenched, her eyes fixed, staring directly at the display of chocolate boxes discreetly wrapped in dull paper with gilded lettering. And then it happened: round the corner of the great wall of chocolate he materialised, Charles Clark-Finn in all his legal glory, a red plastic basket on his arm. Terrible flesh and blood. Holding her breath as she continued to clench her jaw, Margaret continued to stare as if unseeing, but he *was* real. As she prolonged the charade of non-recognition, he appeared to fall in with the game, and, as his step did not quicken, his eyes became fixed on a point over Margaret's shoulder. He moved on, his gaze steady, until he came to a thick display of torch batteries. He dropped several cards of small lithium batteries into his basket and drifted on towards the express lane. Perhaps, in fact, he had not seen

Margaret. After all, why should he acknowledge her? He probably didn't even remember what she looked like – she was just a seventy-something invisible woman, after all. Margaret continued to study the chocolates, careful to observe from the corner of her eye the progress of Charles as he paid for the batteries and headed for the wide open supermarket door. How could she be sure he would not be out there in the street somewhere, haunting perhaps Oliver Lovering's doorway? There was nothing for it – she had to take the risk. She bought the chocolate and made her way outside. If Charles was still around, she didn't see him as she walked back to Bellevue.

'You look exhausted,' Lillian said. Margaret laughed and shrugged it off. She *was* exhausted.

'Ah, but we do have chocolate,' she said.

And thereafter she never again experienced the apparitions on the river walk. There is no way of explaining these things, really. Possibly Evan would have a theory, but Evan was probably the last person Margaret would ever confide in.

The Frog's Mouth

'The living are just the dead on holiday.'
E. R. O'Day

'I think we'll have lunch in the conservatory, Lillian.'

To Margaret there was something magical about the conservatory, where the light was captured for much of the day, where ferns and a shallow pool invited mystery, where a stream of water trickled from the mouth of a stone frog. It was one of the elaborate colonial Edwardian corners of the crypto-Georgian house – the house being a spreading conglomeration of styles and eras. The conservatory was an elegant glass box containing its own air and its own secrets, the only sound being the subtle burble from the frog's mouth. Margaret's favourite delicate begonias, with their graceful stems, spotted leaves and pale pink dangling hearts, traced patterns against the glass. Margaret felt at home and powerful there. This day she would have lunch with Doria, in the conservatory.

When the children were little they used to play a game in the conservatory. It was called 'The Frog's Mouth' and involved whispering a secret to the frog and then having the others ask questions until they could guess the secret. Over the door of the conservatory, in golden gothic letters was the inscription: 'It is the glory of God to conceal a thing: but the honour of kings is to search out the matter.' The glory of God to conceal? The honour of kings to search? Margaret had never really understood it, and now she didn't want to think about it.

'Just a plain omelette and a rocket salad, I think, and some warm strawberries in orange juice. Chilled Sauvignon. Almond bread and coffee.'

When Margaret asked for just a plain omelette, Lillian understood that the guest was someone who gave Margaret no joy, and who was to be more controlled than entertained. It was control by omelette. A sliver here, a sliver there, and a quiet soft squashing with the tongue against the palate. Desultory conversation, meaningless smiles. Plain omelette.

A warm feeling of wellbeing flooded Margaret's veins. Everything was going to be all right; Doria would never uncover the story of Killian and Kitty and poor tragic Ophelia Mary. Never ever. In the quiet of the night Margaret had prayed about it, the prayer formulated as a spell to keep Ophelia Mary safe from harm. Yes, that was it: Ophelia Mary must be protected. Margaret had arrived at her own elegant solution. She would *protect* Ophelia Mary. Like a sister. I knew Margaret would work it out.

So in the silky silence of the conservatory, Doria sat with Margaret. Stone table, clatter of majolica plates, Waterford crystal, family silver. A glass bowl of pale green grapes. Flecks of sunlight between the soft outlines of the vine leaves around the windows. They talked of the old history of the family. Old, old history of ships and marriages.

Margaret's interest in the distant past of the O'Days was sudden and in fact genuine. Doria was a little surprised. But events long, long past were safe enough. The talk was punctuated by the subtle and occasional click-click of silver on the Portuguese surface of the plates. Margaret could perhaps keep the nineteen forties in Eltham at bay by a fascination with sad Irish crimes and convict ships and the lives of long-lost distant cousins. Doria had her iPad forever at her elbow on the end of the table, her iPhone beside her glass.

The phone would ping whenever there was an email or a text. Sometimes Doria would attend to this, sometimes she would not. But there were occasions in the course of the conversation when Doria's fingers flew to her iPad to investigate a file, or to go for exciting journeys into her research. Margaret, the perfect hostess, allowed this startling breach of etiquette, partly in deference to what she saw as a kind of disability in her guest, and partly in the service of her own plan, which was to divert Doria forever into the labyrinths of the long-gone distant past. Margaret could not help marvelling at the way Doria could converse and at the same time keep her attention on both the iPad and the phone, on the present and the past. And perhaps the future.

Margaret was also, in a vague way, afraid that somewhere within the reaches of the World Wide Web there might be a document, or even just a *hint*, that could lead dogged Doria to Ophelia Mary. How to deflect her from catching a wisp, a filament of truth and winding it in until it revealed the baby, the child, the woman in the Greensborough convent? It was one thing, at lunch, to keep the conversation in the realms of ancient history or everyday events, but quite another to hide the facts from Doria at large, forever. Margaret had begun to live in terror of the internet.

'In Tasmania, you know,' Doria said, 'hundreds of records were officially destroyed in the hope of keeping the population free from the stain of its criminal past. This never works totally. The truth has a way of seeping out somehow. It's fascinating, I find. Really fascinating.'

'Yes, fascinating. You are thinking of going to Hobart, then?'

'Oh, I must. There are several Indigenous connections, you know, for one thing. Not only convicts, but Indigenous people.'

'Yes, I realise that. I find it very interesting and very sad.'

Doria was definitely going to Hobart, and to places all across the island where O'Days had left their mark. Perhaps Margaret would care to accompany her? Margaret knew that in her own interests she probably should do this, but when faced with the prospect of Doria's company on the journey her resolve failed.

She drew the line. It was one thing to have Doria round for an omelette; it was quite another to sit beside her and her iPad in airports and on aircraft and in who knew what buses and hire cars. No, she was definitely not free to do that. But she would give Doria introductions to the various family members. Doria didn't really feel the need for such introductions, having as she did the world at her flying fingertips, but she murmured her thanks and accepted. Perhaps those introductions would be useful, in some way. And if it kept Margaret happy to provide them, that was enough for Doria. It was quite a game, really, the game that Doria and Margaret played with each other.

Jean-François and his Blackmail Theory

'Death is really just psychosomatic.'

E. R. O'Day

News of Doria had travelled at least as far as Paris. On their honeymoon KayKay and Evan visited Margaret's daughter Rafaela and her husband Jean-François. When they discussed Doria and her project, Jean-François proposed – and he was the first person ever to voice this idea – that Doria was probably after Margaret's money. Had anyone else ever thought of this? Possibly.

'She hasn't got a hope,' Evan said.

'What about blackmail?' said Jean-François. 'Doria might know something terrible that our Margaret wants to hide.'

'Rubbish!' said Rafaela.

'I just wish she'd go away then,' said KayKay. 'She's always under everybody's feet.'

'Secrets,' said Evan, 'can have an independent life of their own. They make an appearance when they're ready. They float about the universe waiting for their time. And people often don't know they are in fact carrying key bits of information, either. It's like a disease, you know. People die of fact fever. It's incurable.'

'More rubbish,' said Rafaela.

And that was that.

What a little chapter, short and sweet. Is Doria after Margaret's money, then? Surely not. Could Jean-François be right about the blackmail angle?

My Sister is Writing the Family History

> *'Life is one surprise; death is another one.'*
> E. R. O'Day

Doria is still hard at work in Melbourne.

She met Benjamin Ross for the first time at a party. You may remember she sent him a text message some short time before she disappeared. You do recall that she has disappeared? Margaret is dead, and Doria is missing. It sometimes pays to remember these things.

The party was at Clive Bushby's family home. Clive – he's the partner of local priest, Justin Rhys. Seated in the embrace of a blue-green Knole sofa beside Clive's ancient mother, Veronica, Doria felt that she was in a sense holding court. For the assembled throng at Clive's traditional annual April party seemed keen to discuss the mysteries of family history and ancestor-tracing with her, to tell her tales of their own heritage. 'My sister is writing the family history,' they would say, placing themselves at a certain distance from the thing, but close enough to give them licence to ramble on. Doria didn't really enjoy parties such as this, but she was the American expert of the moment, and in demand. She remained somewhat bewildered by her role. Family history seemed to be the fashionable topic among the establishment, artistic and theatrical crowd, but in a manner that was far removed from Doria's cold, relentless tracking. There was a fevered element in the conversation of the people who sat down with Doria and poured out the curious and not so curious facts and fictions of their distant relatives. They presented these relatives as amazing, thrilling characters whose exploits could add glamour to the lives of their descendants. This was seldom the case, in Doria's experience.

Clive's late father had been a High Court judge, and the family home was on a broad and prosperous road known as the Golden Mile. This was not Toorak, but the more conservative suburb of Canterbury. The house was large, fancy Edwardian, set in a rambling English garden where there were ponds and statues of small children, a gazebo, tennis court and chestnut walk. It was a time capsule. You entered the grounds through an elaborate wooden lych gate, and the wide verandah surrounding the house led to a storybook doorway decorated with vintage stained-glass patterns of small squares in heavenly pinks and ambers and greens. In her demeanour Veronica Bushby somewhat resembled Whistler's portrait of his mother, and consequently Clive was often referred to as 'the Whistler' – a nickname that confused new acquaintances, who assumed it referred to something musical. The room where Doria now sat was a large reception area panelled down two walls to resemble Whistler's celebrated blue and gold Peacock Room at the Freer Gallery in New York. Latticed walnut shelving from floor to ceiling, the shelves graced by an opulent and dazzling collection of blue and white oriental porcelain. It was meant to look like the Peacock Room, but it didn't really look like anything more than a crude imitation. As a teenager Clive had added, in one corner of the room, a tiny wiggly copy of Whistler's butterfly signature. All the references to Whistler had been manufactured by the original owner of the house – which was named Nocturne in honour of the artist's series of that name – and Clive liked to think that all this had had an effect on his mother's looks in later years. So there she was at the party, Whistler's Mother.

To Doria, who had visited the Freer often, the room here felt like a small dolls' house ossification, far, far from home.

Clive was lord of the manor now, sharing it not only with his mother but with Maeve Murphy, his mother's younger unmarried sister, who was responsible for the running of the house and the overseeing of the garden. She was a great cook – brilliant, legendary, fabled, etc. – and the party food was, people always said, to die for. At the bottom of the garden Clive had a vast and untidy studio where he painted and frequently entertained. It contained a harpsichord and a glorious old brass bed, curlicued and decorated with porcelain medallions painted with woodland creatures – squirrels, foxes, hedgehogs. The bed was covered with a lavish rug made from the skins of possums. It was probably just as well that Clive didn't live in close proximity to the Church of the Assumption and the presbytery and Bellevue, the better to preserve the discretion surrounding his close relationship with Justin Rhys. His neighbours also lived in similar storybook places, and they had tennis parties and garden parties and – well, all kinds of parties, being people with much to celebrate as well as the time and the funds to do so. The annual party was an event into which Clive put a great deal of thought and effort, not to say money. The April theme meant that everyone came wearing autumn colours, autumn being Clive's favourite season, a time of great beauty in the gardens of Canterbury. The sight of people dancing in the ballroom was like an English wood where all the golden leaves were falling, sometimes slowly, sometimes feverishly, sometimes like burnished snowflakes. Whistler's Mother, who really did always favour dark grey, consented to sport a large cairngorm clasp in autumn tones on her shoulder. She was more or less exempt from the rules of the game. Doria had done her best to comply, and appeared in russet velvet from a Toorak boutique. In fact it suited her very well. Her colouring was themed to the dress in a pale and vulpine way.

A tall thin man in a yellow jacket and scarlet bow tie edged up to Doria and sat down between her and Clive's mother. This was Benjamin Ross. He was a theatrical set designer. His story tumbled out. He was the descendant, he said, of someone called Alexander Ross who came to New South Wales with the First Fleet, on the *Lady Penrhyn* when he was ten. Doria perked up – this was indeed interesting history, and a far cry from the meanderings of the woman who thought she might be related to the original Miss Havisham, and would Doria be able help her to find out more. Alexander Ross was the son of the lieutenant-governor, commander of the garrison.

'In 1791 they went back to England on the *Gorgon*, and it wasn't until the nineteen fifties that my great-grandfather, his name was also Alexander, came here as a ten-pound Pom. My sister's writing the family history. She'd love to meet you, I imagine.'

But Doria said she was about to leave for Tasmania, and so such a meeting was unlikely to take place. They should exchange phone numbers. 'Oh, and, also,' Benjamin said, 'the Ross family is related by marriage to the artistic O'Days.' So Doria pricked up her ears. She gave him her mobile number; he gave her his and his sister's. He had made Doria's time at the party worthwhile. Hold that thought. We are now going way back in time.

In the Summerhouse

'The worst is death, and death will have his day.'
E. R. O'Day

I really need to go back to the days of Margaret's childhood in Eltham. For it's there that we are going to discover the details of the truth about Ophelia Mary, the secret that Margaret must keep from Doria. We can get the general idea of what happened – from the letter Charles Clark-Finn wrote to Margaret. But the actual events deserve a closer look.

It was the spring of 1939, five days after war had been declared on Germany. Muriel, the wife of Dr Killian O'Day, was feeling very pleased with herself as she had just engaged a girl to do the laundry and generally help with the children. The girl was Kitty Sullivan, daughter of Brian and Gwen who ran the local general store. Kitty was the oldest of their seven children. You can tell this is not going to be a happy narrative, but you need to know it now.

The O'Day house was set on a sharp slope in the small town of Eltham in the hills outside Melbourne. Muriel and Kitty were in the summerhouse in the garden beneath a Cootamundra wattle that was a cloud of fluffy yellow blossoms. The summerhouse, a hexagon of green metal and smudged glass, was shrouded in a tangle of shiny boobialla, native honeysuckle and purple wisteria already in bloom. The women sat on a broad wooden seat, drinking tea from pottery cups made by local potters. Through the doorway the land fell away gently before them, and they looked out, every now and again, to the misty blue of the hills on the horizon.

War was far away yet strangely close, and people spoke of little else. In the Toorak house of the funeral O'Days, they were excavating a bombshelter underneath the wine cellar. Yet life must go on, and Muriel needed a girl to do the ironing. Killian spent every spare moment staring at the radio, listening intently to the news as the reality of the war sank in. These days Muriel found herself gazing at the children in a strange mood of deep fear and foreboding, remembering the stories of cousins and uncles who had died in the Great War, recalling fading sepia photographs of handsome young men in uniform, their faces soft and youthful, their eyes steady and glowing, looking into the other eye of the camera as they would one day have to look into the eye of the enemy. Then into the eye of death. So many of the photographs now hung forever on the walls of houses where they had become sacred memorials. The name of Gallipoli far away in Turkey was a household word, a brand across the hearts of the young men in those pictures, like a ribbon won in a terrible gymkhana. The memorials in Australian country towns, the boards of honour in town halls and churches and schools intoned in gold leaf the endless lists of the names of the dead, sacrificed for their country in alphabetical order, lost forever in places far away.

These monuments are the eerie war wounds that would forever scar the surface of Australia. Unlike the scars on other lands, these were not to be the graves of the dead, but the strange forlorn obelisks and fountains in memory of sons and fathers who had died far off in other lands. And Margaret's brother Augustin, a child when Kitty came to help, would die in the nineteen sixties in the war in Vietnam, the coloured photos of him to be frozen in youth alongside the sepia pictures of his long-dead uncles.

'The four children are quite a handful,' Muriel said.

'Well, I'm pretty good with children, too,' Kitty said. Her voice was light and confident.

'I would be so grateful if you could see to them from time to time, as well as the laundry and the ironing.'

It's never-ending, the laundry – the copper is lit every second day, and there are always clothes strung up to air as they hang from the kitchen ceiling. 'It all seems to get on top of me somehow.' Muriel sighed, and then she laughed. 'I'm completely disorganised.' She was.

So Kitty was engaged to help Muriel out four days a week. She would light the copper and stir the sudsy water with a wooden pole that was rough at one end where it had for years been immersed in the water; she would rinse and blue and wring, and lift the sodden lumps of linen into the wicker baskets. Then she would heave them onto the wires that were propped on stakes across the bottom of the garden, just before you came to the hen house. They flapped in the wind and the sun until they were ready to go either into the laundry to be ironed, or into the kitchen to air up above the wood stove that burned all day and all night. Kitty's arms were slender but strong, and she heaved the baskets of wet or dry washing about with a will, her cheeks flushed deep pink, fine rivulets of sweat on her forehead. The tendrils of her russet curls would flatten and stick to her white skin in trailing question marks. Her eyes were always bright and twinkling, blue, her voice sweet as she sang away to herself. Oh, careless sprite! When she spat on her fingers and touched the iron to test its temperature, there was a delightful and dangerous little hiss. She mended and stitched and knitted. She was what Muriel's neighbours and friends called, in awed and envious tones, a treasure. Yes, to be sure, a treasure. Her family was proud of her, the nuns were proud of her, she would one day marry and make a perfect wife and mother. A soon-to-be famous artist painted a picture of her, all rosy cheeked and copper haired, laughing underneath an apple tree in bloom. The children loved her, and she spent many hours with them, supervising bathtime and playing ball games and board games and hide-and-seek.

She knitted a crooked yellow teddy bear and tied a tartan bow around his neck. She played the piano and the children sang along. 'Roses Underneath the Snow'. Kitty Sullivan was mythic, a beautiful stereotype. The house and the garden were filled with her laughter which tinkled as she skipped and ran. It did, her laughter tinkled as she skipped on her small smooth light feet.

It happened the way these things so often happen. Killian found Kitty entrancing; Kitty was smitten from the start. Her employer, the handsome doctor. The wonder of these things is that they don't happen more often. And another wonder in this case was that nobody, in the hustle and the bustle, the hurly and the burly, really seemed to notice. Well, Killian was known to be flirtatious; it was part of his bright and sparkling personality. He had, in fact, a certain amount in common with Edmund, a distant relative, who would later marry little Margaret. And Kitty was just joyful Kitty Sullivan from the general store where her family sold groceries and axes and shoes and balls of wool and home-made scones. Killian – warm and laughing and devoted to his family, wide enough to embrace the world. It was in the rustic summer house under the wattle tree that Kitty and Killian had the fatal encounter that resulted in the conception of baby Ophelia Mary. Kitty felt wicked and also wonderful, more wonderful than wicked, in truth.

Three weeks later Killian left for the war.

Now Kitty refused to say who was the father of her baby. Until, that is, suddenly she was dying. It was then to her priest that she named Killian O'Day. The priest's lips were sealed. For the time being. Killian, as it happened, was home on leave, but he did not visit Kitty, paid no heed to the events until after she was dead, when the priest made discreet contact with him, and he was able to spirit the baby away. Did Muriel ever know the truth of all this? It seemed not. Was it forever a matter between the lawyers and the nuns and Dr O'Day? Killian arranged for the damaged child to be cared for by the nuns in the reasonable expectation that she would die before her first birthday. Did Kitty's family ever hear that the child had outlived her mother? Of course not. The birth with all its sorrow and regret happened at a time when nobody really asked too many questions about still-born babies, when everyone assumed that they were somehow disposed of by the hospital after baptism, their souls in the certain sure embrace of the angels. Kitty's family mourned and buried their eldest child with sad ceremony, but the fact of the baby, believed dead, was left in a cloudy limbo, was never mentioned except in the private whispered prayers of Kitty's mother. This good woman listed the baby's soul along with the soul of Kitty herself in a long litany of the family dead. Imagine if you will, knowing what you know, the *power* of that woman's prayers. It makes you think.

It was Killian, the physician and father, who delivered Ophelia to the convent where the nuns made certain she was given also the name of the Mother of God. And they kept her safe, her care paid for by a fund which Killian set up. Killian could never have imagined that the child would long outlive him, that the fund would have to stretch for seventy-three years, skilfully administered by Colley, Morton and White, and eked out by the Sisters, quietly, indeed silently. Ophelia Mary never thrived, but she was a source of untold joy at the Convent of the Holy Child.

A Good Deed in a Naughty World

'Death is the first and last best friend of the profession'
E. R. O'Day

I drew a comparison earlier between Killian and Edmund. But, in fact, Killian's sexual transgressions were child's play compared to the lifelong career of effortless seduction carried on by Eddy. This next bit might surprise you.

Think of this. It was 1951. The girls from Lisieux and the boys from Loyola combined to present *The Merchant of Venice* from which some of the text had been cleansed of unnecessary innuendo. Edmund O'Day was the lithe, blithe Bassanio and, lo and behold, Portia was played by Cecilia Feeney from Mount Macedon – she who will in later life be known as Sissy Bagwell. Edmund was the gorgeous and muscular captain of the football team, and he had a grand and carrying voice; Sissy was small and, let's face it, exquisite. Don't give too much credit to Margaret's jealous comments. She had large dreaming green eyes with a faraway look, and drifting wisps of ash-blonde hair falling on pale suntanned shoulders. Her teenage breasts were perky and perfect, her waist slender, her tanned legs long and athletic, her backside one of her greatest attractions. She had studied ballet from an early age. No wonder Sister Genesius, the nun in charge of theatre at Lisieux, chose Sissy for Portia. Sissy had an engaging way of slightly tossing her head. And as it happens Sissy had a pleasing voice, with a sweet suggestion of a lisp. The name 'Sissy' was originally the result of her babyish inability to say Cecilia. Sissy's lips and teeth were widely used in magazine advertisements for toothpaste. Curiously, the Feeneys of Mount Macedon were not above selling the children to advertising people, and when the children were very young they frequently used to appear as models in knitting pattern books for baby clothes. The ever-resourceful Mrs Daphne Feeney, a war widow, knew how to exploit every resource at her command in order to support her large family. She is to be admired.

So there was Sissy, on the Saturday afternoon following the final performance of *The Merchant of Venice* on Friday evening, in her best brick-red dress with the white hailspots, a dress made by her mother from a *Vogue* pattern. A long, long zipper travelled down the centre of her back. Daphne was a genius with a zip, and the dress fitted Sissy like a glove. The waist was cinched and the skirt was full. The sleeves and neckline were demure, the breasts their neat pert selves, softly evident beneath the rise and fall of hailspots. Cecilia wore a careful smudge of pink lipstick. No mascara. It was, after all, 1951. White gloves and rather thickish stockings, clipped at the tops to the suspenders that dangled from a clinical white damask suspender belt. Flat black slippers with a small black bow. Sissy was sixteen, flirtatious, innocent; a tease, in fact. A gold cross on a fine gold chain hung around her snowy neck.

Something that marked the Feeneys, as it marked several families in the school, was the fact that their father was killed early in the war. The black and white photograph of John Feeney in uniform hung on the wall above the piano in the house at Mount Macedon, one of those sacred pictures, a terrible and sorrowful family icon.

When she was with Edmund, Sissy was excited but out of her depth. She had heard he took girls for joyrides in the old Edwardian hearse belonging to the family business, and she was horrified but thrilled by the thought of this. But today Edmund had different ideas. They would have simply an afternoon cup of tea with his mother. Goodness! Sissy was surprised, and her pale green eyes were filled with innocent wonder, and, it has to be said, a kind of seductive gleam. Things were going well for Edmund. He drove her to Bellevue, having collected her from the boarding house, in a small black Ford Prefect that smelled of engine grease. He was wearing a navy reefer jacket, a white silk scarf flung around his neck, tasselled fringes dangling down his back. The nonchalance of it. Everything about him was romantic in Cecilia's scheme of things. Even if it wasn't the promised adventure in a hearse, it was not often she was driven around by a boy. She waved to some of the other girls as the car bumbled away from the fancy iron gates of Lisieux, heading for the even more fancy iron gates of Bellevue.

Tea with Mrs Larisa O'Day was a rather stiff and gloomy affair in a small afternoon nook that was decorated in brown and gold velvet. Suddenly Cecilia was nervous, and even Edmund could not quite put her at her ease. Mrs O'Day had a large, tired face and was wearing drab pink crepe with a lace collar – the sort of dress that made Cecilia feel suffocated and intimidated. Mrs O'Day bore a resemblance to the dressmaker's dummy in Sissy's mother's sewing room. Sissy's pert sexiness faded and withered, and she felt small, awkward, and almost crumpled. There were fine pintucks all down Mrs O'Day's bodice, and Mrs O'Day looked at Sissy through the narrowed slits of steady and uncharitable eyes. Terrible changes had taken place in the person of Larisa O'Day, over the years, since the time when the lovely wedding portrait had been painted. Sissy's cup jiggled on her saucer. She nibbled on a small egg sandwich, dropping a few crumbs onto her plate. She dabbed the corners of her mouth with the nervous points of a small white linen napkin. There were gaps and silences in the conversation.

'Mount Macedon,' mused Mrs O'Day. 'How long is it I wonder since I visited Mount Macedon? It quite feels like a lifetime.'

There was still an echo of her European accent. She somehow managed to suggest that nobody would really choose to go to Mount Macedon. To make matters worse, Sissy was afraid to look directly at Mrs O'Day because of what she had heard among the other girls about Mrs O'Day's glass eye. It was true. When Larisa was a child she had had a passionate disagreement with one of her brothers over a violin, and he had stabbed her in the eye with a tuning fork. The consequence of this was that she practised a steady and seemingly stern gaze that was not unkind, but certainly arresting. She had, on her dressing table, a silver box containing three identical spare blue eyes.

As Sissy tried not to think about any of this, Mr O'Day, a large, fat version of Edmund with a red face and enormous gleaming teeth, erupted into the room and the mood changed as he roared: 'Congratulations, children! I did enjoy the play. So this is the real Portia! How do you do, my dear! The quality of Mercy!' And Mrs O'Day began to dissolve and sweeten a little, and before Cecilia knew what was happening, they were all out on the terrace looking at the roses, and then abruptly Mr O'Day whisked his wife away somewhere. Sissy and Edmund were alone in the side herb garden and he quietly but firmly put his arm around her and she thought she was going to faint from intense feelings of pleasure among the rosemary and thyme. There were different kinds of lavenders from France and Italy and England. Urbane Edmund pointed them out. Edmund snipped off a few heads, handed them to Cecilia, who rolled them thoughtfully between her palms and smiled. She breathed in the perfume of her cupped hands, and then Edmund took her hands in his, and he too breathed in the perfume. Beside a large aloe that sprang from the corner of a flowerbed in an astonishment of bluish flesh, Edmund gently drew Cecilia to him and planted a kiss, a rather chaste kiss, on her lips, which tingled and trembled and longed for more. Her eyes were shivering shut. A little more was offered, and Edmund pressed his body against hers. Sissy grew nervous – what if his mother came round the corner – but Edmund was too confident for her to even murmur her fears. And he knew that today the light kiss was as far as he would go. He did not even ruffle Sissy's silky hair. A gentleman, he moved back and straightened the lapels of his jacket, smiled at her a slightly crooked smile, and invited her to tennis the following Saturday. That adorable smile. Tennis. Yes. Oh yes!

The O'Day sisters, as well as two other girls from Lisieux, several Loyola boys – they all turned up on Saturday for tennis. Cecilia in a rather long pleated white linen dress that had also been made by her mother, this time with a string of perfect buttonholes and a row of clear glass buttons down the front. Daphne Feeney was a genius with needle and thread, and no mistake. The Sister on Duty at Lisieux signed Sissy out, the O'Days being a family listed by Daphne as approved for visits.

After the last game everybody gathered under the oak for lemonade and cakes. Somehow, it seemed to Sissy, everybody dissolved and she was suddenly alone again with Edmund. She had longed for this, and dreaded it too. The tingling feeling of the pleasure of Edmund's touch filled her body and seemed to spin into her brain. She had to be back in the boarding house and ready for tea by six thirty. There was a flutter of panic in her heart. But Edmund had this timetable well figured in *his* brain. We are, after all, dealing with Edmund here. Sissy would be back in time. But first they must explore the paths that went round to the outside door, the door to the wine cellar. Edmund produced a key, and in they went. The door was dark green. It was worn and dusty. Yes, it squeaked as it opened. The interior was dark as dark can be. They briefly roamed the gloomy passageways between the rows of bottles. He showed her wines from Bordeaux that were put down when he was born, that would be opened when he turned twenty-one. He grasped a dusty old bottle of brandy and swung it by the neck. She loved the sight of him doing that. And he showed her the door of the bombshelter.

The bombshelter. Who had not heard of the legendary bombshelter in the O'Day house? Thirty-nine steps down, down, down below the cellar.

'Do you want to see? My family had it built at the beginning of the war. Excavated underneath the cellar. It's like a really deep grave.' He laughed. 'Or an Egyptian tomb. Do you – want to see?' His voice was careless, but with more than a hint of expectation and sexual excitement. Sissy lifted her face towards him, opened her eyes wide, slightly pursed her lips while smiling shyly, and nodded. Edmund kissed Sissy ever so lightly on the cheek. He was an artist in these matters.

There was a steel bar on the outside of the door, placed there because the door had a habit of swinging open at inopportune times and hitting anyone who happened to be there for one reason or another. In truth, few people ever ventured into this remote part of the wine cellar. Edmund lifted the heavy bar and swung back the door, flicked on a light, and stood aside to let Sissy go in first. There were cobwebs, and dusty concrete steps leading down to the underground shelter. Then he followed, closing the door behind them. They were beautifully sealed off from the outside world of reality. Never mind the dangers inside the cellar. It was completely freezing down there, and Edmund plugged in an old electric radiator that had a centre like a beehive. It was, in fact, quite effective.

This was Edmund's special place, furnished with broken chairs and a sofa, glasses and ashtrays, everything faintly grimy and covered in a veil of dust. Three gasmasks, like the heads of three terrible insects, hung from a hook high up on the wall. Sissy had heard of the cellar before, but nobody had ever described it to her. The walls were covered with maps of the world, resembling in their pastel colours maps from the Bible. Empty shelves on one wall, a few comic books lying in a heap on the floor. An old stained sink with a tap. The air was stale, there being one tiny dirt-clogged ventilator high up near the ceiling.

'A drink?' he poured them generous glasses of brandy. Sissy was unused to drinking, and so Edmund watered it down for her. She gagged a little, then got used to it. They sat on a sofa and Edmund lit them each a cigarette. Sissy was quite accustomed to smoking, as it happened. They removed their shoes, and Sissy tucked her feet, still in her socks, up under the pleats of her tennis frock.

Before long, naturally, they were lying on the sofa in an embrace. The perfect buttons in their perfect buttonholes placed by the deft needle of Daphne Feeney give way to the deft fingers of Edmund O'Day. And Sissy, her head beginning to spin with the brandy, became a lovely young creature in white socks, chaste white knickers, thick white bra, gold cross on slender chain around her throat. She still *dimly* remembered she was supposed to be a temple of the Holy Ghost, but her will was, in fact, at this stage, growing very weak indeed. The bra and knickers were gone. She had never really been a particularly devout or religious girl, and right now her body was feeling simply glorious. She wanted more and more of the feeling Edmund aroused in her. More and more. She hardly even knew that Edmund was naked, then in a flash Edmund's fingers were inside her, and the feeling was one of almost unbearable pleasure. He was above her. He took her hand and placed it on himself and she began to stroke him, quite softly, and he obviously liked that a lot. She was by now drifting in a little ecstasy of astonishment. He grinned and then he said quietly in her ear, 'Turn over,' and he gently rolled her onto her front. Her backside, remember, was one of her greatest attractions. 'Kneel up,' he whispered and then he pushed himself into her from behind, and in a few miraculous seconds of wonderfully sharp pain and a blissful flood of unknown warmth it was all over – with Sissy flat on her face on the sofa and Edmund lolling back, stretching out full length, obedient to cliché, lighting two cigarettes. If he, in those few minutes, hurt her, the pain was the pain of high pleasure. He took a long draw and exhaled, throwing back his head as he did so. Then he turned Sissy's face towards him, kissed her lightly on both cheeks, and put the second cigarette between her lips.

'There,' he said. Then, 'Oh-oh, there's a bit of the old blood.' He handed her a grubby towel. Cecilia stared in a kind of dumb horror at the sight of her own blood on the towel. She stared and stared. She was beginning to feel ill.

'It's OK – it's normal, you know,' Edmund said. Is it? Is this normal? Nothing was normal. Everything was shifting and spinning slowly. Sissy knew very little about the facts of life.

'Here, have some water,' and he handed her a glass of water that was still tainted with the brandy.

There she was, a convent girl naked except for her socks and her gold cross, bleeding a little, sitting on an old leather sofa deep underground in a bombshelter, gulping down water from a dirty glass. Where to from here, Cecilia?

Well, Edmund, ever gentle, kind and cheerful, got her cleaned up generally, folded his handkerchief and placed it between her legs, and she was buttoned up and in the car and back at Lisieux by six. The bleeding had stopped, a prayer, as fervent as you can possibly imagine, had been answered. There would be subsequent and even more fervent prayers to follow.

Sissy was worn out from tennis, the sun and the exertion, the deflowering, and was permitted to take a bath and have her tea brought on a tray. There were smudges of cobwebs on her tennis dress. The Sister on Duty seemed not to notice a hint of alcohol, if indeed there was one. Not for nothing was she known fondly among the students as Sister Idiotica. Surely she could at least smell the tobacco? But she appeared to be oblivious. And Sissy remained in bed all the next day, receiving small delicious snacks on trays. Sissy wrapped Edmund's bloody handkerchief in brown paper and put it in a rubbish bin. She prayed to the Virgin for forgiveness and help. She took out a card covered in roses that her sister had given her – it was a Spiritual Bouquet, the message on it telling her that her most pious sister had, on Sissy's last birthday, offered up ten Hail Marys for her intention. This was meant to comfort her but, in the present situation, it had the effect of driving home to her the nature and reality of what had just taken place. She fingered her crystal rosary, gazed at the drop of Lourdes water in the centre of it, but her lips refused to frame the words of the prayers. In one of those symbolic gestures life can manufacture, she had eventually lost her cross and chain in the cellar. She saw the loss as divine punishment for her fall, her sin, her few moments of unbelievable pleasure, her strange feelings of exultation and degradation.

She waited for days, which turned into weeks, which turned into months, for Edmund to write to her, or to send her some message, some sign, but he never did. The two of them were sometimes part of the same crowd, and they greeted each other politely. It was as if nothing had ever happened between them; and, for Edmund at least, nothing had, really. He danced with all manner of other girls, and there were reports that he was going out with a really fast girl from the grammar school. Sissy's conscience was definitely coming back, and she considered Edmund's silence as another form of divine punishment for what she had done. Her twisted thinking, the convolutions that would rule her later life, had begun to take hold.

Sissy told the story to no-one except, after some soul-searching, her confessor, who offered her the routine consolation of prayer and chastity. To tell you the truth, he didn't quite understand or care to try.

Her experience with Edmund remained the most beautiful sex of Sissy's life.

What, her whole life? It would seem so. Not until she married Mark Bagwell did she ever do it again, and it was certainly not the same. At school Sissy went into a religious phase, got the prize for Doctrine, and eventually entered a convent, although she came out after a short time. What a powerful and defining moment that was with Edmund on the sofa. Forever after, her energies were poured into good works and prayer, activities that she paraded like a series of banners, each one a good deed in a naughty world. She might have followed the lead of her pious sister and made Spiritual Bouquets for other people, but she gradually developed the ill-mannered and aggressive approach of simply announcing more or less to all and sundry that she was praying for them, and that God would listen to her and so would do her will. The girl in white socks in the bombshelter remained sealed off in her mind, a creature in a strange and long-gone-but-not-forgotten fairytale. Deep, deep in the earth below Bellevue.

It might be hard to believe, but Edmund found Sissy's gold cross and chain in a crack in the sofa one day, could not remember whose it was, and gave it to one of his sisters for Christmas. Oh, Edmund!

The miracle of Edmund's early life and adventures was that he got away with so much. How was it, for instance, that his buttoned-up mother in her pink crepe pin tucks actually let the incident in the cellar with Cecilia happen that afternoon? It seems that as far as she was concerned Edmund, the beloved son, could do no wrong. There was a wonderful glibness, a ruthless expertise, about his romantic life, and if any girl ever fell pregnant no news of the matter ever reached out to trouble the gleeful progress of Edmund's life. It so happened that one of Sissy's sisters did produce a child to Edmund, but the matter was concealed, the child adopted, and it seemed there was no skin off anybody's nose.

Not that you would notice anyhow. Consider, however, the child. Surely he or she was somehow or other damaged by the whole thing? You would think so. But that is obviously another story. Edmund did, after all, marry his desirable distant cousin, the virgin Margaret, and lived happily ever after with little interruption to his rake's progress until he died in the arms of his lovely mistress Fiona.

The Afternoon of the Picnic

'Sweet is the longest slumber of the virtuous man.'
E. R. O'Day

Doria comes to this story as a given, as a presence, and then as an absence. Margaret is the force up against which she is matched, and it's Margaret, and who she was, that really matters here. It's the cumulation of the events in Margaret's life that are going to converge and swallow Doria up. So we need to pay attention to Margaret's history, the irony being that, if Doria had had access to the truth of Margaret's past, she might not have wandered in her way, might not have decided to come up against her. It's possible. Oh, irony!

When Margaret was a child she had a *Children's Bible* given to her by a Methodist aunt. It had a blue cover with gold embossing, and the edges of the pages were gilded, the endpapers, all in shades of blue, showing the image of God as a Michelangelo figure drifting across the top of the picture, rays of bright light radiating from his hands, beaming down through the clouds onto the vague mountain tops of Earth. For some reason the picture did not inspire in her awe but fear, a vague, floating fear that hovered at the back of her mind and sometimes came forward, often for no reason she could discern. It was as if some unknown dread lurked in the darkness behind the pictures, and behind the bright realities of her life. Well, maybe it's much the same for everybody, to a degree. We're not so very far from the primal swamp, are we? Tormenting shapes moved quietly in the shadows of Margaret's imagined world. In times of trouble the memory of the images in the Bible, and the feelings they prompted, would return, bringing the dread. Quickly she would rearrange her thoughts to place the blue clouds, the rays of light, at the front of her mind, but always there was the steady pull of the feeling that darkness threatened, that what was black and hidden was larger and more powerful than what was blue and visible.

There were dark days and there were sunny days.

One sunny day when Margaret was eight, many O'Days and their related families were on a picnic by a river. Killian and various other male members of the clan were absent, away at the war. Margaret pined for her father. So this is a Margaret–Killian anecdote, although it reads as being about the absence of Killian. Margaret longed to go out mushrooming with her father in the early morning, longed to feel his large strong hand as it enfolded her own small hand while they walked along in the misty air. Some uncles and cousins were in fact absent because they had died on the battlefield. One was missing, believed dead. But the tribe knew how to keep its spirits up with food and games and jollity in the open air.

One young woman in a purple dress spent most of her time sitting apart under a paperbark quietly weeping for her lost fiancé. 'Come on, love, come over here and have something to eat.' But she would not. In due course she would waste almost away in her solitary bedroom in a house not far from Bellevue. She finally rallied, however, became a pillar of the Red Cross, and married a farmer. They had no children – the result, the women in the family said, of all those years of pining. They were probably right.

From among the games of cricket and the gossip on the deck chairs and picnic rugs, the bountiful baskets of sandwiches, beer and lemonade and the old uncle with his violin, Margaret wandered away until she was alone on a hill. There were eerie gum trees above the wide, slowly flowing waters of the river, which purled downhill over stones. Staring down Margaret imagined she could see a platypus. Rocks, reeds, platypus – surely that was a platypus? Yes? No? She always longed to see a platypus, but in fact she never did, not even at the zoo where the shy creature refused to appear in public.

In the far distance were hazy blue and violet mountains. She shaded her eyes with her hand and stared out at them. The noises of the picnic were lost up here. There seemed to be no sound, and yet the air appeared to be alive with sound, gently vibrating with sound; the light was constantly yet subtly shifting, the sky huge and wide, a vivid blue where clouds detached and drifted slowly in gigantic puffy balloons, their edges brilliantly backlit.

She lay down on her back under the trees, gazing up, trying to see as far as she could into the sky. For an instant, an instant that seemed to last for a very long time, Margaret realised she understood something very grand, something inexpressible. She seemed to know, for that fleeting moment, and yet forever, the meaning and the reason of things. She was unable to put this into words, unable even to form the thought, but for the rest of her life she carried the knowledge – or was it just a feeling – of the gift she received there above the river on the afternoon of the picnic. The blue of the sky through the spaces of the trees was actively drawing her into itself. The blue pages of the *Children's Bible* were now something flat and childish, crude and unimportant. She was dissolving into the air. In the fleeting seconds it took for her to gain this gift of knowledge, the dark dread ceased to be. It would come back, it would always come back, but there had been a flash of insight that rendered its power less potent, less real.

She told nobody of this. There was, in a sense, nothing to tell. There was no substance. She was lying on the forest floor above the river and she looked up into the sky and felt for an instant that everything was all right. She told nobody. It might now appear to be the kind of thing to put in the *Book of Revelation*, but as we know, she is still incapable of picking up a pen. I suppose you could say that Margaret is suffering from, among other things, writer's block.

The strange thing – or was it so strange – was that forever after she understood that the endpapers in the Bible, and also the stories and the rituals of her religion, and indeed of all religions, were really just that: handmade stories and pictures and rituals created and developed in a vast human effort over many centuries to somehow capture the heart of the gift she received on the afternoon of the picnic. Stories, beautiful stories, terrible stories, but inadequate to meet the glorious truths of the moment above the river, under the broad blue arch of the sky.

The epiphany, if that was what it was, never interfered with Margaret's practice of her religion. She was not really a thinker. The afternoon of the picnic did in fact strengthen somehow her formal attachment to the rituals and rites of the faith. They were part of the story as she understood it. And they were right, too, in their way, she thought. They were a pattern, a context, a comfort. Was that how it should be?

That was how it was.

At Sullivan's Corner

*'All men must take their medicine.
Death is the medicine that gives the greatest ease.'*

E. R. O'Day

Moving on now to the era of Doria Fogelsong. It was to be an afternoon with Doria.

On the anniversaries of her parents' births and their deaths, Margaret would visit their graves in the churchyard in the small country town of Robbins Creek, not far from Eltham. One of the most serene rituals of her life had been to go there with Edmund, oddly enough. He was at his kindest and gentlest on those days. So anyhow, it was the anniversary of Muriel's birth, and Doria, who came round each morning to swim in the pool, ever keen to see physical evidence of family history, asked if she could accompany Margaret when she went to Robbins Creek. Margaret was unable to think of how to say no. She did not want a companion, and particularly not Doria, since this was the first visit after her discovery of Killian's betrayal of her love and trust. She was a tumult of powerful emotions. Remembering Killian, remembering Edmund. Remembering Muriel, Kitty, Ophelia Mary. She was visiting the grave of a father she no longer knew or understood. But all her training and all her grim ability to maintain a façade came into play – she graciously invited Doria to go with her. She took, as always, a large plastic box of flowers from the garden to put on the graves.

On the journey Doria, for some reason a faithful follower of astrology, read out her own stars: 'Put the past in context. Try to get perspective. Seek a cosmic substitute.' That was the advice. You'd imagine an intelligent woman like Doria would take this with a pinch of salt, yet she read it out solemnly, as if she intended to follow its teaching. She read out Margaret's, too, but it was beyond either of them to begin to understand its message, which was: 'It takes one to know one. All else is in the detail. Make your move.' Margaret favoured Doria with a light laugh, nothing more, but she thought that getting things in perspective was quite a good idea.

Margaret was no longer fond of churchyards and cemeteries and graveyards. In childhood she and her brothers had enjoyed playing foxes and ghosts and bushrangers among the headstones, but as time went on she grew to hate everything about them. As an adult, wife of a funeral director, careful always to present the correct face to the world, she would say that she was not particularly affected by such places. Cemeteries had changed, becoming in many cases serene and beautiful parks made of rolling lawns and glorious flower beds and trees and works of art, places where people came to celebrate weddings and births as well as deaths. Indeed, O'Day Funerals, now run by Margaret's sons Joseph and Paul, prosperous and forward-thinking, owned two such places, Evergreen Park East and Evergreen Park North. And then there was Heavenly Days – a funeral park like no other funeral park on the face of the earth. While the cemeteries partly funded Margaret's very comfortable life, they were a dark background undertow, something she tried, fairly successfully, not to think about. In fact the whole enterprise of death into which she had married remained for her an arm's length matter, first managed by Edmund, and then by Joseph. It might just as well have been the business of a chain of fast-food outlets, she would say, for all she understood. Edmund's father and also Edmund and then Joseph, while being very successful businessmen, enjoyed black humour about the business they were in. The O'Days had been in the funeral business back in Waterford in the nineteenth century; it was nothing new.

And Margaret's romantic imagination led her to the desire to travel to her own funeral in the O'Day Edwardian hearse with all its glittering silver knobs and sparkling glass. Sometimes she wished she could finally be laid to rest beside her parents and her brother Michael in the churchyard in Robbins Creek. This would be her final split from Edmund, whose mortal remains were with his own parents and some of his sisters among the dells and glades and statues of Evergreen Park East, not, of course, at Heavenly Days. But she knew it wouldn't be possible for her to go home to her parents – she would end up in Evergreen Park East, with Edmund.

She had been betrayed by Edmund, but she now knew that she had been betrayed also by Killian. She was alone.

Morbidly – her mind ran on – it occurred to her that Edmund might ultimately be followed to Evergreen Park by his beloved Fiona. Yes, that was possible. If so, then so be it. But then it was also on the cards that Fiona would marry, changing everything. None of these things seemed to matter very much any more, not since the discovery of how different the past was from the way she had thought it was. Getting perspective. One lethal letter from the office of Charles Clark-Finn, and all the pieces fell in a new and sorry pattern. Part of the pattern in her mind included where people were laid to rest. And she still felt helpless, lying forever beside Edmund in Evergreen Park East. Well, she did love him, after all.

Once she had briefly considered having Edmund buried at Robbins Creek, but such a notion was out of the question, would disturb the pattern. Edmund had to go home to Evergreen East; Margaret had to go home there with him. Margaret duly visited Edmund's grave at Easter and Christmas – the place was perfectly well cared for without any intervention from her. She went on his birthday and on the anniversary of his death. She never saw

Fiona there. She wondered about that. She wondered where Fiona went, what she thought, on that day. Edmund had, after all, died in Fiona's arms, hadn't he. How did Fiona and the boys remember the day Edmund died? I suppose we'll never know.

Fragments of thoughts about the meaning of Robbins Creek drifted in the background of her mind as she drove through the suburbs, out to Eltham, and on to Robbins Creek with Doria beside her chattering on about the horoscopes. It was a little odd to have a companion on such a pilgrimage, and such a companion. She tried to pretend it wasn't really happening.

You and I know that, horoscope or no horoscope, Margaret herself is soon going to be dead, and Doria is going to vanish without trace. Dead?

The small Catholic church had been lovingly made from sandstone and brick, and had weathered softly down the years so that it nestled among European pine trees, a haven of peace and prayer. The door was locked, in these days of vandalism and lack of faith.

'Why, goodness gracious, how very sweet,' said Doria, 'It's like a churchyard on a movie set, isn't it? So very British, too. Or Irish, do you think?'

'Australian,' Margaret said drily.

There beside the church was the old graveyard, neat but worn, lichen on top of the headstones, slightly higgledy-piggledy gravel paths, fresh flowers here and there, low hedges of rosemary, one large tap where you could fill a vase with water. Imagine the movie stars in some movie or other, in their dark overcoats and veils, their black gloves, their black umbrellas, the soft rain, the thud of the first sod as it falls on the coffin lid, the bowed heads, the grimly grieving wife, the tearful mistress, the stone-faced killer standing by the tree.

'Yes,' said Margaret, 'but the part you never get in the movies is the smell. I do object to the *smell* of graveyards.'

Doria didn't know whether she was supposed to laugh when Margaret said that. She just said mmm and then she said it was just as well you couldn't smell graveyards and various other things in the movies, and they both uttered a kind of grunt that was a sort of laugh.

It was strange, Margaret thought, but the presence of Doria seemed to ease her feelings about Killian. Here she was, bringing Doria right up to where the secret was buried. How strange it felt. But Doria was somehow anaesthetising the pain. Enemies can be useful, that's for sure. The sound of the water gurgling from the tap into the vase was today incredibly loud in the silence of the churchyard, a silence broken every now and again as a text message came through to Doria. All this was so unlike anything that happened at Evergreen Park East where everything was tended daily, and where there was no such thing as a vase of flowers. Lawns and rose bushes and statuary. She filled a vase for each grave, and she and Doria carried them over and put them in place. The whole graveyard came to vivid life when the fresh flowers bloomed in the vases. Muriel, Killian, Michael. Margaret said a silent prayer at each grave, and made the sign of the cross. Well-mannered, Doria did the same. Doria was mentally marking off names on her charts, mentally giving them little headstones. She was used to this, had visited many of the graves of the folk on the vast and spreading family tree. She took dozens of photos with her iPhone.

Afterwards they drove back to Eltham where Doria suggested they have a cup of tea, pointing to a kitsch little tearoom called Sullivan's Corner. Margaret had driven past it many times over the years, but had never even considered going in. It was a café that occupied the much changed building where Kitty's family used to have their corner store. The café was run by a Vietnamese family named Ong. Along the window ledges was an array of cheap china ornaments such as pale lustre swans and smiling squirrels. These were the identical kinds of things Margaret, and almost certainly Kitty, used to collect as a child. At the sight of them Margaret recalled the shadow box that used to hang on her bedroom wall. Where were all those precious objects now? It's quite possible that some of the things on the window ledges of Sullivan's Corner had once belonged to Kitty, or even to Margaret herself.

'Devonshire tea,' said Doria with a kind of breathless triumph in her voice. 'We really must have Devonshire tea. I'm simply mad for Devonshire tea.'

And so it was that a wicker basket of warm scones appeared, scones that were adequate, but nowhere near the standard of those made long ago by Kitty's mother. Doria ate with a keen appetite, but Margaret could feel the things sticking in her throat. The emotion she had held in at the churchyard was beginning to tell. Try as she would to push back the memories, images and thoughts of Killian, of Kitty, of the apparent innocence of the past kept shifting up out of a shadowy nowhere and pricking her eyes, stopping her throat.

'Margaret,' said Doria, 'I think you are sorrowful after our visit to the graveyard.'

'Yes,' said Margaret, pleased enough to be able to admit this much, 'I believe I am.'

'You looked for a moment as if you had lost your way in a wilderness.'

Margaret straightened her back and smiled. What an extraordinary and poetic thing for Doria to say.

'Oh,' she said, 'I suppose we all lose the path from time to time. It's nothing, really. The old memories, you know. I always get a little maudlin when I visit the graves.'

'Who doesn't?'

'Quite.'

'I guess most people never visit.'

'You could be right there, Doria. I have a lifelong habit of going there on anniversaries.'

'You're a good woman, Margaret.'

'Oh, you don't know me, Doria.'

They sipped their tea in a meditative silence.

She was perfectly accustomed to concealing her true feelings from people, but since her discovery of the life and death of

Ophelia Mary, she was finding this more and more difficult. She was so alone. And here was Doria – was Doria a nemesis? Was this how a nemesis worked? But Margaret had done no harm. Nothing for which she should be pursued and punished. She was only really trying to do that thing people talk about, trying to 'come to terms' with the past. Perhaps Doria had been sent to help her? Is that possible? Were people 'sent'? But then she looked at Doria – between her fingers a small portion of scone smudged with strawberry jam and blobbed with cream, her iPhone on her left, her iPad on her right, her pale eyelashes flicking up and down – and she knew that Doria, if she had been sent, had not been sent to help. Were people ever really 'sent'? *She had come to spoil everything.* Without the prospect of Doria discovering the truth about Ophelia, exposing Killian's true nature to the family, to the world, Margaret felt she could perhaps have 'come to terms' with the facts, in the deep sanctity of her own heart. But the light of common day, Doria and the light of common day, that was more than she could bear. Doria had come at the *wrong time.*

Every now and again Doria would make a note on her iPad. Sometimes she had manners, and sometimes she did not. Would she ever realise that the gaze Margaret turned on her that day in Sullivan's Corner was one that concealed deep hatred? And fear. Of course she didn't. Doria was blithely focused on her own important project and her iPad and her iPhone and all the rest of it.

This Much-Travelled Craft Work

'Thou owest God a death. And a funeral.'
                                              E. R. O'Day

Doria has a little more business to attend to before she disappears. Remember the lovely old quilt? It needs to go to the museum in Tasmania. With some relief Margaret heard that Doria was off to Hobart to present the quilt and to talk to members of the family. She may well discover dark and scandalous deeds from the past, but she would at least be far away from the precious story of Ophelia. It crossed Margaret's mind that there might be other members of the family with things to hide from the prying eyes and fingers of their self-appointed family historian, people with more vigorous responses, people who might tell Doria to go jump in the lake and take her iPad with her. That could be good, couldn't it. A week without Doria coming round every day to swim in the pool and drink coffee and maunder on about this ancestor and that would be a week of peace and tranquillity such as Margaret had not had for some time. To be fair, Doria frequently brought flowers from the florist, wine from the local cellars, cakes from the French bakery, but Margaret took no real pleasure in these gifts. Doria showed her a list of names of people she would see in Tasmania, most of whom she had already contacted. Did Margaret have any other suggestions, anyone Doria had missed? Doria had missed nobody. Margaret knew of no other relatives, but gave her a few letters of introduction anyway. Oh, Doria was thorough, so very thorough.

Doria and the quilt were greeted at the Folk Museum in Hobart with open arms, and there were articles in the paper, pictures of the quilt, pictures of the exotic Doria O'Day Fogelsong who had come all the way from Florida to present the historic and beautiful object to the community. People, acting out of kindness, sent some of these news items to Margaret, for her interest. At least they reassured her that Doria was probably safely occupied in Tasmania, far enough away from Greensborough. Was Doria ever *really* far enough away?

The main story about Doria and the quilt was in the Hobart *Mercury*.

> Florida historian Dr Doria O'Day Fogelsong is currently in Hobart visiting relatives as part of the research for her book on the history of the O'Day family. She has brought with her a patchwork quilt that was made by two young women, Catherine and Rosetta Hart, who were transported to Van Diemen's Land in the nineteenth century. It is known as the Rosetta Quilt. Rosetta Hart married James O'Day in Richmond, and eventually the couple set sail for the United States where they settled in Detroit. It was there that Dr Fogelsong discovered the quilt, which she persuaded the family to donate to the Folk Museum. Dr Jennifer Campbell, director of the museum, said: 'This much-travelled craft work is a great treasure for the museum. It is very much part of our heritage, and it must be remembered that such objects are incredibly fragile and rare. We are absolutely thrilled to be able to display it here in Hobart where it will be part of a slowly growing collection of artefacts made by convict women from our past.' Dr Fogelsong will be the guest at a dinner on Friday hosted by the Historical Society, and attended by members of the O'Day clan from all corners of the state.

All corners of the state – imagine!

There was a large colour photograph of a beaming Doria, the lovely old quilt looking its best spread across a table in front of her, behind her a black and white drawing of the ship that had brought Rosetta to Van Diemen's Land.

Sometimes in the middle of the night Margaret would wake suddenly in her bed and feel her heart beating fast. She would try to calm herself, saying she was ridiculously obsessed with Doria, that Doria could never uncover the truth about Ophelia and Killian. But then her sorrow for Ophelia would overwhelm her, and her sadness for the loss of her father's open love would dampen her face with tears. Poor Margaret; she is really in trouble here. She resolves, quite suddenly to resume her writing in the *Book of Revelation*. She leaves out the story of her visit to the lawyer, the matter of the letter, of the shock. Well, I've filled you in on all that anyway. Margaret's journal now flows on. You might think of it as having healing properties for the writer, perhaps.

Speciality of the House:
The Book Of Revelation

'Relax. The sun will shine tomorrow in heaven.'
E. R. O'Day

The day inevitably came when I could no longer put off going to Greensborough to visit the place where Ophelia Mary lived and died. Today was that day. I suppose I always knew I would eventually have to go there. How could I not? But a great fear of knowing and feeling held me back. I wanted to know and I did not want to know. I knew I owed it to Ophelia, knew I must at last keep faith with her, with her memory, with her spirit. But I shrank, oh, how I shrank, from meeting the Sisters she lived with, those good women who cared for her, loved her, I am sure. What must they think of me, her half-sister who never ever visited her, never in all her life? Could they conceive of the fact that I had never even heard of Ophelia until the day in the lawyer's office? Well, after all, I suppose they have seen everything. I often think they know a good deal more about the world than I do.

I had made an appointment with Sister Beth, who seemed to understand exactly who I was and why I was calling. During the long drive out there I felt so solitary, somehow skinless, with the defencelessness of a baby rabbit.

It was Sister Beth who met me at the door when I arrived. And, in fact, she was the only person I saw during the visit. I half expected and dreaded that she would be somebody I knew, but I had never seen her before. She resembled one of the Sisters from school – old Sister Vincent, round-faced and cheerful; she reminded me of a smiling cheese in a children's picture book. Cheery Cheese and her adventures in kitchen and market. Sister Beth was matter-of-fact, no-nonsense, exuding an immense aura of warmth and wisdom. Kindness. I suppose that's what it is they have, those women, a profound kindness that comes with their wisdom and their discipline. It is based on their confident love of God. I say Sister Vincent and Sister Beth were old, but they were probably younger than I am, and they both looked young and pink and ageless. Sister Vincent used to wear the full old habit, her face framed perfectly by her wimple and veil, her shiny black shoes peeping out from beneath her long black swishing garment; Sister Beth wore a dark blue skirt and a white blouse and a brown cardigan. Her hair was short and silver and she had a rather silly cream veil pinned to it. I found that endearing. When I looked at her dark eyes I thought of an eagle, although in fact I have never looked into an eagle's eyes. She saw a lot and she knew a lot. She could maybe see right through me. Yet I felt Sister Beth loved me, as she had loved Ophelia. She did not judge me. She accepted the state of affairs. It's ironic in my case, I can see, that one calls these people 'sister'. I have never really thought about that before. Oh, there have been many such sisters in my life, but never a true sister.

'It is wonderful, Margaret,' she said – her voice was firm and soft and sweet – 'that you have come.'

I found this statement unanswerable, but I surprised myself by saying, 'Oh, Sister, I only wish I had come all those years ago.'

'Ah,' she said, 'but you were not to know.'

'I didn't know. No, I didn't know.'

'Then you must forgive yourself for not coming. It was for the best. You must believe that, Margaret.'

I was choking with emotion, unable to go on to ask her how it was for the best. I suppose she meant that it was best for Ophelia, for the Sisters themselves. But me? Was it the best for me? I realise now that I must put Ophelia first, and also the Sisters. What it all meant to me doesn't really come into it. Oh, but it does. Ah, but it must not.

She took me out to the rows of graves beside the chapel. They were all the same, stating on their low white marble headstones the names and dates in religion of the women who lay buried there. There were three graves to one side, two of them very old, one recent. Ophelia Mary. No distinction made between her and her two companions and all the others in their ordered rows, except for the separate position to one side. My gaze drifted sideways to read the two other headstones – Pauline and Vera Maria. I stood for a very long time beside Ophelia. I wept as I said a silent prayer. Then we turned away and walked slowly back to the convent parlour.

We drank weak tea and ate slices of an orange cake that Sister Beth told me was a speciality of the house.

'It was,' she said with a gentle smile, 'Phelia's favourite.'

It jolted me to hear my sister's name shortened in that familiar way. I could have called her Phelia. Phelia, I said it to myself.

The cups we used were nostalgic for me – green 'Beryl' the same as those used for everyday by my mother. There was in the room that old familiar convent smell of lavender and beeswax and lemon. Sister Beth told me Ophelia's life had been joyful and beautiful, her death so peaceful. I suppose this was true. Could it be true? Well, I suppose it could. Thank God there was no mention of sanctity, no hint that Ophelia was a miracle worker in the midst of the convent. Sister Beth had more sense than to say such a thing. I suppose.

She made no reference to my father's true role in Ophelia's life, but I know the truth was in the background to our meeting. However, she did say, at one point, that my father was a generous supporter of the convent, and that he gave his medical services to them free of charge. I was shocked when I heard that. So I suppose he knew Ophelia and Ophelia knew him. Did he hold the child in his arms when she had chicken pox? Did he soothe her forehead with a damp cloth? This new fact seemed at first to ease some of my pain, but then my bewildered rage at my father resurfaced, and I mourned again my own distance from my little lost sister. He would visit her and then come home to us *as if nothing had happened.*

'Come back, Margaret,' she said, 'come back whenever you wish. You are always welcome.'

I know I will never go back. I will send a cheque.

On the wall of the parlour, among pictures of saints, photographs of the Sisters themselves, and framed prints of a number of well-known Australian paintings, was the print of Nellie Melba as Ophelia. I believe the frame was identical to the one that used to hang over the piano at home. I believe it was our picture. I could have been mistaken. But no, it was our picture all right. My father brought it here to the convent, this reminder of Kitty Sullivan.

Dark storm clouds ruffled the sky as I drove home, thunder rumbling in the distance, tears pricking my eyes, a kind of relief flooding my soul. The very least I can do is send the nuns a cheque – but that seems so inadequate and material. There is nothing else I can think of doing.

'Pray for us, my dear,' Sister Beth said. I will pray for them. Perhaps they will pray for me.

It was not long after this that Isobel gave birth to a baby girl. How she and Hugh have longed for another child. She is to be named after me. This was a delightful surprise, the name, so very gratifying after Charmaine's choice of Ophelia. It was a balm.

Doria produced a most lovely coral bracelet. Where on earth does she get these things? Again she explained it was a family heirloom. So she travels around with an endless supply, on the off-chance that the family tree will miraculously bear new fruit? Baby Margaret. Well, she is a miracle. I truly thought Hugh and Isobel would never manage to have another baby.

The Shadows Close in

'I shall be as secret as the grave.'

E. R. O'Day

Doria returned safe and sound from Tasmania, her iPad replete with more weird and wonderful details of the lives of the O'Days. One of them had been transported for forgery. That was news to everybody. Doria was planning a return visit to Tasmania quite soon.

Margaret was in the garden with a pair of secateurs. She was wearing hat and sunglasses and gloves, snipping swiftly and expertly, dropping the cuttings into the wicker basket over her arm. She was not pruning, just tidying. It was pleasurable, like a moment of light meditation. The sunshine sweet as it spilt between the trees, filtered through the leaves, dotted the gravel. Margaret was thinking about nothing at all.

A shadow fell across the path, and there was the sound of trainers, Doria's trainers, on the gravel. Doria, wearing absolutely enormous sunglasses with reflecting lenses, joined Margaret as she moved about among the grevilleas, snipping. Margaret said, 'This is the rosmarinifolia, once thought to be extinct until they found it growing in the botanic gardens in Edinburgh in 1969. It was actually from a cutting taken there in the early nineteenth century.

Then they realised it was still growing in Australia anyway, not extinct at all. You see?'

So Doria listened patiently and with a certain amount of interest as Margaret delivered her explanation, more like a lecture, on the grevillea.

'I have always loved its tiny pink coils and long soft points, like the horns of a snail, or something under the sea.'

But Doria was in fact distracted, preoccupied, her mind elsewhere. They wandered about, now in the sunlight, now in the shade, snip, snip, and then they came to a handsome garden seat beneath a lilac no longer in flower, and, after taking two or three snips at the ends of branches, Margaret placed her basket on the grass, peeled off her gloves, and sat down. She resembled a woman sitting for her portrait: self-conscious, but in command. Doria took up her place at the other end of the seat and they both looked for a moment into the near distance, silently facing a formal rose garden in the heart of which stood an ancient sundial.

'I do love these dreamy summer days in Melbourne,' Margaret said.

There was a silence. Except for someone down by the river calling faintly, 'Here boy! Good dog!'.

'I have never visited Florida, you know. Do you have days like this where you live? In Florida?'

Doria didn't answer. She was staring into space.

'We must have some tea brought out onto the back terrace. I notice the Ophelia rose up there seems to have decided to pull up its socks. Perhaps it's celebrating the arrival of its little namesake, I wonder. The Queen of Denmark is looking good, too.'

Doria turned her head swiftly, in a way she had, to face Margaret.

'I wonder about that, too; about the namesake,' she said, and Margaret was surprised, a light frown crossing her brow.

'Oh,' she said, 'I didn't realise you were particularly interested in the roses.'

'No,' said Doria quietly, 'not the roses, exactly.'

'What, then?'

'I saw your sister-in-law Mary yesterday. We had a very long and interesting talk about the family. From her perspective. Which is different from that of some.'

'Oh, really? Is it? In what way?'

'Oh, it's not easy to say, but she is obviously still an O'Day, if only by marriage.'

Margaret uttered a quiet and brittle laugh.

'That's Mary for you. She always considered the Fultons were superior to the O'Days in every way. Naturally, she didn't mind Columb's money.'

Doria's eyes opened wider. She was unused to hearing Margaret say such sharp and critical things. Margaret flushed slightly, wishing she hadn't said it. A slip of the tongue. But she was feeling anxious. What might Mary have told Doria? What did Mary know about anything anyway?

Softly, softly, Margaret.

'She was very pleasant. She showed me an old album that had belonged to your brother. It was full of black and white photos of all of you on picnics and in rowboats and in fabulous old cars. Your father was such a tall and handsome man. There are pictures of you on his shoulders. I must say you were a very pretty child. Do you remember a time when you and your brothers dressed up as foxes, with skins on your heads?'

'Yes. We used to do that.'

The odd thing was that there was one picture of a nun holding a baby, and underneath it said, "Sister Bridget with Baby Ophelia". Most of the photos had handwritten labels in white ink. Mary had no idea who the baby was. But I just thought it was a coincidence. The name.'

There was a silence.

Margaret lifted her chin and stared out into the rose garden. When she spoke her voice was soft and apparently thoughtful.

'That *is* a funny coincidence, then,' she said. 'I wonder who it could be. There was no other – er – documentation?'

'Nothing. A photo like that is so little to go on, isn't it?'

'Yes, so very little to go on.'

Margaret's head was spinning, and she thought her heart would stop. She squinted at the sun.

'Of course, our old family photograph albums are full of odd pictures of nuns and priests and so forth. I expect Sister Bridget was some kind of relative. Or she could have been anybody for that matter. Just a photo in an album.' Margaret went on. She needed to stop talking really, or her panic might get the better of her and she might say something she would regret. 'You say Mary had no idea?'

'No, no idea,' said Doria.

Just a photo in an album.

They Talked About Cricket

'God's in his heaven; all's right with the funeral industry.'
                                                              E. R. O'Day

So that was that for the time being, give or take a forger ancestor, and life just went on more or less as usual.

When KayKay and Evan returned from their European honeymoon, they threw a big party to welcome themselves home. The Freud House was again lit up from top to toe, there was a small jazz band indoors, and a barber shop group on the back terrace. Evan loved barber shop. It was winter, so there was less wild activity out of doors. Nobody would drown in the river tonight. The house seethed with people wreathed in perfumes, and wearing bright designer clothes, artistic, original, amusing. There is no need to say that champagne flowed – champagne popped and flowed.

'A toast, a toast to the happy couple!'

And there was no mistaking it, KayKay and Evan were the happy couple. Among dozens of couples, some are more happy than others.

Margaret, who would have preferred to be at home doing patchwork, was elegant in pale green silk, sitting beside one of the older members of the psychiatrists' cricket team on a deep grey sofa. She toyed with her champagne and quietly observed the scene. The man next to her was was Robbie Jellis. He and Margaret had met when they were children in a ballroom dancing class. His wife had died recently. Way back when, his face had always reminded Margaret of a nice dog. It still did. Robbie the Labrador.

'I don't suppose,' he said, 'you fancy a waltz? Not that there's really a waltz. Figure of speech.'

Margaret laughed.

'We could show them all a thing or two.'

'They could show us more than a thing or two, I suspect.'

He was trying to be cheerful, but Margaret could tell that he was sad.

'We might cut a rug,' said Margaret, astonished at her use of such old-fashioned and silly words.

'Ah, let's not.' Then Robbie went on, his doggie face even more wistful. 'The last time I danced with you was a very long time ago, at the party where Monica, no, Marina crashed over the balcony.'

Margaret felt herself jolt at the shock of his words. Nobody ever spoke about Marina. She sat quite still and straight beside him, looking into space.

'I am sorry,' she said, 'I don't actually remember dancing with you. It was a terrible night. I must have blanked most of it out.'

'Oh, quite,' he said, 'quite. I expect you have. Terrible. Yes, terrible. I am sorry I brought it up. It's just that I remember how sweet you were. You were one of the good girls, shy and, I thought, mysterious. Some of them were pretty fast, you know.'

Margaret said nothing. The conversation was impossible. So they small-talked about cricket and about the opera and about life in Toorak today. Old families disappearing, people from all over the world buying up the houses. Knocking them down. Perhaps she did cheer him up. Or perhaps she didn't.

They sat quietly on the sofa watching the tangled movements of the crowd. Sometimes Paul would bob up, or Charmaine, or some neighbour or acquaintance. Justin and Clive were there, and Margaret waved to them across the room.

Among Margaret's talents was the ability to see things out of the corner of her eye, to register them and to process them and to understand their significance. She could do this without showing on her face that she had seen anything at all. What she saw, standing in a doorway, brilliantly clad in raspberry and gold, accompanied by a tall and very handsome Indian man, was the woman from the Windsor, the afternoon companion of Charles Clark-Finn.

'Oh,' she turned to Robbie Jellis, ' do you happen to know who they are?'

'That's the Guptas. Adit and Winifred. He's a brilliant Lacanian. He's just moved into rooms in East Melbourne. They live in the bush somewhere. In a fantastic converted convent. Do you want to meet them?'

'No. Oh no, I just thought her dress was beautiful. You know.'

'Not just the dress.'

He chuckled. Margaret smiled. It was her tolerant smile.

And then it happened. Out of the corner of her eye, again, Margaret glimpsed in the distance, on the edge of the terrace, the tall frame of Charles Clark-Finn, on his arm a lithe blonde woman, probably Sally. Charles the Handsome and Sally the Lithe. Standing with them, deep in conversation, with her back to Margaret, was Doria.

This is a truly horrible party, isn't it.

Surely it was inconceivable that Charles would discuss family business with Doria, with anyone for that matter. But these days tongues were so loose, discretion almost a thing of the past. Margaret couldn't refrain from staring as if stunned in the direction of Charles and Sally and Doria. How long would it be before Doria, somehow or other, put a short biography to the photograph in Columb's photograph album? Was there any point in asking Mary to hand over the album? Wasn't it already too late? At least get hold of it and somehow put a stop to any further damage. Margaret wasn't even quite sure what she meant here. She just knew she had to get her hands on the album. Oh God! How many more photograph albums were out there, not only among family members, but among all kinds of who knew what people? Her racing mind raced on. She had to get to Mary. Get her hands on Columb's album. Slow down, Margaret. The damage is pretty well done.

But as fate would have it – yes, fate – Margaret never even got to speak to Mary.

The Course of Events

'And my large kingdom for a little grave.'
E. R. O'Day

Margaret O'Day was killed in a car crash on the Princes Highway somewhere between Sale and Bairnsdale. Visibility was poor. She was foolishly attempting to pass a milk tanker but misjudged the moment and sailed across its path so that the tanker could not avoid her.

Swift and terrible, the squeal, the crash, the tearing, splitting metal, flying glass, the splatter and flurry, and suddenly the stillness, the moment of complete rest. Airbags could not begin to save the driver of that car. The man who was driving the tanker braked but was helpless to avoid the collision. He was slightly injured. Post-mortem examination of the body showed that the victim had suffered a haemorrhage in the cerebellum prior to the accident. She had lost control of the vehicle.

How shocking and sad it was that Margaret, still so full of life and energy, was so swiftly, without warning, reduced to fragments of herself, to be finally reassembled by O'Day Funerals and placed in a luxurious casket before being farewelled by the sorrowful circle of family and the shimmering blue wings of the Ulysses butterflies.

'I wondered if she really should drive all that way, but I never said anything. She wasn't well, wasn't herself. I should've said. Somebody should've done the driving. She loved to drive. I know she loved to drive. She shouldn't have been driving. I knew she shouldn't.'

This was Lillian, who repeated these thoughts over and over again to anyone who was listening, filling large silent gaps in family gatherings with her soft and tearful waves of speech. The tapestry room, the heart of Margaret's world, was undisturbed, a strangely peaceful, hollow haven now, an abrupt mausoleum where the details, large and small, of Margaret's life lay neatly, silently, in drawers and cabinets. Her Famille-Verte behind glass, a still and perfect porcelain statement of what Margaret had held to be beautiful.

The Church of the Assumption

'Trust in God. Trust also in me.'
E. R. O'Day

Following the release of blue butterflies at Bellevue, a sparkling motorised Edwardian hearse, bearing Margaret's coffin beneath a blanket of greenery and daisies, moved on to the church. The vehicle had been taken from the O'Day Funeral Home Museum for the occasion. Margaret had wished it. With its large glass panels etched with vines and hearts, it was something between a horse-drawn carriage and a very fancy milk van. It had a look of toyland and minor European royalty. Margaret had always loved it. When the coffin had been placed in the church, the congregation began to arrive. Nine grandchildren in sober clothing of black or navy blue. Veiled women all in black, wearing smooth and beautiful gloves, carrying rosaries and tiny handbags. Sunglasses in the pale sunlight. Lace handkerchiefs. The steps of the church were lined with vivid bouquets and wreaths. The organ was softly playing Verdi's *Requiem*. Paul, son of the deceased, played the organ. Speakers were her other son, Joseph, and also the Director of the Victorian Ballet, and the Minister for the Arts. Sister Beth from the Greensborough convent.

After the service, outside the church, when the congregation was gathered in murmuring and moving huddles of dark and stylish clothing, women here and there in their black mantillas, as the coffin with its cloak of daisies was slowly moved on high by six tall sons and nephews, once again a flock of deep blue butterflies was released into the watery sunshine. So many insects had been sacrificed to this woman. The grand notes of the organ still floated out the doors of the church as a young man from O'Day Funerals opened a large plastic box. First there was a flurry of blue, and some of the insects flapped and fluttered out and off.

A sigh of 'aah' and a few people shaded their eyes briefly, looking up, trying to register the fleeting beauty, straining to distil it, to keep it forever in the mind's eye. It was gone. There remained some butterflies that stuck, some with open wings, some with closed wings, to the sleeves of the young man's jacket. Others alighted on black mantillas, on white shirts. Frederick captured one in his cupped hands – then he opened his hands like wings and sent it sailing off into the air. Was there a sound of wings? You don't hear butterflies as they pass; you don't hear the soul as it sails out from the body to wherever it is going.

The cars, filled with so many family and friends, made a solemn processional drive through traffic to Evergreen Park East where Margaret was buried beside Edmund. Beside Edmund, after all, as was correct and as was expected. All was recorded for electronic posterity. Several clips went to YouTube.

Yes, she finally came to rest in the pristine lawns of Evergreen Park East, encircled by her children, her grandchildren, and also by Fiona and the boys, and a vast crowd of other family, friends, dignitaries and acquaintances. Sissy Bagwell, dramatic in black lace and veil, resembled a sorrowing medieval queen.

All Things Considered

'Life is the question; death is the answer.'
E. R. O'Day

In the middle of the afternoon on the day that she would die, Margaret was in the tapestry room, sitting at the desk, with the parcel of Ophelia's sad little belongings lying open in front of her. She sometimes did this – folded open the parcel, took out the medal, the scissors, the photographs. Her mind was almost blank with quiet sorrow, yet always there was the fear that somebody – well, Doria was of course that somebody – would discover the parcel and all that it meant. In these moments Margaret hated Doria, hated her for moving into their lives and threatening to bring to light anything and everything she could discover. Margaret wanted, above all, to protect Ophelia from Doria's searchlight. She wanted to hold Ophelia forever secret in her own heart. She also needed to preserve the heroic public image of her father. She packed the parcel up slowly, and put it back in the drawer.

She stood up and dithered for a few minutes over which books to take with her to read that night after driving to the ski lodge. She had just taken from the shelf two of her favourites, *Journey into the Mind's Eye* and *The House by the Dvina – A Russian Childhood*, when she heard the buzzer on the gate. Damn. Could it be the girl from the kennels coming back for something? She had taken the dogs off for the week. Then Margaret remembered – Tilley's were meant to be delivering a case of wine. Lucky she was still home. Lillian had already gone so Margaret opened the gates.

The sleek burgundy and gold van nosed its way round to the cellar. Since nobody else was there to let the delivery man in, Margaret took the key from the hook in the pantry and went down to open the tradesman's door. She instructed the man – his name, Forest, was embroidered in gold on his burgundy jacket – to stack the wine in the rack. It was a red from the Bedrock vineyard at Woodpecker Point. That was nice; she always like to get wines from the Tasmanian vineyards. They were very popular with the family. When he had gone she locked the cellar again, and went briskly back into the house, leaving the gates open. Her SUV was already out in the drive and her bags were already in it. She held the books for bedtime reading in her hand. She went upstairs and put on her sheepskin jacket and mustard pigskin gloves. Then she remembered that she had meant to get a bottle of whiskey from the cellar. Damn. Then she heard the doorbell – the old brass bell-pull jangled and almost made her jump. Of course, the gate was open. But who was this? She was growing quite impatient with herself for not getting away sooner. Down she went, placed the books on the hall table, and there on the doorstep was Doria. Doria in a long pale sulphur puffer jacket looking like a big scary caterpillar. She was wearing huge black sunglasses, although there was no sun to speak of. Would this woman never leave her alone?

'I'm sorry to trouble you, Margaret, but I have misplaced my iPhone, and I wonder if perhaps I left it here last night? I've simply never lost it before. I must be getting distracted.' She looked agitated, even a little wild.

'If it's here it will ring,' Margaret said, brisk and practical, taking her own phone out of her jacket pocket.

But Doria's didn't ring. The house was silent.

'You could pray to St Anthony, perhaps. Come for a walk while I get a bottle of Powers. I always have to take my own up to the snow. Nobody else seems to be able to remember. The phone will appear by magic. Just relax,' Margaret called as she went through the kitchen, into the pantry, with Doria on her heels, and came to the internal cellar door. She switched on the cellar lights. They went down the six worn stone steps into the cool of the wine cellar.

Doria could not relax, but she followed Margaret.

'Would you like a nice bottle of red to take home? From Tasmania?'

Margaret handed her one of the bottles that had just been delivered. Then suddenly, Margaret said, 'That's the door to the old bombshelter over there. Do you want to have a look? It's quite historic. Full of cobwebs. It dates from the Second World War. My husband liked to use it as a kind of cubby house when he was a boy. Nobody's been in it for years and years, probably.'

Later she couldn't understand what had possessed her to say all that. She was in a hurry, and she had never in her life offered to show the bombshelter to anyone. Well, she was seldom in the cellar for that matter.

'How very fascinating,' Doria said. 'I have never seen such a place. I imagined they no longer existed.'

So they walked down the cold and dusty aisle between the shelves of bottles until they came in the end to a metal door that was secured with a heavy metal bar. Margaret slid back the bar and swung the door out. It was noiseless. She turned on the dim light and they both peered in. There was a chill as if they had opened the door to a huge refrigerator.

'Go in,' she said, 'it's rather musty, I'm afraid. It's completely underground, you see. There are thirty-nine steps down. Look at those gasmasks. They remind me of horrible insects or something.' The masks hung in a row at the top of the steps, beneath the low ceiling just inside the door, masks smeared with dust, their concertina air pipes curving out from between their sinister dark eyes. The chill from below came creeping up towards the two women.

Then something happened. Doria took just one step down, looked up at the gasmasks, and tripped on the rough surface of the step. She twisted and tumbled, falling down, down the whole flight with a gasping, ringing cry. A crash and then silence. She lay there at the foot of the steps, on the dusty concrete floor, sprawled. She didn't move. As in a dream, Margaret could see, by the watery light, a splodge of eerie yellow, face down. Far, far away. The bottle of red had smashed, and wine was spattered on the yellow. It sat in a pool on the surface of the distant concrete floor. Margaret stared down the stairs at Doria for a second, a split second, and in that second a swift and terrible decision was formed. Was it a decision? What made her do what she did? A strange sensation of clarity came to her.

Margaret turned off the light, stepped back into the cellar, and firmly swung the shelter door shut. It closed with the clang of a collision. She slipped the long heavy bolt through the steel slots. The bombshelter was sealed.

As if nothing had happened, Margaret walked briskly down the aisle until she came to the spirits, collected a bottle of Powers Gold Label Special Reserve for her nightcap, and made her way up into the pantry. She collected her books from the table, set the alarm, locked the house, made the sign of the cross as was her custom from childhood, and got into the car. Out the gates, which closed behind her. She drove off with a feeling of unreality, yet with a level of triumph, and drove as in a trance through a maze of many roads that were thickly tangled with traffic until she finally found she was on the Princes Highway. It was three hundred and eighty-five kilometres to the family ski chalet at Dinner Plain.

A woman lay badly injured or dead or dying, trapped in the bombshelter at Bellevue. Margaret had not just left her there, but had locked her in. Fate had offered Margaret the chance to conspire in the death and disappearance of Doria Fogelsong. Or fate had offered her a chance to attempt to save her, or to offer her the dignity of attempted succour. Hand in glove with a cruel destiny, Margaret chose to leave Doria to the whim of fate. Should Doria happen to call for help, nobody would hear her.

Will somebody, by chance, come to Bellevue in the next few hours, go on a search for bottles of brandy and champagne, decide to pay a visit to the old bombshelter, discover Doria, or the body of Doria? If anything is impossible, *this* is impossible.

It will be a week before anybody goes to the house, let alone the cellar. And people who go to the cellar simply never go into the shelter. Ever. Never ever. What will Margaret do when she returns to Bellevue? Is it possible she will walk brightly around her house while Doria rots in the bombshelter? It's a forlorn and forgotten place. How will that be possible? Not just fleeing from an accident, failing to render assistance, but actually walking back and forth, tracking across the scene. Walking on Doria's chilly sepulchre. What of the Good Samaritan? What of Margaret's fine Catholic conscience? Did she in fact even have such a thing? Is she planning to go to Confession?

When is she going to Confession? How can she imagine telling all this to Justin Rhys? Or will she avoid Justin and confess to a stranger somewhere in another parish? How will she choose that stranger? Margaret is under the touching impression that almost any priest she chooses, anywhere in the country, would recognise her, the notable Melbourne philanthropist, patron of the arts, etc., etc. She's wrong, of course, being far less grand than she thinks she is.

What is she telling *herself*?

Margaret was now alone, quite alone, a body and a soul without a context. Perhaps already she was in some Dante-esque circle of the Inferno. I believe she was.

As she drove up the highway towards the snowfields, Margaret had a vivid recollection of the old blue Methodist Bible with its endpapers. There were the vague floating fears that hovered over the radiant images of the clouds. It was late afternoon and squalls of rain were falling now and again through the cold air. The sun pierced the clouds, which drifted in strange three-dimensional puffs and streaks, causing the patches of blue sky to recede, placing the clouds in relief, in a foreground of blinding white. The Mercedes SUV was silver, and a curious fact was that behind it for long stretches of road Margaret could see in the rear-vision mirror a steady convoy of six white cars, all with their headlights on. The sunlight and the rain caused the lights to appear to waver, to produce watery yellow beams that shifted and glowed in the mirror. The cars appeared to Margaret to be sinister and threatening, shark-like, milky, relentless, shadowing her, bearing down upon her. Then suddenly, with no apparent movement, they were no longer there. They had, all of them, dematerialised in the blink of an eye. They had bled away into the landscape, disappeared down a silent side-road to nowhere. When they had been in view they had served the purpose of keeping Margaret's thoughts away from the moment of dreadful decision on the steps of the bombshelter. That blink of an eye, that split second. Now that they had disappeared, the effort of swinging her mind's eye away from the cellar and onto the road became so very difficult. Large pink flat coin-shapes floated across her vision. They shifted about, slid across each other, like the scales of some great and horrible fish. She saw the fish on the white marble fishmonger's slab. Her temples began to throb, her left eye to ache. In the distance she could see the pale weak ghost of a rainbow.

 She was half listening to FM radio playing something vaguely Mozartian in the background, but her thoughts were fixed on what she had done or not done in the cellar, forever questioning the moment of decision. She could go back, go back and change it! But she drove on, relentless through the swiftly fading light. She tried to blot out the lurid and immediate memory of the moment when she slipped the metal bar into the slot. She would imagine herself then quickly lifting the bar, swinging open the door, running down-down-down the thirty-nine steps. There was Doria, lifting her head, dazed, not really noticing that for a few seconds she had been a prisoner in the bombshelter. But always

Margaret's thoughts returned to the fact that she had not lifted that bar, that she had picked up the bottle of whiskey and walked calmly along the row of dark shelves, out into the daylight. She had gone through the pantry and through the house and had just kept walking, one foot neatly after the other, step, step, collect book and gloves, close the front door, step, step to the car. Black boot after black boot, smartly stepping away from the event, the mistake, the incident. The body. Put the book and bottle in the car. She had started the car and driven round the gravel circle and smoothly out the gates, which closed behind her. They were great iron gates, and sometimes, in fact nearly always, Margaret found the last lines of 'To His Coy Mistress' go through her head as she saw them open or close.

> Let us roll all our strength, and all
> Our sweetness, up into one ball;
> And tear our pleasures with rough strife
> Thorough the iron gates of life.
> Thus, though we cannot make our sun
> Stand still, yet we will make him run.

The iron gates of life – it always seemed to her to be a horrible image. Was it sexual? Margaret didn't have a particularly good grip on poetry. The gates themselves, the gates to Bellevue, were graceful, reminding her of some French convent, yet they were iron, and they were gates, and they kept some people out and some people in. And on the afternoon when she left Doria for dead in the bombshelter, she said out loud to herself: 'The Iron Gates of Life,' and as she said that she winced. The gates closed behind her, and that was final.

Where was the point of no return? Was it then, as the gates sealed off the house from the world, as they put Margaret outside in the big silver car, heading for the snowfields, the lodge, the family? As the gates sealed off the big house, locked up, empty, not quite empty?

It was as if she had been taken over by a power, or had discovered another personality that had overtaken her. Her real self? The moment when she did not move back the metal bar was now the defining moment of her life, the split second when everything changed.

The lovely engine of the Mercedes ran quietly, the luxurious tyres rolled quietly, Mozart played quietly. Margaret's head ached and throbbed, and her thoughts went round and round, now screaming and twisting, now purring fuzzily along, flowing in a fog, only to jolt suddenly and burn and flare with a hot bright light. The word she kept thinking was 'anguish' – this was anguish as she had never before known it – well, she had never known the meaning of the word before. The terrible thing was that she did not regret what she had done. She hated herself for her lack of regret, for the abyss where regret should be, tried to manufacture regret but it would not come. At some moments she thought she could smell smoke. Lines from a poem learned in childhood kept singing in her head: 'Can it be the flames of hell, or just the abbot smoking?' They had been terribly funny when she was seven, now they rang and leered and laughed at her. The flames of hell. Or just the abbot smoking. She remembered the drawing of a fat abbot with a huge cigar, smoke billowing out the barred window of the refectory. The flames of hell – how silly. She knew there was no such place as hell, no hellfire. Hell was the absence of God. The loss of goodness. That was it – the loss, the absence of goodness. Not flames. This.

Margaret had always consciously striven to do good, to be good, to practise virtue. She had considered the habits of her aunt who kept a book of her own virtues to be excessive and even amusing, yet she had occasionally found herself, as she visited friends and relatives in distress or sickness, mentally crossing off the order 'to visit the sick, to bury the dead'. She would smile to herself. She was known, she felt, among her family and associates, as a good woman. How then, after all, had she descended to this act against goodness, this act of supreme cruelty, of, in fact – how she had always hated the word – of murder? Was it murder? The arrogance of murder, of judging the life of another to be not fit to continue. Thou shalt not kill. How was she going to confess this unbelievable act, this sin against a fellow human being, against herself? Against every single thing that she held dear? Against everything that she believed, that she knew to be true and good. How had she made the transition, so suddenly – oh so very suddenly – from good to evil? Evil – she tried not to think of the word. She tried not to think 'murder' but it kept oozing into her mind. She had undergone a black metamorphosis. Bless me father for I have sinned. Since my last confession I have committed one act of murder. Is that how it would be? Mozart had disappeared and given way to Debussy's *String Quartet in G Minor*. If one murder, why not more, why not many. Once you have crossed the line, what's to stop you? But it was not like that.

Murder? But it wasn't really murder. No, no, Doria was alive, stunned, uninjured, and somebody would come, and the door would be opened by chance – chance; ah, chance – and it could all be explained. Doria was dead. No, I didn't see her. I went to the cellar but I didn't notice anything about the shelter door. Open? Closed? No. Perhaps the man Forest from Tilley's. It could all be explained. Footprints in the dust of the cellar floor? So many footprints up and down the aisles, in among the shelves, dust disturbed, dust falling day after day onto the dust of the days before.

Footprints. What was that Longfellow poem my father used to say to us:

> Lives of great men all remind us
> We can make our lives sublime
> And departing leave behind us
> Footprints in the sands of time.

Courage, my father said, is the first of all the virtues, the one from which all other virtues flow. Sometimes it is difficult to see the distinction between courage and cowardice, between virtue and vice. He had said that.

Abruptly the image of Lillian, Lillian in her sensible shirt and cardigan, sitting in the tapestry room at dusk. The *Lady with the Unicorn*, the butterfly screen, the Famille-Verte. Lillian can see the distinction between courage and cowardice. Plain as day to Lillian.

Lillian is knitting, clickety, Margaret is quilting, in and out, in and out, the needle and the thread. Needle and thread. They are talking, softly murmuring about this and that. It is clear, as Lillian sits there quietly, bathed in a subtle glow, that Lillian is good.

Lillian, Lillian, race to the house, fling open the door to the shelter, call the ambulance! Help me! Lillian, help me!

But Margaret drove on, her mind and heart a terrible jumble of despair. Margaret had shut the door on Doria because she was afraid, she was sure, that Doria was going to expose the aching wound in Margaret's own heart, the knowledge that her father, her spotless and beloved father, was flawed. He had betrayed her, betrayed Margaret's trust, her all-shining, loving trust. She had longed for a sister, he had promised her a sister, he had delivered that sister, and he had locked her away in a place where she had lived and withered and died, had lived for so many long years, without ever feeling the embrace of Margaret her sister who loved her. Her beloved father had betrayed Ophelia, had betrayed them all. The cruellest act was what he did to Ophelia. But perhaps Ophelia had been happy, after all, safe and sound in the convent, with her scissors and her medal and her fluffy teddy bears. Her cracked picture of Kitty in the orchard. How could she be happy? It was surely impossible.

The image of the painting of Nellie Melba drifts across Margaret's consciousness. The water, the flowers, the little open mouth that seems to sing.

'How could I love her when I did not know she existed? But I did. Perhaps deep inside me I always knew of her existence. Is that possible? Yet now that I know she lived, I love her. But I could never tell her. If I am confined forever to Purgatory, if I am never to see the face of God, I will never be able to tell her that I love her.'

This is a cruel theology. For Margaret, in spite of modern teachings of her church, persists in her belief in Purgatory.

Killian, the paragon of virtue Dr Killian O'Day, had betrayed his devoted wife, his devoted daughter – he had betrayed Kitty Sullivan, the trust of Kitty's family – he had betrayed most of all the baby Ophelia. How is that possible? Whatever the answers to the questions that will never now be answered, Margaret's task, the task of her heart, was to prevent Doria Fogelsong from bringing it all into the light and publishing Killian's sins for all the world to know. And publishing the sad imprisoned life of Ophelia. Margaret had discovered she was capable of doing whatever it took for the story to remain undiscovered. Yet, as she drove relentlessly north to the snow, doubt came twisting up out of the darkness in her heart. Doria was only the first – there would be other interfering family members digging into the secret recesses of people's lives. Was she planning to lock them in the bombshelter too? Oh, dear God, the story would come out one day, in a year, or in a hundred years; one day everyone would know what Killian did to Ophelia, what Killian did to Margaret, that Killian had feet of clay. Feet of clay. The iron gates of life. The fires of hell. The abbot smoking. Saint Killian is the patron saint of rheumatism – they had always laughed about that. Nothing was funny any more. The images, the thoughts and fears swirled round and round in Margaret's mind as the pink discs floated and slid about, as the throbbing in her temples gave way to sharper pains and as the three-dimensional blue skies and the eerie slanting sunlight shifted to a blur of bloody orange and the sudden fall of night.

It takes just over five hours to drive from Melbourne to Dinner Plain along first of all the Princes Highway and then on the Great Alpine Road. Margaret scarcely knew that she was driving.

Once she stopped to use the toilet at a service station. The green and yellow signs had loomed suddenly up at her as she rounded a bend and she pulled in. The place was a blaze of light in the desolate highway darkness, a haven of warmth, an artificial reminder of home. Sanctuary. Margaret bought a bottle of water.

'Cold out there?' the girl behind the cash desk was bright and chirpy. Oh yes, it was cold out there. Her badge said 'Kylie' in fine scarlet letters.

People in parkas sat at tables drinking coffee and eating donuts, steaming up the windows. Bright racks of chocolate bars, gleaming refrigerators of drinks, ice-creams on sticks lying in snowy vats, neatly packed in like exotic fish.

'Heading for the snow?'

Yes, Margaret was heading for the snow.

'Reckon there's some good falls. Where you headed exactly?'

'Oh, Dinner Plain.' Exactly.

'Not much snow there yet. My sister's up at Hotham. She just texted me. Here, look.'

From the pocket of her yellow uniform the girl pulled out a phone and handed it to Margaret. There was a small gleaming picture of a laughing girl in a pink parka, her face ringed with white fur, cradled in her red-mittened hands a big and glistening snowball.

Everything was so normal. The world was spinning on its merry way. Life goes on. Nothing had happened, nothing had changed, Doria was not lying in the bombshelter. On her way to the washroom, Margaret spied Doria sitting at a table in her sulphur caterpillar coat sipping steaming coffee from a tall brown paper cup. Her black woollen mittens lay on the table, her freckled hands were curled around the cup, her iPhone rested on one of the mittens. So that was where the iPhone was, on top of a black mitten in a café on the highway to the snow. What a lot of fuss for nothing, after all.

Margaret left her mustard gloves behind on the side of the hand-basin in the washroom. Never mind. There was no going back. Margaret gripped the steering wheel with her bare hands, and there was something unfamiliar and somehow comforting about the immediate contact with its curved surface. It was meant to be gripped. Margaret gripped the wheel and clenched her teeth and squinted into the darkness, which was cut by the slicing yellow of her headlights. She was now moving in a dream, and the sharp pains in her head were coming and going in waves. Her deep anxiety had taken control of her body. She sipped the water from the bottle.

She should not have been driving. She could kill somebody.

Up ahead the milk tanker. Somebody crying over spilt milk. The lights of the far distant village sprang into Margaret's vision quite unexpectedly, like the twinkling lights in a Christmas scene, like a Swiss fairyland in a department store window. The lights in the window of the O'Day lodge, the lights of home. The lights of the old house in Eltham glimpsed through the blossom of the apple trees. The bosom of the apple trees. Margaret felt suddenly warm and safe and unafraid, the horror in the cellar far behind her in a pocket of unreality. Nothing was going to happen. Nothing had happened. Doria was OK, after all. Margaret had just imagined everything, just imagined it. Everything was fine. She would call on Mary and insist she hand over the photograph album. She would have the kitchen chairs painted green after all, a rich viridian. Some table napkins the colour of cabbage leaves, somewhere something carved from malachite, a glass bowl of fragrant roses, Blue Moon. The Famille-Verte was so exquisite, wasn't it, placed there on the shelves of the cabinet? Margaret in a white pinafore picking violets under the trees with her father, her fingers digging down into the heart of the plant to nip the stems off where they are soft and white. In the distance somewhere her mother sang a haunting song:

> The snow is fast falling, the winter is here.
> Yet I, Robin Redbreast, have nothing to fear.

The dangerous water rises until it reaches her armpits. Scarlet poppies in her hair. She clutches the fragile reeds with her left hand. Jack-in-the-box. Two lone sorrowful stars.

Then this is what happened:

There was not much traffic on the highway. Margaret gripped the wheel tightly, missing the feel of her gloves, wishing she had returned for them. But as the lights of Dinner Plain danced towards her in her imagination, the slippery pink discs moved in across them and Margaret's hands seemed no longer able to hold on to the wheel. She glanced down at her right hand; it didn't seem to belong to her. She thought she was trying to pass the tanker, its great white whale of a shape resembling a huge milk bottle. Somebody, somewhere, crying over spilt milk. Her foot on the accelerator pressed down hard as her head jerked up and the SUV sailed at speed across the path of the tanker.

By the time the police and the ambulance had arrived Margaret was dead in the mangled car. She had not even reached the beginning of the Great Alpine Road.

The Snow Is Fast Falling, the Winter Is Here

'In Heaven an angel is nobody in particular'
E. R. O'Day

At the wake, which was held at Bellevue after the requiem, a sorrowful but ever-efficient Lillian in charge of the proceedings, waiters served elegant finger food and poured wines from the cellar, including some of the new Pinot from Woodpecker Point. There were slender slices of Lillian's Perfect Fruit Cake and plates of Lillian's Tiny Sage and Saffron Scones. As well there was catering from The Friary of Toorak. Throughout the house there was a clear sense of the absence of Margaret. Everybody received an exquisite jar of Margaret's Honey of Roses. Lillian had emptied the pantry shelf.

Dr Bing Honey from across the road was there with his glamorous young wife, who looked amazing in black lace and velvet, like a teenage vampire. Was there the ghost of a satisfied smile on the chiselled features of Dr Honey? Was he taking pleasure in the disappearance of one more old matriarch? It's a sad irony that he and his lovely young wife – her name was Mickey – were killed in a skiing accident in Switzerland before the year was out. Ah – the twists of fate. Dr Honey had written his last prescription. The funeral and burial of the couple took place at Heavenly Days – no irony there. It probably wasn't a suicide pact, although Bing had recently celebrated a birthday, and stranger things have happened. The man was fifty-six, after all. Perhaps it was time to go. The big black box of his house would stand empty for a few months. Then along would come a Chinese manufacturer of toys to demolish the box and to put in its place a kind of nineteenth-century Danish hunting lodge. Times change.

'Margaret would have loved the butterflies,' KayKay said, her face grave but also smiling at the memory. 'They were such a success. And Paul playing the organ. She would have been so proud of him.'

'Justin was obviously very emotional. He really loved Margaret. I have never seen him like that at a funeral before.'

'It's the end of a era.'

'Sissy Bagwell has aged.'

'Whose baby was that – crying all the time?'

'I don't know. I don't think it was baby Margaret. Could have been Ophelia, I suppose. There's always a baby crying somewhere or other.'

It occurred to Evan, of all people, suddenly to wonder aloud where Doria was. Nobody seemed to know, or really to care.

'She was going to Tasmania again, I think. Yes, Tasmania – for some unfinished business,' Lillian said. In fact Lillian was scarcely able to speak. Her voice came out as a controlled whisper. She was bereft. It felt to her, although she did not form the words, that when she lost Margaret she lost not an employer, and not just a friend, but that she lost her dearest sister.

'Would she know what's happened?' Evan asked.

'Possibly,' said KayKay, 'Doria knows everything.'

'Possibly not,' said Evan. 'Maybe we should text her or email her or something. I think if she knew she would be here. She would want to be here, if only because it's the end of an – um – era. In the family.'

'Or she would send flowers. Oh, what does she matter, anyway,' KayKay said. 'She'll be back to pester everyone again in due course. I find her so heavy, the way she fidgets with her iPad, on and on and on in the roots and branches of the holy O'Day family tree. She asked Charmaine for a copy of Charm's birth certificate. And Charm's only a holy O'Day by marriage. Well what could that possibly have to do with anything?'

'She's a type,' said Evan. 'She has to know – um – everything about everybody, just in case. A total ber-busybody.'

'Just in case what?'

'Oh, they think they might need the information one of these times. It's – um – a bit like being a crocodile.'

'What?'

'You know, crocodiles drag their live prey into their lair and – um – h-hoard it there, in case they need to eat it later on. Doria's like that with information about people.'

'I didn't know that about crocodiles. I don't believe you.'

'It's true. I think of Doria as a kind of crocodile. Charmaine's birth certificate is, for Doria, just part of the whole picture. It needs to be – um – filed in the lair.'

KayKay laughed her loud and barking laugh. 'You're so mad, Heaven Keene. But seriously, I wonder why she isn't here. I would've thought it was just her thing.'

'Actually Charmaine said she thought she saw her at the church.'

'Well, there you are, then, she's about somewhere.'

As indeed she was. And, strange to record, KayKay then said, 'Well, just so long as she keeps her distance. I simply can't stand it when she gets underfoot.'

But Life Goes On

'Life is not a spectacle or a feast; it's a predicament.'
                                                    E. R. O'Day

A few weeks after the funeral, baby Margaret is baptised. In the prevailing spirit of invading one's own privacy, not only the baptism but indeed the birth itself is recorded in various ways and made available on YouTube and Twitter and Facebook and so forth. Life in the future might be so much simpler for family historians. Perhaps more complicated for me, the talking skeleton in the wardrobe. The weather on the day of the baptism is cold, so the party following the ceremony is held indoors at Isobel's house, which is not far from Bellevue. Isobel has taken in the border collies Venus and Jupiter, much to the joy of the children, who add them to their own collection of tabby cats, long-haired guinea pigs, flop-eared rabbits, white rats, the snake called Uncle, the canary called Coalmine, and the red-footed tortoise called Manuela. This tortoise was acquired when Isobel, volunteer at a wildlife rescue centre, read a rather puzzling news story about Manuela the red-footed tortoise who disappeared from her home in Rio de Janeiro, in 1982. Her family believed she had run away when builders working on the house left the door open. The father of the family died in 2014, and they began clearing out his second-floor workshop that was filled with old and broken things. The workshop had always been taboo to the rest of the family. They discovered Manuela alive inside a box of old seventy-eights. Perhaps truth is stranger than fiction after all.

One day this menagerie will move in to Bellevue.

Smith the nanny is kept very busy, one way and another – not least in the care and nurture of all the animals. The interior of her little car reeks of animal, and is always littered with straw. Hugh delights in pulling bits of it out of her hair and her clothing and flicking them into the air.

'Clean straw for nothing, Smith!'

'I don't get you. What's that mean, exactly?'

'It means you've been knocking back the gin (don't deny it) and soon now I'm going to provide us with a dear little haystack where we can both sleep off our hangover.'

'Whatever.'

At baby Margaret's party, Ophelia Rose takes her first steps. Some child knocks over and smashes an Émile Gallé vase. St Michael the Archangel and George the Family Skeleton stand guard inside the front door of Bellevue.

Bellevue lies forlorn and empty, waiting for the revolutionary residency of Isobel and Hugh, who love it and plan to live there forever and ever. Well, nothing is forever. But for the time being Lillian, with the help of Paul, is in charge of organising Margaret's effects and possessions and has moved into a guest room.

Ophelia Rose's quilt lies unfinished on a table in the tapestry room, which is the saddest, the stillest room of all – the butterfly screen, the *Lady with the Unicorn*, the Famille-Verte are the silent witnesses to the eerie absence of Margaret. Ophelia Rose inherits the Verte, to join her collection of the Rose. Lucky girl. The grandly titled *Book of Revelation* lies unfinished in the drawer of the desk. Was there more to be revealed? Were there things that would be forever dormant? What is forever?

I suppose journals are always unfinished. An interesting thing about them, nearly always, is not so much what is there as what is not there. I have been through *The Book of Revelation* – the writer has no problem revealing her true attitude to Charmaine and KayKay and Sissy and Evan and so on. The central and devastating thing for Margaret was the betrayal by her father. It's pretty horrible, I think, that Ophelia Mary was in residence at the convent at the same time as Muriel, the dying wife of her father. I wonder if Margaret's mother really knew about Ophelia. Ah – coincidence, destiny, irony – all that. The tight-lipped nuns knew, of course.

In the late afternoons Paul plays the piano at Bellevue, Chopin's *Ballade in G minor* filling the quiet hollow of the house; but he is soon to leave for a new life in Milan with Gerard. Rafaela has returned to Paris, and she calls and texts and emails and skypes the family sometimes with her thoughts and questions and ideas. Jean-François still insists that Doria is a blackmailer. Everyone is on Facebook – which keeps them abreast of all the family news. Fiona and the boys are very helpful of course, as are Justin and Clive.

Benjamin Ross and his sister tried to call Doria's mobile a few times, but it was always switched off. Then the police discovered it anyway. A traveller, on her way to the snowfields, is wearing Margaret's pigskin gloves. Happy traveller.

Lillian walks in the garden, feeling the non-presence of Margaret, as she observes the subtle changes in the trees, the flowerbeds, from day to day. How quiet everything is. Sometimes she goes down to the river, where she sits near the old boatshed and watches the melancholy wind as it ruffles the surface of the water.

In the outer reaches of the city, at Heavenly Days, where the ferris wheel turns, and where the trees are sweet with the songs of electronic birds, where Bing and Mickey Honey will quite soon be laid to rest, life goes nicely on and on and on.

Yes, life goes on very nicely. Until one day at an auction, somebody, some stranger, buys Bellevue.

And decides to demolish the house or maybe just renovate the wine cellar.

'O death, where is thy sting? O grave, where is thy victory?'
E. R. O'Day

EPILOGUE BY THE STORYTELLER

That's all from the wardrobe for now. Life goes on. I still have my own teeth – but I believe I already told you that.

Lightning Source UK Ltd.
Milton Keynes UK
UKOW03f0603190117
292353UK00001B/153/P